The flute player was etched into the smoke-blackened ceiling above him. The curve of the walls made him look as if he were crouched, waiting, watching Mack in the dark of the cave.

Mack began waving his arms like a lifeguard calling everyone out of the sea. "Hey, get up here! I've found it! I've found it!" Grier and Rick lifted their heads, looking slightly stupefied. At the raft, Harry set down his fly rod. They either didn't believe him or were too tired to move.

"God damn it, you guys, get the lead out! It's no joke..."

For a second Mack nearly lost his balance, but he grabbed the top of the ladder to steady himself. Grier and Rick and Harry pushed up over the rocks like resentful converts moving slowly to the altar. They met at the base of the ladder. Mack stared down at the sunburned, skeptical faces.

"Start climbing, you lazy bastards, I'm going to make you rich!"

JAMES MAGNUSON

MONEY MOUNTAIN

A Critic's Choice paperback
from Lorevan Publishing, Inc.
New York, New York

MONEY MOUNTAIN

Copyright © 1984 by James Magnuson

Reprinted by arrangement with Doubleday & Company, Inc.

ISBN: 1-55547-176-5

First Critic's Choice edition: May 1987

From LOREVAN PUBLISHING, INC.

Published by arrangement with Tom Doherty Associates, Inc.

Critic's Choice Paperbacks
Lorevan Publishing, Inc.
New York, New York

To my mother and father

ACKNOWLEDGMENTS

I would like to thank some of the people whose generosity and intelligence have been crucial to the writing of this book. They are: Ulu Grosbard, Bill Mauldin, Michael Martin Murphey, Alfonso Ortiz, Fred Smoler, Doug Terry and, once again, Wendy Weil. The staff of the State Supreme Court Library in Santa Fe I would like to thank for friendship and shelter. For the legend of the flute player I am indebted to Frank Waters's excellent *Book of the Hopi*.

GOODBYE MONEY MOUNTAIN
by Michael Martin Murphey

The spirit's willing, but the flesh is weak
when a man sees colors in a muddy creek
A few specks of gold dust in a sandy stream
will stake a claim on your wildest dreams . . .

I said goodbye, Money Mountain
I can't live here any more
So it's goodbye, Money Mountain
it's not you I'm looking for

MONEY MOUNTAIN

Chapter One

THE SOUND of pebbles spattering against the window woke Mack out of a dead sleep, out of what felt like the saddest of dreams. He propped himself up on his elbows. The first traces of dawn streaked the Sangre de Cristos. Still befuddled, he scanned the shadowed room. His eyes drifted across the electric guitar propped in the corner, Annie's clothing draped across the jaws of the half-filled suitcases, the photo of the three of them taken on Kaia's second birthday, all beaming in their paper hats. He stared at the yawning closets with their clutches of empty hangers, the piles of what would go and what would stay, the ordering of a dismantled life. The clock on the bedside table said it wasn't even six yet.

There was a loud pounding on the door downstairs. Mack was drawing blanks, but even without knowing what it was, he felt accused.

"Mack! Mack!" The call was hushed and urgent, the voice familiar.

All at once it came back to him. It was Rick. Today was the day. Mack dropped his head back into the pillow, furious. He had never said he was going. He'd said he'd see, he'd let him know. He should have known that wouldn't be enough. There was no such thing as the polite brush-off with Rick. Rick never could get it through his head that people had real lives that had to be tended to. Some people didn't have time for fools' errands.

There was another round of urgent pounding and then silence. Mack waited a couple of minutes more, slid quietly out of bed, and moved to the edge of the window.

Rick was still there. Mack stared down on the thatched, unruly blond hair, the tense, angular features. Rick paced up and down the patio, hunched up against the morning chill, his hands jammed deep in his pockets. Mack didn't recognize the jacket; he must have borrowed it from somebody. Mack remained perfectly still, hidden by the shadows of the curtain.

He knew Rick about as well as he knew anyone, and yet there was something about the figure below that was herald-like and vaguely threatening. On the street beyond three or four stray dogs trotted in and out among the garbage cans, scavenging. Rick came back to the door and rattled the knob. People got shot as prowlers for less.

Finally Rick gave up. He searched his pockets until he found a pen and a piece of paper. Using the adobe wall as a writing surface, he scribbled furiously, then knelt down and slipped the note under the door.

As he rose to his feet he suddenly looked up, staring directly at the window. Mack, caught off guard, took a couple of quick steps back. He wasn't sure whether Rick had seen him or not. Mack leaned against the closet and waited. He heard the latch close on the patio door, Rick sprinting up the hill, and, after a minute, the growl of a car engine turning over.

Mack bent over and picked up a roll of reinforced packing tape. He whirled and threw it at the picture of Kaia's birthday party on the wall. It hit a couple of inches high, bounced back, bounded across the floor as if it had a life of its own.

Mack lay down again for a half hour but couldn't go back to sleep. He finally went downstairs and retrieved the note from under the door. He unfolded it.

Where were you? Coronado was a quitter and so are you, creep. Take care, Rick.

He backed his pickup into the strange driveway, careful to avoid hitting Annie's car. He swung to the ground, let down the back of the truck, seesawed one of the boxes of packed linens toward him.

The walk to the house was lined with old lilac bushes and there was a dirt yard filled with weeds and some apple trees. A wire fence in need of repair separated the yard from the dry riverbed. He wondered how safe it was. Imagining Kaia playing in this yard didn't make him feel good at all.

He climbed the steps to the house, the box of linens in his arms. He heard movement inside and then Annie appeared, pushing the screen door open for him. Her face was flushed and she had a rolled-up bandana tied around her forehead to hold back her long red hair.

"Kaia's asleep," she said.

Mack said nothing. When Annie had said come at two, he assumed it hadn't been accidental. Kaia would be taking her nap; it would save a little awkwardness, a little pain. He moved sideways past her into the house, their eyes sliding past one another's.

He stood in a tiny room with slanting floors and cracked adobe walls. Bare pipes, hookups for some long-departed washer and dryer, jutted out of the ancient linoleum. Annie was using the room for storage. There were the familiar duffel bags, the car seat, the woven basket stuffed with Kaia's toys, a pile of quilts and blankets.

"Tell me where," he said.

"Anywhere," she said.

He set the box down. He could see into the kitchen. A round wooden table shone with sun from the skylights; a bucket of soapy water sat in the middle of the floor. Annie rubbed the corner of her nose with her wrist. Her hands were still wet. He had to give her credit for being a trouper.

"Where is she sleeping?" Mack said.

"Back there." Annie nodded down a narrow corridor running off the kitchen.

The floorboards creaked under even his most cautious steps. He leaned into the first doorway he came to. His daughter lay curled up in the far corner of the crib, away from the streams of afternoon light. There were no curtains on the window yet. Kaia's red McDonald's tennis shoes were on the floor. Babar and the stuffed mouse leaned against one another in a rickety hand-made bookshelf. Mack pushed himself away from the door.

"Six-fifty a month you're paying for this?"

"That's what places cost in the summer. In the summer, that's a deal."

"You mind if I look around?"

"No," she said.

She let him go on his own. The house was only partially furnished, a jigsaw puzzle of impoverished rooms. The framed poster of one of Mack's concerts leaned against a battered Baldwin piano. There seemed to be light switches everywhere. The first two that Mack tried didn't work. An overgrown rosebush rested against the living room window. Every detail seemed a condemnation, an accusation of failure. It was hard not to take it all personally. Mack ducked his head coming through doors.

Annie was in the hallway, cleaning a long mirror. She saw the reflection of him standing behind her. They stared at one another, their gazes locked.

She let the paper towel drop to her side. Her blue-green eyes were unwavering. The house was still.

Looking at her in the mirror, he felt as if he was seeing her with perfect clarity. He knew why she got angry and why she got silent, what it was she wanted and needed. It all made sense and was no reflection on him. The only terrible thing was that she was still such a part of him.

Neither of them moved for almost a minute. He came up behind her and put his arms around her. She shut her eyes. She didn't want him to do this.

She opened her eyes and saw the sadness in him. She put her hand over his. They were still not beyond giving comfort to one another. He felt her finally relax into him.

She rested her red hair against his short blond beard. Everyone had always said what a handsome couple they were. There was a low, shuddering moan above them.

"What's that?" Mack said.

"The skylight," she said. "It's the wind that makes it do that."

Mack released his hold on her, stared up at the milky plastic sheet in the ceiling. In the square of the skylight someone had mounted some faded stuffed songbirds on a slender branch. Again the wind moaned through the rippled plastic.

"I don't know why we're doing this," Mack said.

"Yes, you do, yes, you do," she said.

"It's crazy, I don't want my daughter living here. She should be in her own room. If we're really going to go through with this, let me be the one to get a place."

"It was my idea. I made the decision."

His voice began to rise. "So what does that matter?"

"You're going to wake her up," Annie said. She walked away, dropped the crumpled paper towel in the wastebasket. Mack could see the muscles tightening around her mouth. A *ristra* of bright red chilis hung on the far wall. "I'll fix the place up. Nothing's perfect."

"Now that's true about just about everything, isn't it?"

It wasn't the right tone. There was a grocery bag full of plastic cups and plates on the kitchen counter. Annie began to lay them into the empty shelves, not facing him. There was a snatch of the amplified voice of a tour guide, the sound drifting in from somewhere out on Canyon Road.

"You said we couldn't afford anything more. You said that."

"So we're fighting about money?" Mack said. They were both struggling to keep their voices down. "Is that what we've come to?"

"That's only part of it," she said.

"But it is part of it," he said.

She turned back to face him, furious. "I can't stand it. I feel as if everything is always my fault and I can't stand that feeling anymore; I feel as if I'm always failing you. That's why I'm here. You know that, Mack, don't try to pretend that you don't . . ."

The first fitful cry of the child froze both of them. They waited in silence. The skylight moaned briefly, and then came the longer, sustained cry from their daughter. It sounded like she was up for good.

He had been a golden boy, whether he ever admitted it or not. The older men on the country-western circuit, the ones in the cheap imitations of Marty Robbins's sequinned jumpsuits, would watch his act and shake their heads. What he was singing was country, but it wasn't *country*. It wasn't gospel, but it was about as sincere as you could get. Whatever you called it, cross-over, cosmic cowboy, or outlaw rock, there was an audience for it.

Mack felt as if he had a bright secret in his heart in those days. The secret was that there was no secret, you just sang from the heart about those things that you cared about. If you did that you couldn't go wrong. There were songs about old men haunting the railroad stations in small Kansas towns, about an Indian cafe in Winslow, Arizona, about elk driven down out of the mountains by winter snows.

He really believed he was going to have it all. He was going to be rich, famous and honest all at the same time. He was going to be the one exception; he was going to be the lucky one. There were a couple of hit singles and for about a year he was touted as the next Kris Kristofferson. The first album didn't do that well, but it really didn't matter, because he knew that the next one would.

He had met Annie at a Fourth of July party at a friend's house in Taos. She was a painter, working as a waitress at Ogilvie's, sharing a place with a girlfriend. Mack's first impression was that she was filled with a lot of dubious notions about astrology and holistic medicine, but there was an astonishing directness to her, a gracefulness. She claimed she had never heard any of his songs. They took horses and rode to the end of the freshly mown pasture and back, Mack's eyes watering fiercely from the pollen.

That night there were fireworks in the backyard—someone's teenage sons scheming in the darkness, setting off bottle rockets and twelve-dollar-and-fifty-cent extravaganzas that fizzled wildly, spinning erratically across the grass. The adults huddled under blankets, leaning against the adobe wall, passing a wine bottle. Coming out of the house, Annie made a place for herself next to Mack. She made that seem like an easy thing to do. After the fireworks someone brought out a guitar and Mack sang. He sang only Woody Guthrie and Hank Williams. On the Fourth of

July anything else would have been sacrilege, but he did sing them to her.

The next two albums did decently, nothing terrific. When the baby came, Mack cut down on the number of concerts he was doing so he could spend more time at home. After a year, when he started to get panicky about money, it wasn't so easy to get those concerts back. Even in a year musical tastes had changed. People had stopped chanting, "Take me high-er, high-er . . ." in packed stadiums. Mack felt as if he was being pigeonholed as some sort of sixties throwback. Integrity was an act that people had stopped buying. "It may be, old buddy," his bass player told him, "that all our ideas have gone to the great bunkhouse in the sky."

For the first time he had to hustle for dates. There were glowing times that seemed so simple and deep, sitting in his chair playing his guitar while Kaia scooted and bulled her way around the kitchen in her walker, or the three of them strolling down to the plaza after dinner for ice cream, Kaia strapped to his back.

There were also times that were not simple at all. Mack would come in at two in the morning after a concert and Annie and Kaia would both be asleep. He would pace the dark house trying to unwind, knowing that the child would be up in four hours. Two or three times he made the mistake of waking Annie, just to be able to say a word to someone. She would stare at him, groggy and confused, too exhausted to speak.

They were being pulled in different directions. There was a new edginess to him. He was worried and brooding and he was taking it out on Annie in ways he scarcely realized.

Fights began over the smallest things, a letter he'd said he'd mailed and then forgotten, a pecan pie catching fire in the oven. "If I want things done I will have to do them myself," she would say, and the remark seemed to contain as much despair as it did determination.

They would always make up, try again, there was no question of their good intentions; and yet there was a growing sadness, some acknowledgment that not all wounds heal perfectly.

He slaved for months over the tape for his new album. Songs that would have come effortlessly before he now worked and reworked, willing them into existence. The trick was, how could he sing what was in his heart when he didn't know what was in his heart? The day he sent the tape in he took Annie out to lunch to celebrate. He told her he knew it was the best stuff he'd ever done. He didn't even know if he believed it or not.

A week later he got the nonstop phone call from his agent. "I know you busted your balls on that tape. I told you, I *like* the songs, I'm just telling you what they said. They don't know who the audience is. The songs are nice, Mack; it's just that nobody's got time for nice. I'm not saying you've got to go around with paper clips in your nose or pretend you're a robot. May I be frank? For a minute? Times have changed, but your music hasn't. O.K., some people don't have the ear for it. People want songs about mountain streams, they got John Denver, what can I do? How am I going to get people to dance to a song about Spanish land grants, for chrissakes? It's not like your life has ended. You still got your band, right? Cancel? So they cancelled. It's just semantics. You come up with something terrific, we'll go in there and bust ass, we'll knock their socks off . . . One big score, buddy, and what's happened today, we'll just be laughing about it . . ."

He didn't tell Annie, but it worked on him, which meant it was working on her. Several days later she started up about unwashed dishes left in the sink and Mack felt rage welling up in him. He walked away, trying to control himself, then swung blindly through the hangers in the hall closet, sent them scattering like frightened birds. "I can't stand it," he said, "most of the time I feel like I'm just holding on."

She was shaken by his outburst. She knew this was something different from anything they had gone through before. After he calmed down he tried to modify what he'd said. He hadn't meant, "most of the time." He had overstated things; that's what anger does to you. They had things to work on, sure, every couple did, but he loved her more than anything. His efforts at reconciliation didn't work. She had seen something. "We were wrong about things," she said. "You shouldn't have married me." The next day, over breakfast, Annie said she thought it would be a good idea if she moved out, at least for a time.

The skylight shuddered again. "I'll go in and get her," Mack said.

"I can go," Annie said. Mack hesitated, not sure whether she was saying she didn't want him to go. The silence hung darkly between them. Kaia cried out again. Mack went ahead, not waiting for permission.

Kaia was standing up in her crib. One of her cheeks was a bright red from being slept on. She stared blankly, surprised to see him. He felt her sizing him up.

"Hey, Kaia," he said softly. "How are you, honey?"

She still didn't reach out for him. He lifted her up. Her blue eyes widened and she raised her arms to her neck, trying to wake up.

Mack carried her back into the kitchen. Annie was down on one knee, laying pots and pans into the shelves under the sink. She rose slowly and Mack could feel the anxiety in her.

"Juice," Kaia said, pointing to the refrigerator.

Mack balanced her on his hip, got out the juice pitcher and poured some into her Donald Duck cup. They sat down together on a chair, Kaia still clinging to him. It was an old routine. She raised the cup. His hand covered both of hers. Half her face seemed to disappear into the cup and she drank for a long time. Annie moved warily across the sun-dappled room. She stood behind a chair, ran her hand along the worn wooden back of it. She raised her eyes to meet his. It wasn't any easier for her than it was for him. A motorcycle roared past on the street. Kaia pushed the cup away, put her arms between her legs, snuggled up tight against her father.

"So what are you up to today?" Annie said.

"I'm going to the party at the museum. You were invited too, you know."

Annie pushed the chair back under the table. "Have you seen Rick?"

"Yeah, as a matter of fact. He's starting to get on my nerves."

Kaia slipped out of his lap and went around behind her

mother. She stuck her head between Annie's legs, staring back at Mack, still trying to figure things out. All Mack wanted to do was shout back at Annie, don't you realize what a precious thing is at stake, how dare we risk it, how dare we . . . He said nothing, just picked up the plastic Donald Duck cup, swirled the orange juice around in it.

Kaia ran suddenly back into her room. She came back with her red baseball cap with the Little Slugger emblem on it. "You gave me this," she said.

"That's right," Mack said. He reached out and drew her to him. She stood patiently between his legs as he fixed the baseball cap on her head, smoothed her blond hair. "Your Daddy gave you that."

She twisted around and squinted up at him. "Are you still my Daddy?"

He picked her up quickly, held her close. "Yeah, honey, I'll always be your Daddy."

Cradling his daughter to him, he made a vow. He was not going to lose the two of them. He was going to find an answer. Rage welled up in him. He remembered Rick's note. Rick had been wrong. Mack was not a quitter, not this time.

From somewhere behind him he heard a flurry of sharp tappings against glass. He whirled around, chilled by the same sound that had wakened him that morning.

At the far window of the living room he could see the overgrown rosebush nodding and swaying, thorns raking across the glass. The huge bush lolled about like a shaggy eyeless head. The sound was like a cat trying to scratch its way in. Uncertain light flickered through the dark, bowing mass. It was as if something was trying to claw its way into his life.

He handed Kaia over to her mother. "Your Daddy's got to go, honey, Daddy's got to go."

Chapter Two

IT WASN'T until the first clean notes of the flute that Mack looked up and saw the golden plume of dust moving along the dirt road, still a mile off. For a second it seemed as if the music drew the car onward. Mack squinted into the glare of the falling sunlight, made out the familiar green Datsun, coming much too fast. He couldn't be back. Not already. Mack squeezed the empty plastic glass, heard it crackle in his hand. He wasn't going to let Rick trap him.

Mack stood at the top of the hill, under the edge of the party tent. He was talking to a tall, healthy-looking girl in a long silk dress. She was back from Hollins College, visiting her mother, a local gallery owner. She recognized Mack's name and was sure that she'd heard some of his songs, but then she made the mistake of asking him if "Desperado" was his. He had to say no, that was the Eagles.

Trying to be polite, Mack glanced casually past her and saw Rick angle his Datsun in behind the long staggered line of cars at the bottom of the hill. Rick climbed out, arched his back, stretched the way you do after a long drive, halfway across New Mexico and back in the same day. Rick's problem had never been a lack of energy.

Mack watched as Rick shielded his eyes with one hand and stared up at the party. Mack was still under the shadow of the tent; Rick couldn't see him, not yet. There would be a story, there always was, and Mack would be the one Rick had to tell it to. Rick had always counted on Mack's being a sympathetic listener. What Mack needed now was a few hours' reprieve, a chance to get his bearings. It was time to split.

He looked back at the lovely young girl. He hadn't quite caught what she'd said. No, he said, "Rhinestone Cowboy" wasn't his either.

Mack excused himself as graciously as he could. Walking away he gave the sculpture of the Navajo goatherd a light tap with his knuckles. It gave off a nice, hollow bong. So what if the girl hadn't recognized him? She probably wouldn't have recognized Willie Nelson if he'd come up and put his pigtail in her drink.

Santa Fe was out in all its comic-opera splendor. There was a chamber music quartet playing in the patio of the museum and there was just about any kind of artist you'd ever dreamed of meeting. There were Navajo impressionists, quarter-blood Sioux neorealists, Pueblo potters and a California Indian in a Hawaiian shirt and red sneakers who did Coyote paintings in acrylic and glitter. A pair of young aides came out of the museum carrying a piñata. It was shaped like a bull, and bright strips of paper fluttered in the breeze as they hoisted it, tied it to one of the trees. A world-famous anthropologist held forth on the meaning of Qaddafi's sunglasses to a group of museum benefactors while just behind them a blond Mill Valley divorcee in three-toned Foster Grants who claimed to be a medicine woman cruised the crowd. A New York *Times* journalist was hunkered down in the sculpture garden, teaching the retired president of a major airline how to drink Tecate with lime.

Harry seemed to be doing fine. Harry Dakota was Mack's buddy, a Cheyenne carver who did ceremonial pipes and shields. He had his dark hair in braids and with his gold tooth, orange San Francisco Giants baseball cap, raffish smile and the white sandals he'd found rummaging under Mack's porch, he looked like a coyote.

He was still backed up against the buffet table, right where Mack had left him fifteen minutes before, nodding sagely, listening to a young woman in an eight-hundred-dollar Navajo shawl explain how she knew she was the reincarnation of a Hopi princess. Harry always enjoyed the show.

Mack dropped his plastic glass in a trash basket, paused for a second until he caught Harry's eye and gestured that he was leaving.

Mack looked down the hill one last time. He saw Rick's lean figure laboring up the slope, among the low juniper. Around Mack clean-boned women glided like swans, flattered by the fading light. Rick scrambled over the loose rock, always in too big a hurry to take the main path. In the tricky, ever-shifting light, the lone figure toiling up the slope seemed like a messenger from another world.

Again there was a flurry of bright notes of the flute. Mack turned and saw the flutist, diminutive, red-bearded, in his tuxedo, sitting in a folding chair. The other members of the quartet watched as he bent over his instrument, closed to everything except the sound of his own music.

Mack couldn't wait any longer. He began to move through the crowd. If he went around the museum and circled back to his car he could manage to avoid Rick.

The sunset was spectacular. It lit up the mountains a blood-red. That was where they got the name, *Sangre de Cristo,* "blood of Christ." It cast its spell, shifting, red, purple, gold, lighting fires down on Cerrillos Road, turning that strip of motels, gas stations and hamburger chains into a string of gleaming diamonds, bathing the desert and mountains beyond in haze.

There were some who had stopped to stare out across the desert at the sunset, awed into silence. Others kept talking, as if by some witchery the glowing light was spurring them into excess. Mack slipped through the crowd, catching snatches of the talk.

"Man sold more gems in Europe last year than Harry Winston and no one knows who he is . . ."

"A genuine out-of-the-body experience, right there at the public pool . . ."

"An abandoned airstrip in Florida, eight million, you can't beat it . . ."

"Sawed the house in two, took pictures of it, and that was it, that was his art . . ."

"An option, plus he does the screenplay and I heard he was going to suit up for the football sequences . . ."

Mack slipped behind the museum wall, moved down under the piñon and juniper. He felt slightly ashamed, sneaking off, but it was better this way.

He made his way to the dirt road. He saw his pickup, wedged between a Mercedes and a Volkswagen camper bus with all the right stickers. It was going to be a trick getting out. He reached into his pocket for the keys.

"Hey, Mack! Mack!"

Mack turned and saw Rick standing at the top of the hill. The intensity of the light made Rick's gaunt figure, silhouetted against the party tent, seem like an ancient sentinel. Mack leaned against his truck, dropped the keys back in his pocket. Rick loped down the hill toward him.

Rick was tall, with the aristocratic good looks of a pro tennis player. He was also looking a little scared these days, not so sure that people were glad to see him. Rick was a man of a million schemes and every one of them, Mack had to admit, had flashes of brilliance. Every one of them also failed. Rick was going to build utopian communities in the desert, collect medicinal plants in the Amazon, start genetic engineering firms, produce films. He was attracted to long odds.

He claimed to have blown a two-million-dollar inheritance on his projects, and he may have. When he first came to Santa Fe he was a dazzler. He *looked* like the young heir. Three years later he owed money to half the people in town. There were endless stories of him bumming cigarettes, credit cards, places to stay, free trips to England. He still managed to be charming enough to avoid being labelled a deadbeat, but it was getting close. His lean good looks had started to turn a little cadaverous and haunted. Some people said he was drinking too much.

He had the kind of mind that could entertain any notion. Mack loved that about him. Rick saw things fresh, he made your mind stretch. He could convince almost anyone the first time and usually the second. The problem was that Mack and Rick had gone way past that.

No one could be promising forever. That was something

Mack knew all about. Promise had its darker side. There was shame in Rick now. Imagination was a tricky business. His schemes had become progressively more outlandish and the latest one was the maddest of all.

Rick came up to Mack a little out of breath, with that feverish excitement that Mack had seen so many times before.

"Rick, how you doin'? Look, Rick, I'm sorry about this morning, but I've got to run check on something for the band . . ." Mack pulled his car keys back out of his pocket.

"I'm not going to keep you long, man. Not long at all. I just want you to look at something." Rick reached inside his jacket and lifted out a dirty, yellowing piece of paper. It was folded over a half-dozen times. There was the steady look of triumph on Rick's face.

"You drove all the way down to Roswell?"

"Yeah." Rick began to carefully unfold the piece of paper on the fender of Mack's pickup. A stinkbug tottered bravely across the rutted dirt road.

"That's a hell of a drive, Rick. That didn't give you much time. Did the old lady even see you?"

"I got what I wanted."

"You did? And what was that?"

"Take a look." Rick smoothed the paper out with the flat of his hand. Mack just stared at him. He wasn't going to make a friend feel like a fool, even if he was being one. Life was hard enough.

He looked down. The discolored paper had lines of dirt at the seams; it was falling apart. It had to be at least twenty years old. For a second Mack didn't know what he was looking at. A child's drawing, he thought at first. It was nothing but faded lines, scribbles, uncertain doodling. He glanced up at Rick.

"You're not seeing it," Rick said. "Look again."

Mack stared a second time and then he saw that there was a single figure, a small hunched form bent over a reed or a stick of some kind. This figure, or attempts at it, was repeated a dozen times on the tattered sheet. Mack found the figure oddly repellent.

"So what is it? Some kind of inkblot test? I'm supposed to tell you the first thing it reminds me of?"

"Tucker drew these, Mack. The last three days he was alive. Lying in that hospital in Albuquerque and he couldn't talk, this is what he did. He drew these pictures."

"Thirty years ago."

"That's right."

Mack folded the paper delicately, handed it back to Rick. "You're crazy. I'm going home." He tried to open the door to the pickup, but Rick put his hand against it, preventing him. Mack's eyes widened in surprise. "Hey," he said.

Roy Tucker had found gold. That was the one thing no one could argue about. There was forty years' worth of evidence, from a prewar snapshot of Tucker in front of an Albuquerque pawnshop, holding a gold bar up for the camera like a proud father showing off his newborn child, to the now famous TV clip of G. Ferris Hall, the country's most flamboyant lawyer, placing an ingot on the desk of Nixon's chief domestic advisor.

Tucker had been an Indian trader and small time prospector, a handsome fellow who always dressed in an all-black cowboy outfit and carried a gun, a man who had served a little time in the state penitentiary for minor offenses.

In the late thirties Tucker claimed that he had found a cache of gold bars stacked like cordwood in one of the canyons of the Rio Grande. He had found something. For a number of years he would show up in pawnshops around the state with a gold bar or two, carve off a piece with his hunting knife, sell what he could, and go on a drinking spree till his money ran out.

Tucker played it close to the vest. He was afraid of robbers on the one hand and law enforcement on the other. He moved from one town to the next, selling a bar here, a bar there, trying not to attract attention. There was a story that went around about Tucker hiring a plane to fly gold into Mexico at night, the plane crashing and killing both pilots.

Then Tucker accidentally blew shut the entrance to his cave in a dynamite explosion. That, at least, was what he would claim later. For more than a year he hauled timbers up into the canyons on the sly, trying to reopen it. Then came Pearl Harbor. The entire area, along with White Sands further south, was condemned and sealed off as a military test site.

Desperate and penniless, Tucker disappeared into Texas for a couple of years. When he came back he had a partner who had loaned him twenty-five thousand dollars to renew the effort. The two men penetrated the test site at night. Tucker took the man to several caches, fifty bars near the remains of an old ranch, thirty more in a shallow arroyo. In spite of this, the partner was convinced that Tucker was holding out on him. Tucker had told him of thousands of bars. The two men fought, and Tucker ended up with a bullet in his skull. He died three days later in an Albuquerque hospital.

The story was a long way from over. In the early sixties Tucker's widow filed an affidavit with the state land office complaining that the Army was mining her claim. The Army denied it and refused her access. Within the month there were four more affidavits. A group of men, sneaking into the test site at night, had seen jeeps and bulldozers, mining wedges and electric generators, cables running into caves.

After a year of wrangling between the state and the U.S. Army, a team of archeologists, reputable academics, was granted permission for an expedition to prove or disprove Tucker's claim of a cave full of treasure. They found nothing, no tailings or slag heaps, no signs of ancient mining sites. Their report concluded, "If a treasure was or is here, it was brought from some other location or stored here by persons as yet unknown."

An archeologist's report wasn't enough to keep people from dreaming. In New Mexico there had always been stories of lost treasure, there had always been legends. In the beginning there had been Coronado and Cortez, mad Spanish expeditions in search of the Seven Cities of Cíbola, El Dorado. There was the Lost Dutchman Mine. There were the stories Harry Dakota had told Mack of the Indians fleeing Santa Fe during the Spanish Reconquest, taking treasure and hiding it in the canyons. There was the fortune of the deposed Mexican Emperor, the puppet Maximilian, gold and silver sent north by the wagonload, captured first by ex-Confederate soldiers, and then by Apaches. There were tales of renegade priests hoarding gold under abandoned churches. The stories seemed to feed on themselves; in New Mexico it was part of the air you breathed, the Southwest's longest running dream.

In the mid-seventies the story of Roy Tucker surfaced again, hatched out like some seven-year locust, and in spectacular fashion. A group of well-financed adventurers from Atlanta went to work gathering information from all the previous claimants, including three men who had actually seen the gold. They hired G. Ferris Hall to get the government to open the canyons to them. On the first go-round the government refused.

Then during the Watergate hearings the White House counsel testified that the Attorney General had told him that G. Ferris Hall had a client with access to an enormous amount of gold and was trying to make a deal with the government. The next day Hall, in a press conference on the steps of the Treasury Department, told reporters that his people had actually witnessed two tons of gold being removed from the New Mexico test site. He had notified the Secretary of the Treasury of this and no action had been taken. "The law, gentlemen, is not being enforced."

The press went wild. The government had no real choice but to yield. The bargain struck was that Hall's group could have eight days to prove their claim.

The exploration turned out to be an eight-day fiasco. Reporters flocked in from all over the country and the first thing they discovered was that the Army had just completed bulldozing dozens of the caves, sealing them off with metal doors. The Army's only concern, their spokesman said, was for public safety.

Every morning convoys of thrill seekers and news teams bumped over the dusty dirt roads into the canyons. Network cameras tracked the explorers into spectacularly barren crevasses. The National Guard was called in to issue press passes. The explorers had the most advanced electronic equipment, including ground radar powerful enough to penetrate the core of a mountain. Tucker's widow, in her seventies, sat in a rocking chair at the mouth of the cave, waving people away. "Please step back, sonny, the man's going to take my picture." She admitted that Tucker had never actually taken her to the cave, but she was sure this was it, this was just the way he had described it. Camera crews scrambled up and down the rocks behind her, sound men tottered on the slopes, their long-stemmed mikes waving before them like witching sticks. The figures being bandied about were fifty to a hundred tons of gold. Excitement grew as signs were discovered that others had been in the cave before them. There were collapsed timbers, old dynamite caps, a rusted pickax.

Then their luck turned. On the third day one of the men was seriously hurt in a fall. On the fourth day the leader of the expedition claimed that they had found a bar of gold, but the claim was withdrawn within twenty-four hours. An accusation was made that someone in the expedition had planted the gold to keep the exploration alive. The networks packed up their cameras and melted away like critics in the second act of a musical that doesn't have a chance. The adventure sputtered to its end.

Mrs. Tucker was furious. She swore that the gold was there. She had seen it with her own eyes, all those years she and Tucker had stayed up, talking into the night, scheming how to get back to it. Tons of gold couldn't vanish into thin air. A couple of the local broadcasters and the stray freelancer were the only ones who bothered to listen to her now.

Mack watched the whole thing on television along with everyone else. Did he buy it? He didn't *not* buy it. Still, a person would have been a fool to talk about fifty tons of lost gold with an utterly straight face. Nothing had been proved, one way or the other. Like every story that lacks an ending, it just dissolved on the back pages of the local newspapers, and Mack forgot about it.

He forgot about it until two weeks ago when, over coffee at the Palace Bakery, Rick brought it up. At first Mack was sure Rick had to be putting him on. He wasn't.

"Listen to me, Mack, now listen to me . . ." Rick knew the

story front to back. He had gone to the museum to read the archeologists' report, talked to the local lawyers and geologists who'd worked on the case.

Rick had a gift for persuasion. Too many people had seen some part of the gold—some, a bar or two, others, caches of sixty or seventy bars. They couldn't all have been liars. Something had been overlooked. Rick had run across a piece of testimony from a Mexican worker who swore he'd seen Tucker riding *in* to the cave site with full packs on the backs of mules, and riding out with empty ones. Maybe Tucker had discovered gold on a claim that wasn't his. Maybe Tucker had been moving gold from one site to the next, then staged its discovery.

It almost sounded plausible. "So what are you going to do?"

"I'm going to see if I can find any of these people."

"Rick, come on, they're probably all dead."

"Maybe. Maybe not." Rick's hand trembled over his coffee cup. His lean, tanned face suddenly had a hard set to it; the fact that people had ceased to believe him had made him bitter. "I want to know what you think."

"Honest opinion?"

"Honest opinion."

"I think it's ridiculous. I think it's cornball. Boy Scout stuff. It makes me think of decoder rings. I always thought of you as such a forward-looking guy. This is total regression. Go back to microchips. Lost gold—that's the creakiest old story in the world."

"Yeah. But I'm trying to get you to look at it in a new way."

"Rick, it's a waste of your intelligence."

Rick didn't like that much. He left then, pretty sullen, sticking Mack, as usual, with the check. Rick didn't enjoy honesty much.

Lost gold was from another age. It was a throwback, an anachronism, the daydream of everyone's grandfather. It was a Hank Williams song in a John Denver world. It was trying to sing "Tumblin' Tumbleweeds" when everyone was shouting for more reggae. Mack knew there were still local eccentrics going out every weekend with their maps and Geiger counters, but they were crackpots and everybody knew it. What was Rick thinking? The week before he'd been sitting there, at the same patio table, in his LaCoste shirt, telling Mack how they were going to make their fortunes in synthetic DNA. Lost gold. You might as well believe that spacemen were coming down in UFOs to dissect cattle with their special surgical instruments.

For a week Mack didn't hear from Rick and assumed the lost gold scheme had gone the way of all the others. Then Rick called Mack to tell him he had found Tucker's widow and was driving down to Roswell to see her, and did Mack want to go with him? Mack had waffled, thought he had put Rick off. Mack should never have underestimated him. Now Rick showed up with the fevered scratchings of a man who'd been dead for thirty years.

Two couples in evening dress were getting out of a baby blue Lincoln just down the road from Mack and Rick. Rick stared at the folded piece of paper in his hand. The sinking sun cast long, magical shadows through the sagebrush around them. Rick wasn't letting Mack go.

"Don't you see, Mack? He was trying to tell her something."

"What was he trying to tell her, Rick? This dying man keeps drawing weird little pictures of some hunchback, or whatever the hell it is. What is it, Rick?"

"I don't know."

One of the women coming down the road toward them had on a tight shimmery black dress; it almost looked like fish scales. She had to take dainty little steps across the dirt road. Her husband, beefy in his black tuxedo, was giving her a hand. The sunset bathed their faces; their laughter rang like tiny bells. Their wavering shadows stretched twice as long as their bodies.

"It's sick, man. A poor old guy, he's as paranoid as hell, spent half his life trying to hide a few gold bars from Wells Fargo and bandits, half his brain's been shot out, he puts some scribbles on a paper and you want to make it into something."

"It already is something, Mack. She'd never shown it to anyone before."

"And why didn't she?"

Mack caught the flash of a bird sailing into a low juniper just beyond the pickup. It was a camp-robber, a fat black and white magpie.

"She didn't think it was important." Mack saw the terrible need in Rick's eyes, the need to believe what he was saying.

"Rick, Rick, come off it . . ."

The two couples moved to the far edge of the road as they passed, staying out of harm's way. The woman in the shimmery black dress glanced discreetly, not quite sure how serious the disagreement between Mack and Rick was.

"She opened up for me, Mack." Mack looked away; the outline of the mountains to the west was as unstable as a mirage. The magpie hopped from branch to branch, sharp-eyed and impatient.

"Sure. And the next time you go down there she'll probably have a real Treasure Island map that she's discovered in the handle of a knife. She's lonely. She liked having someone to talk to."

"It's out there somewhere, Mack. I swear to God. When I talked to her today I was sure of it. It was just a hunch before, but today . . ."

"You're in the wrong movie, Rick. That one's over."

The mountain behind the museum was glowing. Mack could still hear the chamber music, the laughter drifting down from the party. The scavenger magpie scolded them from the safety of the juniper.

"I'm tired of being nobody, Mack."

"You're not nobody, Rick. Don't get dramatic on me, man."

"You know what I'm talking about. You should be doing something great, a guy like you, and you're not."

"You want us all to be great, don't you, Rick. We're all going to be great . . ." Mack yanked open the door to his pickup.

The sound of oohing and ahhing at the top of the hill made Mack turn his head. The crowd had gathered in a circle. The girl in the long silk dress, the one he'd been talking to, stood at the center, blindfolded, a six-foot pole in her hands. She swung wildly, missing the piñata by a mile. Everyone laughed. The tuxedoed musicians folded up their chairs, locked their instruments, and came to join the fun. The last stragglers hurried up the hill. The girl swung two, three times, then nicked the foot of the papier-mâché bull, spun it on its cord. With her next swing she hit it straight on, split it; the prizes scattered everywhere. There was a great cheer, children and adults alike scrambling for treasure on the blood-red hill.

Mack climbed into his truck. "You're not going to get me to believe it." He flipped down the sun visor to block some of the glare, and slammed the door shut. The magpie, startled off its perch, glided out of the tree, the black and white thief winging its way into the low haze. "Not this time, Rick, not this time."

Chapter Three

THEY WERE old men, bare skin painted in black and white horizontal stripes, their hair woven into horns of cornstalks. They shuffled in and out of the long lines of dancers, their laughter eerie, inhuman, a hoarse mechanical gobble. They were koshare, sacred clowns, and when they got thirsty they danced sucking sno-cones snatched from unwary vendors. Mack had trouble taking his eyes off them.

He and Harry Dakota stood side by side on the adobe rooftop, looking down on the maze of dancers. The back of Mack's neck burned from the hours of sun. The August heat made him dazed and a little sick. The singing of the men rose and fell; the drumming kept on, relentless. The flag bearer, one end planted in his groin, let the heavy pole and its banner of fox pelt and eagle feathers bend and weave over the painted dancers, its rhythmic dipping a blessing, a prayer in a code unknown to Mack. He glanced over at Harry. Harry stood with his hands folded over his chest, his orange Giants hat pulled low to shade his eyes. He was not giving out clues. Mack was on his own.

There were a couple of hundred others, almost all Indians, on the rooftops around the plaza. Kids scampered fearlessly up and down the rickety wooden ladders. In the plaza there were at least a thousand more people. Some of the Indians had set up folding chairs at the front and sat with umbrellas raised to protect them from the sun. The sun was still almost directly overhead and within the foot or so of precious shade along the pueblo alleyways people crowded in like sardines.

At the near end of the plaza there was a bower of some kind, covered with branches of evergreen, but Mack couldn't see into it. They had been dancing since mid-morning. The men, their long, black hair glistening, were naked from the waist up, their bodies painted ochre. They had foxtails hanging at the back of their belts, bells strapped to their legs and ankles. In their left hands they carried seed rattles. The women were barefoot, dressed in black mantas and elaborate silver and turquoise jewelry, their faces framed by *tablitas*, tiara-like painted headboards, and carried sprigs of evergreen. The men's steps were higher, more insistent, almost leaps, the women's more submissive. No one seemed to grow tired. They danced on, utterly absorbed.

As remarkable as the dancers, at least to Mack, was the attentiveness of the Indian onlookers. No one seemed fervent or particularly pious, but they just kept watching patiently, hour after hour. No one seemed restless. Mack wondered what they were waiting for, what it was that held them.

Mack watched too, but there was too much he didn't know. The small turns of the dancers, the merging and breaking of lines, the sudden cries, were part of a pattern and he lacked the key. He felt shut out. His attention wandered.

There were other outsiders there too, outsiders of every degree. There were two Indian women in their mid-twenties, clearly urban and educated, standing by themselves, wearing designer jeans and tasteful straw hats. They must have grown up here, Mack thought, or maybe their grandmothers are here, and they're not quite sure if they belong or not. There was a cluster of European tourists, all blond and wearing sandals, speaking German. A longhair in lavender overalls with a macaw on his shoulder strolled barefoot among the booths. A toothless old gringo with a cheap medallion around his neck wandered through the crowd, trying to start a conversation with every pretty woman he saw. The nuns and the priest from the church stayed on the edge of the crowd, greeting friends. An English poet and his teenage daughter stood at the booths, examining the T-shirts with the pueblo designs.

The day gradually burned away the circus fringe. Mack's

head started to throb; the battered cowboy hat he wore didn't offer protection enough from the pitiless light. Wind came up, swirled dust through the plaza; the onlookers raised their forearms to shield their faces. A crippled old Indian woman dragged herself on her hands along the wall of one of the buildings to find a better place to see. The chanting and the rattles and the drumming were working on Mack.

There was a moment, just before noon, when a couple of clouds drifted overhead and there was a brief sprinkling of rain. A murmur had run through the crowd, but in minutes the clouds were gone; there hadn't been enough rain to even settle the dust.

When the sprinkling of rain came, one of the koshare grabbed an umbrella from someone in the front row and hid himself under it, drawing a big laugh. As far as Mack could tell they were the Indian version of the Marx Brothers and yet they were more too. They prowled in and out of the dancers like aged black and white striped cats, stopping to straighten a child's costume or retrieve a fallen strip of bells. They mimed the gestures of the dancers, mocked unwary tourists with lewd remarks, sat in the middle of the plaza thumping on watermelons like Barnum and Bailey clowns. They seemed to Mack to be fantastic creatures, malevolent and foolish at the same time, utterly fluid, without boundaries. On this day, at least, anything was permitted them.

Early in the afternoon there was a great ruckus on the outskirts of the crowd. A koshare had overturned the cart of one of the vendors, apparently for refusing him food. Dogs sniffed at the ice-cream bars melting in the dust. People were laughing. Mack watched the koshare strutting triumphantly away.

Harry watched, smiling, without making any effort to explain. He was Mack's closest friend. They fished together, went dove hunting in Colorado in the fall. Mack admired Harry's painstaking carvings in stone and wood and Harry was one of the few people he didn't mind talking to about music. Yet there were some subjects Mack knew better than to go near.

It was Harry who had asked him to come. He thought it would take Mack's mind off of things. There was no way Mack

was going to get his mind off of things. On the way out to
Harry's he had driven past Annie's new house. Her car wasn't in
the driveway. It struck him as odd, their not being there at
eight-thirty in the morning. He tried to tell himself they were
out doing laundry. Still, it was the kind of thing that stuck in
your mind.

It was mid-afternoon now and Mack needed to get out of the
blazing sun; he felt curiously light-headed, as if he might faint.
He told Harry that he was going to get something to eat.

He climbed down the ladder and moved through the narrow
passageways, a mangy dog slinking away before him. Glancing
into the adobe houses, he could see the shadows of Indian
women moving inside, hear them speaking in a language he did
not know, smell the cooking food.

Mack moved past the temporary booths that today ringed the
outside of the pueblo. One of the young girl dancers—she
couldn't have been more than twelve—stood in line behind a
dozen other children, waiting to play Pac-Man. She waited patiently, her painted *tablita* framing her face, her two quarters
pressed firmly between thumb and forefinger. Inside the small
curtained booth came the warlike bleeps and explosions of the
electronic game, the sharp sounds cutting into the deep chanting still going on in the plaza.

Ahead of Mack in line for hamburgers was a very prim and fit-
looking woman in a tennis hat. "Well, I suppose it works," she
said to her friend, "if you believe in magic."

Mack got his chili-burger and lemonade and stood at the edge
of the mesa, staring out across the desert. Sun gleamed off the
narrow ribbons of water in the nearly dry riverbed. Far to the
south the wind was whipping up a dust storm. Everywhere else
the air was so clear that Mack almost felt as if he could reach out
and touch the distant mesa that he knew was thirty miles away.

Indian children raced on the slopes below him. They were
playing Cowboys and Indians, darting from bush to bush, using
sticks as guns. One boy, shot, clutched his chest and rolled down
the hill. Two other boys argued about who had been shot first.
The smaller boy waved his stick gun in the air, protesting. "You
didn't get me. I'm not dead yet, I'm not dead . . ."

Mack ran his finger across his lips. They felt cracked in the parched air. He rattled the ice in the bottom of his plastic cup, drained it. Not dead yet. No, sirree, Mack could buy that. He could still hear the chanting men's voices coming from the plaza. I suppose it works, the lady had said, if you believe in magic.

The question was what was magic and what wasn't. One part of Mack had always thought there was something a little pathetic about whites who came to Indian dances looking for enlightenment. Maybe they were a cut above the Santa Fe seekers who were into Tibetan Buddhism one summer, soul travel the next, but it was the same impulse finally. They were all people who had thrown off the shackles of whatever religion they'd grown up with, declared their own traditions bankrupt. But they still had the appetite for wholeness. So they tried to piece together spiritual well-being out of whatever broken fragments happened to be at hand, fitting stray bits of myth together like so many pottery shards. It was a pot, Mack had noticed, that did not hold water for long.

Mack had been to these dances before, he had seen these people, you could pick them out a mile away. They waited and watched, sometimes sitting cross-legged in the more conspicuous spots, as if they believed that if they were only steadfast enough there would be a breakthrough, some blessed rain would fall in their lives. The ironies were endless; the great-great-grandchildren of the conquerors waiting on pueblo rooftops for spiritual rebirth. The fathers had come as missionaries; now their children came back as pilgrims.

Their efforts were doomed to failure. They were locked out. It was not their language; they hadn't lived on this land for a thousand years. It wasn't their magic; it never would be. Mack didn't want to be too hard on them. He was here too, after all; he was one of them, in his own way. He understood why they wanted to believe. Hell, he even understood why Rick wanted to believe in the scrawled figure of a hunchback on a crumbling piece of paper.

Beyond the jumble of parked cars there were rides for kids, a merry-go-round and a Ferris wheel. Mack stared hard, not be-

lieving at first what he was seeing. A pair of koshare sat in the
Ferris wheel, sucking on sno-cones, riding around and around,
rising into the brilliant blue sky, waving to the children as they
came down. They were everywhere, their shapes endless. Mack
threw the last of his ice out onto the dusty slope.

When he got back to his place on the rooftop there was no
sign of Harry. Something had changed. The sun was beginning
to drop. The dust raised by the dancers hung like a golden haze.
Some of the big-bellied older male dancers looked tired, but
they were too proud to give in to it. Their faces remained
masklike. Drained by the heat, Mack was more susceptible to
everything. The steady throbbing of the drum fell in with the
beating of his own heart, became one with it, and the alterna-
tion of the drum carried him, tripped him, carried him further.
There was yearning in the air and even though Mack couldn't
pinpoint why, he felt himself growing more emotional. Mack
was vulnerable, more than he would have ever liked to admit.
He had grown up believing that Jesus would speak to his heart if
he only listened hard enough. He had never heard, not the way
he was supposed to hear; that was part of the problem when you
were a morally scrupulous child. It had, however, put him in the
habit of listening to the smallest of voices.

Once again there was a change, visible this time. The winter
clan, rather than leaving the plaza after their round of dancing
ended, took places on the ground in front of the front row of
spectators. It made the plaza even more tightly packed; even
the air seemed suddenly denser. The summer clan filed in,
following the drum, the chorus of old men chanting, the tireless
koshare moving in and out, waving their black and white
striped arms, sacred mimes cutting the air in age-old patterns.
Long shadows stretched across the plaza. An Indian woman
standing next to Mack on the roof put her hands on her young
son's shoulders and strained forward to see. Both of their faces
were alert, expectant. The deep singing of the men, the vast
cumulative effort of the day, was pierced by cries. The rattles
hissed like rain in the wind. The dance was over.

A hush fell. There was only the soft sound of ankle bells as the
dancers formed in two long lines. Everyone was silent and wait-

ing. Everyone was looking down toward the pine-covered bower. For the first time Mack realized that it was a shrine.

Four of the dancers emerged from the shrine, carrying a small, doll-like saint on a cushioned platform. The entire line of Indian dancers knelt, crossing themselves. One of the elders raised a rifle, fired into the air. The sound was brutal. Behind it came the ringing of a huge bell in the church at the far end of the pueblo, calling them all. The procession moved down the corridor of dancers toward the church. There was a rustling as others in the crowd behind the line of dancers began to kneel and cross themselves while the tiny saint, a delicate porcelain hand raised in blessing, passed by.

Mack felt a chill run through him. The past and the present suddenly existed side by side, available, time laid open like a side of beef. It could have been three hundred years before, long lines of Indian dancers kneeling before a saint and a gun. Mack knew the history, knew that the only way the ceremonies had been allowed to continue was by submission, by embedding them in Catholicism. Knowing it was one thing, seeing it another.

Yet there was reverence in those kneeling figures. One thing had not negated the other. If there was resentment, Mack didn't see it. Mack was stirred, almost upset. Maybe it was just the shock of seeing that diminutive painted figure emerge from that bower of cut green boughs, as though those hours of dancing had brought more than one god to life.

Their families gathered around the dancers. Vendors folded up their tables. A round, middle-aged Indian woman hugged another and wept; someone from her family had been unable to attend. "But he wanted you to remember him, all the same, he wanted so much to be here . . ." One of the older male dancers brushed stiff-legged past Mack, sucking on a Seven-Up.

Mack wandered through the crowd. He still did not see Harry. He hoped that nothing had happened to him. He squinted into the low, blinding sun.

He wound his way through the narrow passageways, slipped past one of the long, wooden ladders. Suddenly he saw, twenty yards ahead of him, a small blond girl standing alone. Her back was to him. One of the koshare stood a few paces in front of her, offering his hand, the aged black and white striped clown beckoning her on.

Mack stared for a second. It wasn't possible. The child took a hesitant step forward. Mack couldn't see her face, but there was something familiar, he was sure of it now. It was Kaia. The child toddled out of sight around the corner of the flaking adobe wall.

Mack began to run. At the corner he stared wildly in one direction and then the other. The child had vanished. Four or five dusty passages forked off like spokes off a wheel. Mack ran from one to the next. Insane thoughts whirled and darted past one another like fighting birds. How could Kaia be here? And where was Annie? Yet he had seen what he had seen.

At the fourth of the narrow alleyways, he saw the child again. She had taken the hand of the koshare. They had left the shadowed maze; the clown led her into the bright sunlight. Mack could still not see her face. Again the two figures slid out of sight around the corner of the building. Mack was suddenly in the grip of overwhelming terror and loss. "Kaia!" he cried out.

Again he ran. As he came out of the narrow passageway there was suddenly a hand on his elbow. Mack whirled angrily. A mild-looking Indian vendor in a turquoise shirt with ribbons shrank back. He hadn't meant any harm. In the man's outstretched palm was a silver bracelet.

"I'm sorry . . . I'm sorry," the vendor said.

Mack said nothing. Thirty yards ahead of him, in the open plaza, the little girl was rushing into a woman's arms. The woman wasn't Annie. As the girl squirmed in her mother's embrace, Mack could see her face for the first time. It wasn't Kaia. Mack stared, stunned at how utterly foolish he had been. Except for the blond hair, there was no resemblance to Kaia at all. The koshare tilted his head to one side, perfectly harmless, waving goodbye to the little girl.

"Would you like to take a look?" Mack shook his head no. The vendor still held out the bracelet, almost pleading.

Mack took it from him, stared at it. There was a dark figure engraved on the silver band, a small, hunchbacked figure bent over a slender reed. It was the same figure that Rick had shown

him. Roy Tucker's fevered scribblings had been more precise
than even Rick would have dared guess.

Mack looked up at the Indian vendor. His creased, brown
face was innocent, devoid of any conspiracy. He was just trying
to make one last sale for the day. The little girl had her arms
tight around her mother's neck, happy to be reunited. The two
of them made their way slowly down toward the snarled traffic.

"This figure," Mack said. "Where does it come from?" Mack
heard someone call his name. He recognized Harry's voice, but
he didn't look up.

"From all around here," the old man said. He gestured to the
mesas that swept the horizon. They were glowing in the late-
afternoon light. "In the caves all around here."

Mack turned the bracelet over and over in his hand like an
amulet, considering, staring at the hunchbacked figure.

"And does it have a name?"

"A name? Of course." The old man smiled, as though he
thought Mack was joking with him. "He's called the flute
player."

Chapter Four

MACK CAME across the Hopi tale on his first day of looking. It was a story any musician would have loved.

The Hopis had started their migration from one world to the next and were climbing a mountain. Travelling with them were two of the insect people, the flute players. An eagle blocked their way and would not let them inhabit the new land until they passed two tests.

The eagle took an arrow in his talons and told the flute players that he would jab the arrow in their eyes and if they did not flinch, they and the Hopis could stay.

The eagle jabbed the arrow within a half-inch of the eye of one of the flute players and he never even blinked. The eagle was impressed, but he warned them that there was a much more difficult test remaining.

The eagle picked up his bow, put the arrow to the string and shot the first flute player through the chest. The flute player made no effort to pull it out. Instead he lifted his flute and began to play. "They are much more powerful than I thought," the eagle said to himself, and he took a second arrow and shot it into the second flute player.

Both wounded now, the two flute players lifted their flutes toward the sky and played with such tenderness that the vibrations healed their pierced bodies.

With that the eagle gave the people permission to stay on in that land. He gave them his feather to use whenever they wanted to speak to their Father Sun, the Creator, and forever after the eagle would serve as their messenger.

The flute player was not an easy figure to pin down. Mack read that he was the oldest of the Pueblo supernatural beings, going back possibly as far as the Mayans in the first century. One of the accounts he read claimed that the flute player was the archetype of the earliest trader and that his hump may have been a basket of birds or a sack of seeds. He appeared all over the Southwest, in the cave drawings and pottery designs, and still existed in Hopi dances.

He was a trickster figure like the koshare, straddling the worlds of good and evil. He was an enigma, a shape shifter, associated with rain and fertility. He was as phallic as all get-out. His favorite pastime was seducing women, whom he would favor with blankets, babies or seeds from his hump. At the library Mack would sit staring at the photographs of the ancient petroglyphs. In one the flute player looked like an insect or a turtle, in another like a phallic Pied Piper or a feathered jazz-man.

Staring at photos in a library was one thing. Trying to unriddle the relation between the flute player and Roy Tucker's drawings was another. It seemed like an impossible leap. Why had Tucker drawn that figure again and again? Tucker scarcely seemed like the myth-mongering type.

Mack hadn't told Rick anything. He wasn't quite sure why. Maybe it was just that he didn't want to look like a fool, and maybe it was just that he wanted to explore by himself for a while.

It was an hour's drive south to the test site. He knew he wasn't going to find anything. He was just curious. That's what he told himself. He had no plan, though it wasn't a half-bad idea, beginning where everybody else had gone wrong.

He was driving against traffic, a steady stream of day workers whizzing past on their way home. The mesas had started to glow in the afternoon light; a few scattered cattle foraged on the bone-dry flats. As the highway began to wind into the mesas,

Mack began to see the wire fences with the blue government signs, an occasional water tower or warehouse set back off the road.

By the time Mack reached the junction there was almost no traffic at all. He pulled his car over on the gravel, as far off the road as he could get it. He stood by his open car door for a minute, just staring at the highway. A lone bread truck rumbled past and then there was no one.

Mack strode through the wheatgrass to the high wire fence. The sign was standard stuff. WARNING: Restricted Area. All persons and vehicles entering are liable to arrest and search.

There was a certain dread Mack always felt around this place. For forty years this area had been closed off. What had been top secret was no secret now. The forces they had unleashed had changed the world, changed even the way people dreamed. The possibility of universal annihilation had started here. It was impossible to even stand next to the chain-link fence without feeling a little prickle of contamination.

The place still did have its dangers. Every so often there would be an article in the local papers about some teenager wandering across an unexploded mine and getting his leg blown off.

Mack stared through the wire mesh fence at the scrub juniper and piñon, the low ridges beyond. He wasn't sure what he'd thought he'd find. Maybe the old roads or signs of mining, some clue. It was really too much to expect that he'd just stumble blindly onto something. Still, he felt let-down. It had been a long ride for nothing.

Mack reached up and curled his fingertips tentatively through the wire mesh, considering what to do. What came next was sheer impulse. He found a toehold in the mesh, lunged upward, chain-link rattling beneath him, and in two moves had a grasp on the top of the fence. He could feel the wire cutting into the palms of his hands. He took a deep breath and with one final scramble he mounted the fence, then dropped quickly to the other side.

He rose from his knees, breathing hard, dusted off his jeans. He heard the sound of a car. He waited for several seconds until a pickup came into view, loaded down with firewood. It rambled past without ever slowing up.

Mack began walking through the brush. His palms were bleeding and he pressed them to his shirt to relieve the stinging. He had no goal, except maybe to get out of sight of the road. He half shuffled and half slid to the bottom of an arroyo and then followed its erratic path.

Mack squinted at the rock outcroppings all around him. The fading light made it easy to imagine whatever he wanted to imagine. He couldn't help it; part of him really was watching for a flute player carved on a rock, just the way it happened in all the adventure stories he'd read as a boy.

After about a mile he climbed out of the arroyo. The thought of someone spotting his car and reporting him gave him a brief spasm of anxiety, but he tried to put it out of his mind. He would go five minutes more. A jackrabbit loped slowly in and out of the juniper, not sure whether to flee or not. A stillness had come over the landscape. It could be 1940; there was nothing to tell him that it wasn't. There was a steady singing of insects and the blooms of the low-growing cactus glowed blood-red in the setting sun. The folds of the ancient rock were as worn as an old robe.

He came over a rise and looked down at the old roadbed. He felt his heart leap up. He stared down the road in both directions. At first he tried to convince himself that he recognized it from the old TV clips of caravans of gold seekers and news teams bumping through these hills. But then he realized that it was ridiculous, there was no way he could be sure. It looked like no one had been over this road in years.

He moved along the dirt road, unconsciously picking up his pace. Some rusted metal cable snaked across his path for a couple hundred yards. Far above the dark blue line of the mountains he could make out the trail of some distant jet. The road forked and forked again, became more deeply rutted. He had no idea where he was and there was no more than a half hour of sun left. He promised himself he would turn back at the next ridge.

As he trudged up the incline he heard the yipping of a coyote.

It didn't sound that far off. He stopped to scan the surrounding brush, thought he saw a gray shadow slide into the piñons. It could have been a jackrabbit, a dozen things. It was then that he saw the giant metal door set back in the ridge, no more than twenty yards away.

He wiped his mouth with the back of his hand, not quite ready to believe what he was seeing. There were the old marks of earth-moving equipment, furrows and embankments, dirt bulldozed up against the gleaming door. Mack ran his hand over the bright metal surface, still hot from the afternoon sun. There may have been gold here, there may not have been, but this was where a hell of a lot of people had thought it was. That was plenty for Mack's imagination to run with.

He tapped it with his fist and then hit it harder. There was a faint echo. He hit the metal door harder still and the sound came booming back, reverberating like a tomb.

"What the hail do you think you're doin'?"

Mack whirled around at the sound of a voice. The sun was right in his eyes. He could make out a mounted figure, maybe fifteen yards away, silhouetted in the stabbing light, with a rifle trained right on Mack. For a foolish split-second it occurred to Mack that he was staring at Tucker's ghost. He shaded his eyes, ducking to one side, trying to see more clearly.

"Nothin'," Mack said.

"Nothin', huh?" The man pulled his rifle up, rested it on his saddle. He was awfully fleshy-looking for a ghost. He looked like he was about sixty. His belly came down over his silver belt buckle; he had a meaty, sun-reddened face and lots of things jammed in his shirt pockets. "You can't read signs?"

"I didn't mean any harm," Mack said. "I just came to look."

The man laughed. "I've heard that before," he said. The horse snorted impatiently.

"Well, I'm sorry. I'll be going, then. No offense."

"I hate to tell you this, son, but you're under arrest."

"Arrest? For what?"

"Trespassing on government property." He swung one of his legs up, rested it across his saddle.

"Well, damn," Mack said.

"You got any identification on you?"

"Driver's license."

"I better have a look at it."

Mack got out his wallet and fumbled through his cards until he found his driver's license. As he handed it up to the man, Mack saw the badge of the U.S. Army pinned to his chest. The rider examined the license for several seconds, flipped it over to see if it was signed. He looked back at Mack.

"Mack McLaine? You the singer?"

"Yeah."

There was a trace of amusement across the rider's face. "You the one who sang 'Lookout Mornings'?"

"Yeah."

He glanced quickly to see if Mack was putting him on. "Hell, that was a damn good song." He looked at the license one more time, shook his head. "Hard to believe, a man of your caliber . . ."

"Beg pardon?"

He leaned forward and handed the license back to Mack. "I guess people never do learn, do they? Now what are you going to do with all that gold when you find it, huh? Or ain't you thought that far yet?" He laughed again, jammed his rifle back in its scabbard. "I like your music, though, I really do." The horse yanked on the reins and the rider let them out enough for the animal to graze.

"I'm going to tell you something. I was raised around here. I knew this fellow Tucker growing up and my father knew him real well. You know that cave where he said he found all that gold? I was down in there dozens of times when I was a kid. There never was anything down there. Except a lot of bat shit." The rider gazed down at his horse tearing away at the wheatgrass. "Mack McLaine, amazing. My wife is not going to believe this when I tell her. Now just what the hell am I supposed to do with you?"

Mack was silent. The light had faded from the metal door.

"Oh, Lord," the old man said. He swung down off his horse, shook his legs out, trying to get rid of the numbness. He sat

down on a rock and pried a pack of cigarettes out of his shirt
pocket, jabbed it in Mack's direction.

"Smoke?" he said.

"No, thanks."

"Got to look out for the voice, right?" the old man said. He
tapped a cigarette out of the pack. "Biggest liar I ever met,
Tucker. Ever meet anybody who just loved to lie? Well, he loved
it."

"You saying there never was any gold?"

"Not saying that." The old man stuck the cigarette in the
corner of his mouth, searched for a match. "But if there was
any, it sure as hell didn't come from where he said it did." He lit
his cigarette, took a long drag off of it. His horse wandered back
into the brush, stripping the low branches of leaves, but the old
man didn't seem concerned. "You know, you could do me a
favor."

"What's that?" Mack said.

"My wife would be just tickled pink if you could sign your
name to something. She loves your stuff and she'd never believe
me otherwise."

"You got something to write on?" Mack said.

The old man stood up and once again went through his pockets. He came up with a wrinkled deposit slip and a pen. "Just
make it out to Edna Springs, that would be nice."

Mack used the metal door as a writing surface. He made the
inscription warmer than usual, handed the autograph back. The
old man read it and seemed pleased. He folded it carefully and
put it in his shirt pocket.

"I hope you weren't serious about this," the old man said.
Mack stared at him blankly. "This gold business."

"Oh, no, no," Mack said.

"I'm only telling you these things because I hate to see a
quality-type person like you get mixed up in something like
this. I don't suppose you'd be old enough to remember, but
there were stories in the papers back in the forties, when this
first came up. Well, hell, Tucker claimed he found this gold in
thirty-eight." The old man took off his battered hat and ran his
finger around the sweatband. He was nearly completely bald

and there was something oddly touching about that pale white crown sitting on top of the tough, windburned face. "I know for a fact he came into my father's office a good year before that. Daddy was a lawyer and he never would tell me everything they talked about, but Daddy claimed Tucker put a bar of gold on his desk and wanted to know how to get rid of it. One year before he claimed to have found anything." The old man put his hat back on and flicked his cigarette away, end over end.

The light was about gone. The horse crashed its way in the heavy brush. Mack leaned against the metal door, just staring at the old man.

"I really don't know how you do it," the old man said. "Get up there and sing in front of all those people. That would scare me to death."

"You been working out here a long time?" Mack said.

"I've been a range rider for the Army since they closed it off in forty-two."

"That's a long time."

"Sure is. Harold Springs is my name." He leaned forward, offering his hand.

"Nice to meet you, Harold," Mack said. The old man's grip was a crusher.

"I'll tell you, I've seen about every kind of nut there is up here. Mostly I just try to keep people from breaking their legs, falling into holes. Caught me one spy."

"You did?"

"Yeah. I could tell he was a spy too. You can tell by the way they walk."

"They say the Army was mining the gold for themselves up here. I don't know. That's what they claim. They say that's why the Army bulldozed all the caves shut."

Mack saw the range rider's jaw tighten. "I can't comment on that. That's the Army's business. Who said that, anyway?"

"I guess I read it in the paper. I think there were a number of people who said they had seen generators and lights up here at night, cables running into some of the caves. As a matter of fact, I think Tucker's wife was one of them."

"Well," Harold said. "She claimed she was Tucker's wife." He kicked one boot against the other, looked up for a second, whistled for his horse.

"You telling me she wasn't?"

"If she was then Tucker was a damned bigamist on top of everything else. I know. I saw that woman on TV too, ranting and raving. She never was from here. She was some woman Tucker met in Texas after he left. She didn't know diddly. She just believed what Tucker told her."

"There was another wife?"

"I guess he was married to her. Back when my family knew him, Tucker was a trader and he was living with some Indian woman. When things got rough, Tucker just ran off and left her."

"And where is she now?"

"Dead, probably. That was a long time ago." He walked toward the brush, whistling again for his horse. "Come on, girl, get out of there." He glanced back at Mack, a look of disgust on his face. "God, I sure as hell hope you're not serious about this."

Chapter Five

Roy Tucker's other wife wasn't something that Harold
Springs had made up. It was a matter of public record. All it
took was a couple of hours running his finger down a list of
names at the county clerk's office before Mack found it. On
February 20, 1936, Roy Tucker had married Antonia Vigil. It all
stared up at him from the certificate: her birthday was August 8,
1917; birthplace, San Carlos Pueblo.

His run of luck couldn't go on forever. At the San Carlos
Pueblo he stopped at the police station, persuaded a priest to let
him look through old church records, and after several hours,
knew no more than when he'd started.

He pulled his car over to the side of the road and asked a
courtly old man sitting on his back porch if there were any
Vigils in San Carlos. "Sure," the old man said, "fifty or sixty."
"Do you know any of them?" Mack asked. "Sure, I'm a Vigil
myself." The old man seemed more interested in the four dogs
playing tag around his woodpile. "Never heard of anybody
named Antonia, though. That an English name?" Mack began
to feel as if he were going about things in the wrong way.

The San Carlos Artist's Cooperative seemed like a long shot,
but it was the only place he hadn't tried. Before he got out of the
car he reached across the seat and scooped up the silver bracelet with the curve of dark flute players etched into it. He put the
bracelet in his back pocket. It couldn't do any harm.

The place was empty. Mack stood alone in an immense,

spanking-clean lobby full of floor-to-ceiling display cases. There
was an insistent hum of air conditioning and no sign of anyone.
Toy bows and arrows were mounted above the cash register and
a Sidney Sheldon novel, cracked open, lay facedown on the
counter. Taken aback, Mack hesitated, sure he must have made
some mistake. He ran his hand along the display case. There was
row on row of turquoise jewelry, the names of the artists on slips
of paper. The old man had been right; every third name was
Vigil. What he was looking for was impossible, he realized that.
It was all buried too far in the past.

The sound of women's laughter made him start. The laughter
fell away and rose again. Mack tracked the sound, walking past
the display cases to the end of the lobby, pushing aside a
brightly painted curtain.

He stared into a cavernous, gymlike room. It had the feel of
something built with federal money. Four women sat at a long
table, weaving baskets. Bright red cans of Coke dotted the
corners of the table.

The youngest of the four, no more than eighteen or nineteen,
looked up and her eyes widened in surprise. The others turned
in their chairs. A middle-aged woman in a pale green pantsuit
rose from the table.

"Can I help you?" she said.

"I was just looking, thanks," he said. He rubbed the back of his
neck. "There are some lovely things out there. It's hard to make
up your mind."

The two youngest looked like sisters, both in T-shirts. One of
the T-shirts had YALE blazoned across it; the other, the name of
the local high school. A slender, straight-backed woman of
about seventy sat at the end of the table, working the sharp
point of her tool into the tightly woven basket. Her silver hair
was pulled back in a bun and she had an almost regal reserve
about her.

Mack took the bracelet out of his back pocket. "Tell you what
I've had my eye out for." He handed it to the woman in the
pantsuit. "You ever seen anything like this?"

"Oh, yeah." The woman nodded. The table was filled with

coiled strips of fiber. She smiled and passed the bracelet to one of the sisters. "Where'd you get it?"

"I bought it from a man at San Pedro a couple of weeks ago."

"The Hopis make a lot of things like that," the woman said. The two sisters examined the bracelet together, too shy to look up at him.

"That's what I heard," Mack said, making it up as he went. "I liked it and wanted to see if I could find something to match it. So I was passing by and I just had a hunch . . ." The silver-haired woman worked on, not missing a stroke with her awl. "If you know anyone . . ."

The woman in the green pantsuit considered for a minute. "My cousin, he does silver. I don't know if he's ever done anything exactly like this, but I know he could make you one, it would be beautiful."

"That would be great," Mack said. The bracelet was passed on to the silver-haired woman. "You'll have to give me his name and number."

The middle-aged woman thumbed through a stack of notepaper on the table until she found a clean sheet. One of the sisters handed her a pen. The silver-haired woman rolled the bracelet over slowly in her palm.

Mack leaned against the table while the woman wrote out the number. "Maybe you could help me with something else too," he said. The older of the two sisters reached into the bag of chips that lay on the table. "I'm trying to locate a woman who was born here a long time ago, Antonia Vigil. If she is still alive she must be, oh, over seventy. Her married name was Tucker."

The middle-aged woman stopped writing for a second, glancing swiftly at him. The silver-haired woman set the bracelet gently back on the table. The two sisters shared a handful of potato chips. It hadn't registered on the two of them at all.

The woman in the pantsuit pressed down with her pen, scribbling to get the ink flowing again. She handed the note to Mack.

"You can call him at night," she said. Maybe it was just Mack's imagination, but her voice seemed much cooler than it had been before. "He gets back about seven."

"Thanks." He folded the piece of paper and tucked it in his

shirt pocket. The silver-haired woman had gone back to work, splitting a long strip of fiber. Mack stared at the gentle, imperturbable face. For the first time it occurred to him: he could be looking right at her.

"You may have heard the story," he said. "It was all on television about five years ago, a group of people suing the government to open up the test site. They claimed there was lost gold in there."

The older of the sisters licked her fingers of salt, peeping at him, not quite sure whether she should laugh or not.

"I know," Mack said. "The whole thing was incredible. But they claimed there was tons of it in there somewhere, Coronado's gold, who knows?"

"I think I saw something about that," the woman in the pantsuit said.

"This fellow Tucker claimed he had found it, way back in the forties. Ended up getting shot for his trouble." The oldest sister couldn't help herself any longer; she giggled.

The silver-haired woman concentrated on her weaving, each tuck and pull of fiber coming even more swiftly than before.

"This Tucker was married at one time to a woman who was born here," Mack said. The middle-aged woman drummed her pen in the palm of her hand, the corners of her mouth pulled downward. She wasn't sure of him anymore.

"And why are you looking for her?" It was the first thing the silver-haired woman had said, and the calm, precise voice took Mack by surprise. One of the sisters handed the bracelet back to him. Mack jammed it into the back pocket of his jeans.

"I think I might have come across something that belongs to her," Mack said. The silver-haired woman ran her hand around the rim of her basket, checking for imperfections. She was making it clear that she had nothing more to say.

"I never knew anybody by that name, uh-uh," the middleaged woman said, shaking her head. One of the sisters took a long swig of Coke, still watching him. Her eyes were bright. She was ready to hear more of the story.

"Well, thank you," Mack said. He stared at the silver-haired woman, but she wouldn't raise her eyes. He patted his shirt pocket. "I'll give your cousin a call tonight. If you don't mind, I'll just look around for a minute."

He browsed through the half-stocked shelves in the huge room, playing for time. Even with his back turned, he could feel the silver-haired woman watching him. He wanted to give her a chance to make up her mind. It was her, he knew it; he should just turn around and ask her. He heard the two sisters laughing and bantering back and forth in Tewa.

He finally picked out a couple of three-dollar ornaments. He wasn't quite sure what they were, crisscrossed Popsicle sticks wound with bright yarn and adorned with feathers and glitter. They looked a little like South American God's-eyes.

He turned back to the table of women. "I think I'll take these," Mack said.

The woman in the pantsuit started to get up, but the silver-haired woman waved her back down. She would take it herself. Mack waited for her, held the curtain to one side to let her pass, then followed her into the lobby.

"Would you like a bag for that?" she said.

"No, thank you." Fluorescent light gleamed off the display cases.

After she had rung up his purchase she looked steadily at him for several seconds. "Do you mean any harm?"

"No harm," Mack said. "No harm at all."

"You're not with the government?"

"No, I'm not with anyone."

The silver-haired woman tucked the dollar bills deep down into the cash register, pushed the drawer shut. "She has not been treated well by people. I haven't seen her for a long time. The last thing I heard was that she was living in El Rancho by herself." The brightly woven God's-eyes lay untouched on the glass counter. The silver-haired woman picked them up and handed them to Mack. She took his hand and Mack felt an unexpected pressure, a sudden urgency in her grip. "If you find her, you tell her that Maria still thinks of her and sends her blessing."

Even at twenty miles an hour it felt like the washboarded road was going to tear the bottom out of his car. El Rancho was a collection of trailers and shacks along a dry riverbed, a place where bad times had never left. Along one stretch of the river there were twenty or thirty crushed car bodies mysteriously half-submerged in the sand. Mack drove slowly in and out of the cottonwoods, leaning forward on the steering wheel, straining to make out the names on the battered mailboxes. A pair of mules stared back at him over the top rail of their corral.

Just beyond the corral there was a long-haired kid standing on top of an adobe house, smashing at the roof with a crowbar. Dust pulsed higher around him with every blow.

Mack got out of his car. "Excuse me!" he shouted. He waved his arm over his head. "Excuse me!" The boy finally looked up vacantly, wiped the grime off his face with an elbow. He was naked from the waist up.

"I'm looking for a woman named Vigil," Mack said. "Pretty old. Indian woman." He raised his voice another level. "Her name could be Tucker too. Supposed to live somewhere out here."

A young German shepherd had roused itself out of the shade of the house and was padding down toward Mack at a good pace. The long-haired boy poked absently at the roof with his crowbar.

"Would you know anyone like that?" Mack asked. The German shepherd jumped up on him, wanting to play. Mack pushed him away.

"I don't know many people out here by their names," the kid said. He slapped at the back of his arm as if a horsefly was bothering him. "But there's an old Indian woman who lives over on the other side of the arroyo. The place with all the chickens."

The boy wasn't kidding about chickens. The small adobe house was set back under some massive cottonwoods and behind the house was a maze of coops and pens. From the road Mack could see birds strutting in the backyard and even a half-dozen hens roaming in the weedy dry arroyo. When Mack got out of the car a large white goose came full-speed out from behind the withered lilac bushes, ruffling its wings and honking, warning him off.

Mack moved toward the house, keeping a healthy distance between himself and the irate goose. He knocked at the door. There was no answer. He knocked again. The goose stood planted a few yards off, its beak raised to the sky, threatening an all-out attack. Mack stared back across the arroyo, saw a rusted icebox in the brush.

"Hello? Hello!" As he stepped back from the door he caught the movement of the curtain in the window. He turned his back and waited. A giant tom turkey appeared at the corner of the house, deep thrumming coming from somewhere inside the gaudy, puffed-up chest. He could hear faint sounds of movement inside the house.

He didn't turn around until he heard the bolt slide. The door cracked open no more than six inches. He could just make out an old woman's face staring up at him.

"Yes?"

"Mrs. Tucker? My name's Mack McLaine."

"What do you want?"

"I'd like to talk to you if I could." Through the narrow slit in the door it was impossible to get a good look at her. All that he could tell for sure was that she had a red kerchief in her hair and that she was dead set against him. "About your husband."

"I have no husband." The door began to close.

"Mrs. Tucker? I just want to show you something." He pulled the silver bracelet out of his back pocket and thrust it through the door. "If you could just tell me what this is."

"A bracelet."

"I know. But the figure on it."

"Some old Indian thing, I don't know." She didn't sound impressed. He could hear her TV going inside the house. He had interrupted her soap opera.

"You're sure you don't?" Leaning against the warm adobe wall, talking through the narrow passage, he was beginning to feel ridiculous. "It doesn't have any special significance to you, say?"

"No," she said.

"If you would give me five minutes, ma'am, I could explain. I drove all the way up here from Santa Fe . . ."

"Why would you want to see me? Go away. I'm an old woman. I didn't ask you to come here. I don't believe in bothering people."

Mack looked down at the bracelet, considered it for a minute. "No, ma'am. And I don't either. I'm sorry. I don't know what got into me."

Mack put the bracelet back in his pocket and headed back to the car, swatting lightly at the lilac bushes as he passed.

He pulled open the door to his car, the handle hot to the touch. He looked out. She had finally come out on the porch of her house.

She was slightly stooped, not a large woman. She wore a long faded black skirt and a blue checked shirt with the sleeves rolled up to the elbow. Her black hair was streaked with white, but she did not look seventy. She had the kind of full, round face where everything registered, and what registered now was worry. She squinted down at him, still holding on to the door behind her.

She made an impatient swirl with her hand. "Come on, then," she said. "It's a long drive back. At least I can give you a cup of coffee."

The house was just two rooms, a small living room where she must have slept, and a kitchen in the back. Everything was neatly organized and yet it had the smell of poverty about it, too many things packed away or jammed beneath worn couches. Side by side on the wall of the living room were a cedar crucifix and a likeness of JFK done on black velvet.

Mack sat at the kitchen table while she heated the coffee on the massive black iron stove. Sitting on a wooden platform in the corner were two pails of water, one with a dipper floating in it. Over the sink was an old photograph of an eight- or nine-year-old girl. She was beautiful, with long, black hair and dark eyes, and she sat on what must have been the photographer's pony, a patient beast decked out in a fancy white saddle and bridle.

She brought him his coffee, then after a moment of consideration, got down a plate of cookies and set it in the middle of the table. She sat down opposite him and began to sip her coffee. Mack sipped his, preserving their truce. It was the strongest coffee he'd ever tasted.

"You don't look like the others," she said.

"What others are those?" Mack said. Her face seemed remarkably young; the only place her age showed was in the folds around her eyes.

"The others who come to see me," she said.

"And what do they look like?"

"They look crazy. You don't look crazy," she said. She broke a cookie in two, a smile beginning to form. "But I guess you must be. All the same."

Mack smiled back at her. "All the same." She laughed, the sound so musical and playful it took Mack by surprise.

"You want to see it?" she said. "You want to see what I got? Sure you do. You come all this way. I showed the others, I can show you, a fellow with nice manners . . ."

She got up and went to a low pantry behind the stove. Mack stood up to help, but she paid him no mind. She tossed aside egg carton after egg carton and finally slid out a dirty cardboard box. When she tried to lift it, Mack took it from her and carried it to the kitchen table.

"Don't be in such a rush, now," she said. "Just sit down and let me show you."

She opened up the box and yanked out a heavy, jagged piece of slag, yellow and flaking. It was two feet across at the widest point. "This is what you're looking for?" It thumped down on the kitchen table.

She stood with her hands on her hips, waiting for his reaction. Mack ran his hand over the rough surface. When he pressed into it with his thumbnail, he could feel how soft it really was.

"Spillover gold," she said. "I was right there when he found it." Mack picked it up for a second. The weight of it caught him off guard.

"And these other things too," she said. She pulled out a silver cup, held it up to the light so Mack could see the date on the bottom: 1819. Next came an old Spanish sword, a rusted pair of spurs, a napkin ring. "He took all of this out of the cave. And people try to tell me there was nothing there. It was there all right. All gone now. Government took what was left. See this? Here's some real old letters that were down there in a chest, you can read them yourself."

She tossed the letters down in front of him. Mack thumbed through them, then set them aside. He heard a rooster crowing outside. He reached out and touched the jagged fragment of gold. It was hard to believe that he was looking at it. She had plunked it down as matter-of-factly as if it were no more than a skillet for supper.

"You have any questions?" she asked.

"Yeah," Mack said. "Who's that a picture of?"

She glanced over her shoulder at the photo over the sink. "My daughter."

"Where is she now?"

"She died."

"I'm sorry," Mack said. She pursed her lips for a second, the lines tightening around her eyes. He straightened the letters and set them back in the box. "Thank you for showing me these things," he said.

She picked up the silver cup, blew into it, cleaning it of imaginary dust, then set it back into the box. She walked to her back door. "I have chickens to feed," she said.

Mack followed her, catching the back door before it slammed shut. She had given him no sign whether she wanted him to go or stay. There was a big oil drum where she kept her feed. She took a big coffee can and scooped down into the drum, filled the can with corn.

Chickens came running in from all directions, like firemen on a drill, lurching from side to side. She tossed a handful of feed and the chickens darted this way and that, fighting over the nuggets of corn, afraid of missing out on anything. There was a pen of ducks further back and they pressed against the wire, quacking and complaining. The old woman came down the steps and flung another handful of corn.

"I have a little girl," Mack said. "She's almost three."

Mrs. Tucker glanced at him, her eyes dark with distrust.

"Well, you take care of her," she said. "Whatever else you've got on your mind. It's the most important thing."

He walked silently by her side, careful to avoid the whitish droppings in the grass. The chickens fussed and flapped around them. The rooster made runs at the others, trying to scare them off. Mack stepped over a plastic ice-cream container half-filled with yellowish water. She threw the corn underhanded, in long, loose arcs; it spattered like rain in the weeds.

When she came to the duck pen she stooped down and let herself in, pulled the door shut behind her. She poured corn into a long metal trough and the ducks flocked around her ankles, grateful as dogs. Mack stood on the other side of the wire.

When she started talking again, she didn't look at him. It was as if she were talking to herself. "We had gone fishing together. Way south of the mesas, down below the dam. He had never taken me there before. We walked up and down, up and down, and I said, 'You go on, I'm going to rest here.'" She straightened up, shooing the ducks out of her path. "So he went on by himself. In an hour he came back. I saw him stumbling over the rocks with this funny look on his face. I could see he was carrying something under his shirt. Almost like he had a baby under there."

As she walked to the door of the pen, Mack kept pace with her, the tight diamond pattern of chicken wire flickering between them.

"He kept falling down. I knew it was heavy, whatever it was. He knelt down next to me and just let it tumble out. This bar of gold."

She let herself out of the pen, fastened the wooden handle. She looked up at Mack.

"I just couldn't believe it at first. And he was acting so strange about it, he just looked so worried, like he wasn't sure what I'd think. But there it was. He took me to the cave where he had found it and I looked in, but I couldn't see anything, even with the flashlight, it went so far back." She turned over the coffee can and shook out the last kernels of corn. "But there was gold stacked up like firewood, he said, and skeletons tied up to stakes. He said he would never, never take me down there. I said that was all right with me." She laughed to herself, set the coffee can down on one of the low coops. "I mustn't ever tell anybody, he said. The more he talked, the more excited he got. All the way home we talked about how rich we were going to be. But every so often he would just get silent. 'I don't think you realize just how careful we're going to have to be,' he said. Then he was quiet for a while. Then he said, 'You trust me, don't you?' I said, 'Of course I do.' 'You're going to have to trust me a lot,' he said, 'trust that I'm trying to do the right thing.' "

She moved along a series of nesting boxes, checking each one. There was a frantic chorus of chirping from the cageful of chicks at the end of the row. She found three eggs, rolled them over in her hand, rubbing the shells clean with her thumb.

"At the beginning he would take a bar down to Albuquerque to sell it. We had a little more money, not a lot, you know . . . I told him he should file a claim, but he was afraid of what would happen if people found out." She slipped the eggs into the pocket of her skirt. "You see, in those years it wasn't legal to own gold. We wrote a letter to the U.S. Mint and they wrote us back, I've still got the letter somewhere. They said that if we would show them the gold they would tell us how much of it we could keep, if we could keep any of it at all. We didn't write to them again."

She picked up a piece of stray firewood and tossed it back on the woodpile. She sat down on the chopping block, lost in thought for a moment, gazing back at the chickens.

"So he went on, selling a bar here, a bar there. Then he started being gone a few days at a time, and when he came back I could tell he'd been drinking and he'd say he'd lost the money in a gas station or somewhere. He tried to blame it all on me. He was so scared somebody was going to take it from him. It started to make him a little crazy in the head. It got so all he could think about was how much was down there and how he couldn't take out more than a couple bars at a time." From behind them Mack heard the beating of trapped wings against wire. "Then he told me one day he was going to make his move. He'd gotten all these mules and hired this young Mexican boy to help him, he was going to take it all out at once. But the boy got scared when he saw what was there. He ran off and he must have told everybody he ran into because suddenly there were all these people up in the canyons looking around, following Roy everywhere he went. He tried to sneak out there at night, being more careful, but even that didn't do any good." She stared out across the arroyo. Mack could hear the sounds of the long-haired kid, out of sight behind one of the next ridges, still mauling his house. "He had gone down to sell a couple more bars and they came into his hotel room at night, ten men with guns, three or four he recognized as sheriff's deputies. They wanted him to take them to the cave where the gold was. They took him out into the desert and fixed his fingers up to the spark plugs of their car, they burned him with lighted cigarettes. He knew if he told them they would kill him so he just held on. They told him, 'You better tell us, because we're going to follow you, no matter where you go.' After he came back, the next day we packed up everything and moved. Didn't tell anyone where we were going."

She took the kerchief out of her hair, worked on the knot. There was an old hay rake next to the woodpile and Mack leaned against the curved, rusted seat.

"In the next couple years we must have moved five, six times. It was so hard on our little girl. We'd just get her in a school and we'd have to pull her right out again. He was so sure people were following him."

"And were they?"

"I guess they were," she said. "Every now and then I would see men driving by the house with guns in their cars. Once some man from the Secret Service came. We would get phone calls in the middle of the night."

There was a little breeze in the cottonwoods. The chickens had returned to their foraging, heads jerking, eyes shining and vigilant.

"He just got crazier and crazier. It got so I never knew if he was telling me the truth or not. And we were poor. All that gold and we had no money. He would sell a bar here or there, and then he'd drink it up or lose it or people would steal it from him,

I don't know." She smoothed the kerchief out on her knees. "He came and told me the cave was filling in with rock slides. The gold was getting harder and harder to get to. He said he was going to have to do something or he'd lose it for good. All day there had been those trucks driving by the house, back and forth. He'd made up his mind, he said. He was tired of living like a coward. I remember watching him back out of the driveway."

She went on in a gentle monotone. It was no longer as if he was being confided in; he had been appointed to bear witness.

"I'd kept Lillian home from school that day with a stomach-ache. I didn't think it was anything important. But in the afternoon she started to have a fever and it went up and up. I gave her aspirin and cold rags, but nothing I did helped. There was no one to call on; we were way out in the country then, we didn't have a phone. He came home from town about six o'clock. He had the dynamite packed in the back of his truck under old blankets. She was burning up and crying from the fever. He was all edgy and wound up. 'This is it, this is it,' he kept repeating. I said 'No, we have to take her in to the doctor, she's sick, she's never been sick like this before. Go in and look at her yourself.' But he wouldn't go in and look at her. 'I have to do this,' he kept saying, 'you don't understand, I have no choice.' And then he just ran out of the house."

Mack kicked at a splintered piece of firewood, glanced over at her. Her voice remained dispassionate; it was all a story now.

"All that night I tended her. I bathed her, rubbed her with ice. She started throwing up. I heard the cars going back and forth on the road and I knew they were looking for Roy. I remember holding her and her crying out and I turned around and I saw these men's faces at the window and I shouted at them, 'Go away, don't you see there is a sick child in here, go away . . .' She was quiet for about an hour. Then she said, 'Mommy, give me an orange.' I said, 'Honey, we don't have an orange, I'll get you one in the morning.' She said, 'But I won't be here in the morning, Mommy, I'll be gone to be with Jesus . . .' She died that night. I remember the car lights passing on the windows. If we'd taken her to the doctor that day we could have saved her. We could have."

The white goose paraded through the yard, lording it over the other fowl. Four or five hens explored a pile of tin roofing and old boards with the nervous intensity of looters.

"He came back that morning, all white and shaken, all cut up. When he first came in I didn't tell him nothing. There had been an accident, he said. He hadn't used the dynamite right. Instead of blowing it open, he blew the whole thing shut. I didn't say anything. 'What's wrong?' he said. 'You go and look at her,' I said. 'You got the time now, you go look at her.' We buried her the next day. He was around the house a couple more weeks. In and out. He was trying to figure out how to haul timbers in there, I'm not sure what. Everything gone between us. Nothing to say. Three weeks, he was gone. I never saw him again. I read in the papers where some man shot him, years after."

Across the yard, here and there among the weeds, were pockets of soft down and stray feathers like patches of spring snow.

"But when they all went into the test site looking, you must have heard about that?"

She smiled, folding her kerchief. "Yeah, I saw that all on TV. I saw that woman sitting there, talking about her gold, all the stuff he told her . . . It just made me laugh. She didn't know nothing about it." She waved away a fly and stood up. "They say he married that woman. That's all right. He wasn't my husband no more anyway."

She walked toward the porch. Mack followed her into the kitchen. She poured herself a cup of coffee, not even looking at him.

Mack stood by the table, ran his hand over the slag gold.

"Go on," she said. "Haven't I told you enough? You thought I had some secret, huh? You know all of them now. Just go!" she tried to wave him off.

"No," Mack said. He caught her off guard. She turned to face him, set down her cup of coffee. Mack found himself suddenly taut with emotion. "You have to tell me one more thing. Then I'll go." She was silent, her face stony with resistance. "Do you hate him?"

"No," she said.

"But how could you not hate him?"

She didn't answer. She took Mack's dirty cup off the table and set it in the sink, turning away again.

Mack brushed off his hands and moved to the door. "I'm sorry," he said. "I had no right."

"Don't be sorry," she said. Mack waited at the door, staring out at the chickens scratching in the yard. "When I met him he was a trader, very handsome. He always dressed in black, had a big pistol at his side. He had gone to all these places, you know, Alaska for eagle feathers, Montana for hides. He would come to us to trade for jewelry. He had so many stories, we would just listen and listen. I thought it would be so wonderful to go to all those places."

Mack turned back to face her.

"One day I asked him if he would cut my grinding stone. It was too heavy and I was forbidden because I was an Indian, that's what I told him. He was a white man, he could do it and nothing bad would happen to him. He sawed and sawed all day and he broke five, six blades. He never did get through . . ." She smiled for a second, then looked at the picture over the sink.

"I remember when Lillian was born. We had gone back to San Carlos to be with my mother and sisters, so they could help me. A week, the baby didn't come. Then the second week. Roy, he was getting so restless and cranky. Too many Indian in-laws around for him. So one morning he went out hunting and was gone all day. Then the baby started coming. My mother ran over to get the midwife. The labor took all afternoon and into the night and I kept thinking how mad I was going to be when I saw him and then I started worrying that something bad had really happened to him. Then the baby came. She was so beautiful and tiny, all red, her hands closed tight, cryin' and cryin' . . .

"Then he came back. A half hour after she was born, maybe. He was all covered in a white dust and his clothes were torn. He didn't have his gun, I guess he had lost it somewhere, but his eyes were shining, they were shining so bright . . ." Her hands were locked on the edge of the sink. She closed her eyes and Mack could see the tears on her cheeks.

"Everybody went out of the room then and left us alone. He came and got into bed next to us. He just lay there, stroking Lillian's head. Her hair was so wet and dark. 'This is going to be the luckiest girl in the world,' he said. And he squeezed my hand so tight. 'Where were you?' I said. 'You were gone so long I was scared something had happened to you.' 'Something did happen to me,' he said. 'Horse got away from me and I had to walk all the way back, through the canyon. It started to rain and I went for cover in one of the caves by the river, the ones with all the rock writing. You know what I saw? I lay on my back in the cave and looked up and there was a flute player, carved in the ceiling . . .' He patted the baby, you know the way they close their fist right around your finger. They grab at anything right when they're born. He said, 'I know it was a sign, it was a sign that we were going to be lucky.' "

She went to the buckets in the corner, took a dipperful of water, sipped at it, tossed the rest back. "He couldn't live without hope. Who can hate a man for that?"

The dipper bobbed on the surface of the water. "It can't be true," he murmured. "It can't . . ."

She gave no sign that she heard him. She stood at the table, putting things back in the box. If what she'd just told him was true, her whole life with Tucker had been built on a lie and she still didn't know it. From the moment their child had been born, he had been holding out on her.

Mack watched her jam the Spanish sword crossways into the old cardboard box, making it fit. No, he wasn't going to believe it. The road here, travelled by so many others, had been too treacherous, too full of blind turns and abrupt dead ends. It didn't seem possible that, in the end, it could be so utterly simple.

Chapter Six

"So DON'T tell him," Harry said.

"How can I not tell him?" Feet up on the dashboard, Mack took an imaginary jump shot through the window of Harry's pickup. In his mind's eye, his release was picture-perfect. "But I'm just afraid he'll go bananas once I do. You know how Rick gets."

Harry wheeled the truck across the bridge. "Doesn't look like we'll have to worry about picking up a fourth," he said.

Mack glanced across at the courts. There was a familiar figure squatting patiently on a ball under the near basket.

"You've got to be kidding me," Mack said. "You call him?"

"You know me better than that, Mack. I just come out here for recreation."

As Harry wheeled the pickup into the parking lot, Grier pushed up from the ball, raised a hand in greeting. He moved slowly across the grass toward them, proud-bodied as ever, basketball tucked under one arm.

Mack and Harry got out of the truck. If Grier was uneasy, he was determined not to show it. With one hand he whipped the ball across the grass on one slick bounce. Mack made the tough catch.

"Rick told me you guys were playing," Grier said. "Hope nobody minds."

"Hey, we got an open game here, Grier. You know that," Mack said.

Mack flipped the ball back to Grier and they moved onto the asphalt courts. Harry knelt to retie his laces.

Grier dribbled the ball twice, getting the feel of it. "Been awhile," he said.

"Sure has," Mack said. He looked across the playing fields. Rick had just come out of the trees, waving wildly. He had brought a ball too.

"Too long," Grier said.

Rick began to run in his loose-jointed, tiptoed way, his head down, apologetic.

Grier put the ball over his head, banged it off the board, leaped to get the rebound, softly banked it in. After eight months, it looked like Grier had pretty much the same game.

There had always been stories about Grier. Some were the ones he told himself, how he'd been a smoke jumper in Montana, a frogman in Vietnam. He'd worked on offshore drilling rigs in Louisiana, had a tryout with the Chicago Bears and lasted until the final cut. A person could pick and choose what to believe; Grier didn't seem to take great offense. But Mack's story about the first time they'd met was as good as any of them.

Late one night after a concert, Mack stopped at a bar on the way home to drop off some equipment for his drummer. Grier came over and introduced himself, insisted on buying Mack a drink.

That was fine. Mack had heard friends talking about Grier and he was curious. Grier had the rough charm to disarm anyone. They were having a good time when two man-mountain types came up staggering from too much to drink. They'd heard about Grier too, and how tough he was. He didn't look like much to them, they said, sort of pint-sized. Maybe they could all go outside and see just what everybody was talking about.

Mack was ready to try and smooth it over, but Grier stopped him.

"I won't fight you," Grier said, "but I will kill you." He spoke very calmly, very distinctly. "So if you and your friend want to die, here is what you do. My buddy and I are going to pay for our drink, then we're going to get up, go out to our car. You follow us. I'll drive down the road a quarter of a mile and then I'll stop. If you still want to die, you just blink your lights twice."

Mack was petrified, staring into his beer. Two men stood towering over them, mesmerized. Grier put a handful of crumpled dollars on the bar, clapped Mack on the shoulder.

"Come on, let's go," he said.

When they were both in Grier's car, Mack took a quick glance behind them. There was no sign of anyone coming. They drove down the road, neither of them speaking. After a mile, the highway was still dark behind them.

Mack's voice shook a little when he finally spoke. "Grier?"

"Yeah?"

"What would you have done if they had followed us?"

Grier turned, smiling brilliantly in the half-light of the car. "Are you kidding? I would have floored it."

Mack was silent again. He had never seen a bluff that good. It was so good, in fact, that when he thought about it later, he could never totally convince himself that it had been a bluff. It was the beginning of a brilliant, if short-lived, friendship.

It was the wrong matchup. Rick had always had trouble covering Mack. Mack hit a couple of jumpers from the outside, then faked Rick into the air and ducked underneath for an easy lay-up. He dropped the ball off to Harry going backdoor. The score was eleven-seven before Rick and Grier made the inevitable switch.

It got harder in a hurry. Grier shadowed Mack, denying him the ball, boxing out on rebounds. White-jacketed karate students tumbled over one another at the far end of the softball diamond. The game closed to eleven-nine, then twelve-eleven.

Mack forced a shot and then, angry at himself, ran into Grier going for the loose basketball. "My foul," Mack said, handing the ball over.

"No, man, I hit you. Go on, take it," Grier said.

It was as if Grier knew where Mack was going before Mack did. Grier was a physical player and so was Mack, their games almost mirrors of one another's.

It was impossible to back in on Grier. He was too strong and too quick; there was always a knee, an elbow, a chest—Grier's blocking moves all borderline fouls. Mack would have had to call all of them or none of them. He bumped back, giving as good as he got, trying not to let it get personal. The intensity escalated. When the ball rolled out of bounds and Rick retrieved it, the other three leaned forward on their knees, trying to get their wind back. A couple of high school kids shooting at the far basket stopped to watch.

Rick hit a circus shot to tie the game at thirteen and then Harry came back with a reverse lay-up to get them one up.

Mack tossed in to Harry, then slid into the pivot. He put his hand up, calling for the ball. Grier was like a wall behind him. Harry bounce-passed the ball in, drifted to his right. Grier was on Mack's back; Mack could feel the unresolved anger between them. It was game point. The only way Mack was going to score was by doing something Grier hadn't seen before. Grier wasn't giving him anything to his left; Mack faked left, then whirled right and was alone for a second. Grier recovered enough to get a hand on the ball, but Mack forced it up. The ball hung on the rim, bouncing twice, three times. Mack and Grier were shoulder to shoulder for the rebound. It never came. The ball dropped through, almost as an afterthought. The game was over.

Grier swatted the ball in frustration, caught it, flipped it skeptically back at the suspect rim. His anger dissolved in a second. When he looked back at Mack he seemed to be filled with nothing but good humor.

"Nice game," Grier said. He slapped Mack on the shoulder. "Tough shot."

Mack shook his head. "Wasn't pretty, was it?"

"A piece of garbage is what it was," Rick said.

They all walked over to get water. Rick squatted next to the fountain, his head down, his blond hair matted with sweat. Harry took a long drink of water, spat it out. Grier kept looking as if he was about to say something. Mack waited, hands on hips.

"I enjoyed that," Grier said. "I haven't been in a game like that in a long time. You and Harry will have to give us a rematch."

"Any time," Mack said.

"You need a ride home?" Grier said.

"No thanks," Mack said. "I've got a bone to pick with your teammate here and I thought I'd take him out to lunch." Rick glanced up, taken totally by surprise.

Rick and Mack walked along the river under the big trees. The river had gone dry and there was only a shadow of damp sand among the smooth rocks. Fluff from the cottonwoods floated in the air. Mack dribbled the ball from one hand to the other.

"Never saw you play so tough, Mack," Rick said.

"It was a tough game. You were the one that told Grier about it?"

"Yeah. He asked me if we were still playing. I wasn't going to lie to him. I didn't think you'd mind. That's over between you two, isn't it?"

"I guess it is," Mack said. He rolled the ball around behind his back. "You know those drawings you showed me, Rick? You ever figure out what they were?"

"No."

Mack held the ball in his hands, spun it, stared at the label like a player before a key free throw. "Well, I did."

Over a beer and a sandwich at the Washington Street Deli Mack told Rick the whole works. He told him about the bracelet at the dance, the range rider, Tucker's Indian wife, how Mack thought it all fit together. If Mack expected Rick to fall to his knees with thanksgiving, he was off by a mile.

"I don't get it."

"What do you mean, you don't get it? All that hullabaloo about the test site never mattered. It was one big smokescreen. Tucker lied to everybody, to his wife, both wives, to his partner. He was moving bars all that time. The real lode is north, somewhere in the canyon near the San Carlos Pueblo, in a cave with a flute player cut in the ceiling."

Rick squinted into the sun, his face pinched with contrariness. "Maybe. Sounds like a long shot to me." Mack rolled the basketball out from under his chair. Rick was giving him a little of his own medicine.

They walked out into the street, waited for a break in the summer traffic.

"You found all this out on your own?" Rick said.

"I guess so. Yeah. On my own."

"Sounds like you've been busy."

They crossed in front of a red-bearded biker straddling his Harley-Davidson, threaded their way through the crowds under the portal of the Palace of the Governors. The Indian vendors, mostly women, sat on their folding chairs, their turquoise and silver jewelry, their pottery and sand painting, laid out on blankets in front of them. Tourists three-deep moved in a slow side shuffle, necks craned, looking for a bargain. Mack could tell the ones who were looking at Indians for the first time. They stared with glazed eyes, as if the Indians had been painted on the wall.

"So how long have you been onto it?" Rick said.

Mack shifted the basketball from one arm to the other, slipped around a languid teenager in a Hook 'Em Horns T-shirt. "The dances were when, ten days ago? I started looking right after that."

"And you didn't tell me anything."

Mack's face reddened. "I didn't know if I would find anything. I didn't want to get your hopes up."

"Really."

They stepped out into the street to avoid the impasse under the portal. Mack's legs had stiffened up from the basketball game; he could feel the pinging in his thighs and rump. He was getting too old for this.

"I thought I'd look pretty foolish, after what I told you . . . I wanted to be sure what I had."

"And are you sure?" They stepped back up on the sidewalk. "You weren't going for the cheap steal? You weren't trying to sneak backdoor on your old buddy?"

Mack stopped and just stared at him. "The hell with you, man."

Mack pressed on through the crowd of people. Rick stayed

where he was. A white-haired woman in an expensive suede vest was down on one knee, turning over pieces of pottery, checking the prices. All around were people in all the poses of scrutiny. A man in a madras jacket leaned back, holding a silver necklace away from him, turning it to look at it from a new angle. Some of the Indians had official-looking plaques that said American Indian Vendor or Authentic Pueblo Jewelry or Navajo Sand Painting—All Natural Colors. Everyone was after the real stuff, everyone was afraid of being taken. It wasn't just Rick.

Mack looked back at him. Maybe he'd made a mistake, maybe he shouldn't have told Rick anything. Rick looked stranded. He shook a raised hand at Mack as if to erase what he'd said, his face in a scowl. Rick was upset. Mack waited for him to catch up.

"O.K., I'm sorry," Rick said. "My problem. The occasional touch of paranoia, you know? It was just that I couldn't help thinking when you were talking . . ."

"Thinking what?"

"Well, that the reason you hadn't told me till now was that you hadn't made up your mind. That you were saying to yourself, 'Lord, this could really be something, and old Rick, he's bright and entertaining, but maybe he's too crazy for this . . . he's a bit of a fuck-up, after all, a bit of a loser . . .'" Mack looked down, not meeting Rick's eyes. One of the Indian vendors had a copy of *Personhood* on her black jewelry trunk. "You needed some time to think about what to do. You didn't exactly come rushing over to the house, right?"

Mack had no answer. Rick was a smart guy. "Jesus, Rick, stop it. You're my friend."

They moved on in silence, side by side. Shame was in the air. Rick was taking this all wrong. A woman in a wide straw hat and a turquoise-colored skirt haggled over the price of a fifty-dollar bracelet. The Indian vendor kept shaking her head no, leaning back against the restored adobe wall. Mutual distrust was everywhere; negotiations went on up and down the line.

Mack was burning up inside. This was the place where three hundred years ago the Indians had revolted; these were the very walls they had stormed, driving the oppressors out. The Spanish had abandoned what treasure they had, all records had been destroyed, the trail had been lost. If Mack was right, he was the first person in a long time to pick up a fresh scent, a new lead. The only thing holding him back was Rick's hurt feelings. That was what you called really being nickeled and dimed to death.

Then, without warning, Rick tapped the basketball out from under Mack's arm, reached up and caught it. It was a reckless gesture, adolescent horseplay. Rick intercepted the ball a couple of inches shy of the straw-hatted woman's head. Everyone in the vicinity looked at Rick with alarm. Rick didn't care. He suddenly had his grin back.

"I think it's damn great, man, I do. You're as big a sucker as I am, aren't you? But it all fits now, doesn't it? What you were telling me . . . I can see it. Of all the people to have come up with this, Mack, who would have thought it? You really took the ball and ran with it, didn't you?"

Rick's switch caught Mack by surprise. "I'm sorry, man, I should have told you before."

"Hey, Mack, I'm fine. I was just kidding. No, forget it. I'm great." Rick wasn't watching where he was going. He stepped onto the edge of one of the blankets of jewelry. A toothless old vendor with a red ribbon around his head rapped Rick on the back of a calf with his slender wooden stick. Rick stepped off, too keyed up to take offense. "We'll take helicopters, we'll get the best electronic equipment there is. Grier can get us whatever we need."

"Hold on, Rick. I don't want Grier in on this."

"Grier's already in on this."

"What do you mean?"

"I told him about it. Back when you didn't want any part of it. I figured if you wouldn't go for the long odds, Grier would. He's been checking with the Bureau of Mines and the courthouses, looking for the sites of old claims. Grier's in on this, no question."

The woman in the straw hat was finally opening her wallet, fishing for bills.

"You tell anyone else?" Mack said.

"No. Did you?"

"Harry," Mack said.

"Harry. What did you tell him for?"

"Harry's my buddy. Somebody I could trust. You have a problem with that?"

They looked at one another, both cool-eyed for a second, men considering terms. Then Rick's disarming smile crept back, rescuing them.

"No problem. Four's just as good a number as two, right?" The woman with the straw hat leaned forward, bills in her fist. The plastic Baggie and the money changed hands. "And if we find what I think is out there, there will be plenty to go around. Why quibble?"

They had come out from under the portal, had run the gauntlet, and were back out in the sun. Rick raised the basketball over his head, spun it up into the blue sky, caught it again with one hand. "Besides, it'll be great to all be on the same side for a change, right?"

Chapter Seven

STANDING ANKLE-DEEP in the water, Mack and Grier steadied the raft between them. Mack could feel the tug of the slow-moving current on the huge black rubber craft. Harry and Rick scrambled down the incline with the cooler. The sheer walls of the gorge curved away like the open jaws of a trap.

Grier broke the silence. "So welcome to *The Wild Kingdom.*"

"You watched that too?" Mack said.

"Every Sunday afternoon. I sat there on the edge of my seat waiting to see if they could put a radio transmitter in a beaver's ear. Hell, that was exciting. Not as exciting as this, of course. 'Fess up now, Mack, you made up this whole thing, didn't you?"

"I guess we'll see if I made it up or not, won't we?"

"See? I knew it, I knew it all along."

Harry and Rick heaved the cooler into the raft. The bottom of the boat grated on sand. Mack had never seen the river this low; exposed sandbars rose up like the tawny backs of ancient beasts. Most of the canyon was still in shadow, even at ten in the morning. A few scraggly juniper clung to the hundred-foot walls.

Once everyone was in, Grier pushed them through the shallow water, then hopped aboard, perched for a second with one knee on the soft rubber side, poised like a runner in the blocks. The raft scraped over small rocks. Grier clambered in, took the oars.

Harry leaned back among the fly rods, arms folded across his chest, baseball cap pulled down over his eyes, playing Mr. Casual. Mack trailed his hand through the warm water, watching the thickets of willow and tamarisk slide by, the canyon unfolding before them.

It still felt odd, being teamed up with Grier. It was not an arrangement that any of the four of them would have chosen. Not that it was such a serious matter. It still had to be treated as an afternoon lark. What was the other choice?

They had agreed that a raft was the least obtrusive way to get down into the canyon. The other choice was to take a jeep through the San Carlos Pueblo and out across the flats. They wanted to arouse as little suspicion as possible, look as much like tourists out on a sight-seeing float as they could. That was why Grier had insisted on their bringing fishing equipment. It seemed like a ludicrous and transparent bit of make-believe to Mack. On the one hand no one was willing to admit there was a chance they could find anything, and on the other, they were already thinking like a bunch of second-rate bandits.

It took them almost two hours to get down to the San Carlos cliffs. The ancient cave dwellings were honeycombed in the soft volcanic rock like a colony of swallows. Shining in the midday light they seemed dreamlike and impenetrable, a sleeping fortress. The cliffs were abandoned now, with the exception of the stray pilgrim and the Indians who came, one day each fall, for ceremonies to honor their beginnings.

Mack knew the stories that had always swirled around the San Carlos cliffs. The Indians had always considered it a holy place, the ancestral home of several of the Rio Grande pueblos. When archeologists came to excavate in the thirties they used Indian workmen and several of them died. Whether the cause was their own bad consciences or the action of angry, violated spirits, one thing was certain: they died in terror.

There was a story, repeated for years afterward, of the Indian workman who claimed that a hand had reached up out of the earth and grabbed his leg. A voice spoke to him saying, "Brother, do not disturb us." Two days later the man died in his sleep, and he was just the first. Mack didn't believe in ghosts, but his conscience was less than clear. The thought of disturbing those cliffs bothered him too.

Grier steered the boat over to the bank. Harry leaped out into the shallow water to help pull them in under some cotton-woods. The canyon was wider here, with real woods along the river. There were probably deer in it. There was a wide, grassy expanse where a thousand years before the Indians must have grown their corn. Mack could see why they had chosen to settle here. It was a beautiful, peaceful spot. Sheltered by the cliffs, it could have made do for Eden.

The four men walked across the meadow with the wary for-mality of men crossing an empty parade ground. Halfway across Rick broke into a trot, a pair of flashlights banging at his side. He moved ahead of the others, then turned back to grin at them like a kid at an Easter egg hunt.

They stared up at the cliff walls. They were pocked with caves. There must have been several hundred of them, stretch-ing up and down the canyon. Mack's heart sank a little. The immensity of what they were attempting suddenly hit home.

The closer they came, the more fantastic the caves seemed. Centuries of erosion had worked the mouths into all kinds of distorted shapes. Mack, for a second, imagined them as great dark sockets staring down on them. There was no way to gauge the depth of their recesses. Even in the bright afternoon sun Mack had the unmistakable sense of something being withheld, something poised and waiting.

"Oh, mama!" Grier muttered. He shifted the coil of rope he had slung over his shoulder. "Well, it wouldn't be much fun if it was too easy, right?"

Five or six old wooden ladders were scattered about the cliffs, leading from level to level. At least a couple of them looked usable. Mack could make out now the winding trails of foot- and handholds in the soft rock, worn-white sluiceways, gentle curv-ing stairways leading into jumbles of boulders, leading no-where.

They began, marking out rough divisions of territory for each man. They each took a flashlight and water, then fanned out, laboring over boulders. The open rock was hot to the touch.

Most of the chambers were small, filled with a soft, fine dust, the ceilings blackened from centuries of smoke. In a few there were connecting passageways, interior rooms carved out by their ancient inhabitants, and Mack had to crawl on his hands and knees through the narrow openings, roll on his back to shine the beam of his flashlight over the walls, searching for some sign.

It was hard, methodical work and all the joking quickly died away. There was not one of them who was indifferent now. On a ledge above Mack, Harry threaded in and out of a series of exposed chambers, stooping low, then craning his neck to peer up a long crevice. Grier, twenty yards below, rolled boulders aside, clearing a blocked entrance. He was singing. "Every time I go downtown, somebody's kickin' my dog around . . ."

The sun radiating off the walls turned the canyon slowly into a kiln, hardening shapes, reducing everything to its simplest elements. Hope ebbed and flowed. There was a momentary flare of excitement when Rick found a wall of petroglyphs. He waved the others over, looking like a ghost himself, his arms and face covered with cave dust and streaked with sweat. It was a false alarm. After twenty minutes of examining every etched spiral and cross and lizard, they found nothing that even remotely resembled a flute player.

The heat worked on them all. After a couple of hours they took a break down below. Grier, his boots off, carefully peeled the sticky cellophane from a squashed Ring-Ding. Rick stretched out on the ground, exhausted, an unfinished sandwich on his belly. Mack had snapped off a long, dried weed and was breaking it into small pieces, wondering what he'd gotten them into. Harry glanced over at him.

"Want a Slim Jim?"

"Sure."

Harry handed it over. Mack bit off a piece of the slender, tough sausage. Rick propped his head up on an elbow.

"You don't think that Indian woman could have been lying to you, do you?" Rick said.

"Don't think so," Mack said.

"You know sometimes they'll tell you whatever they think you want to hear."

"Isn't that the truth?" Harry said. "Bunch of lyin' savages."

"It wasn't like that," Mack said. He batted the dust from his jeans. Insects were singing in the grass.

"Maybe she wasn't lying," Rick said, "but, Jesus, we could look every day for a month and still not be sure we'd covered everything."

A lizard clung frozen to a nearby rock; the only sign of life was the tiny pulsing in his throat. The slender reptilian head was cocked to one side as if he was listening.

"Hey, ease up, Rick," Harry said. "You guys didn't really think we were going to find anything, did you? Not really."

"I did," Grier said. He pushed himself back to his feet, brushed the dirt and twigs from the bottom of his socks. The lizard disappeared in one quick flash. "Still do. Don't try to blame it on Mack. We all came here of our own free will. I think there's something out here. Mack wouldn't lie. We still got a couple of hours of sunlight; I say we give it our best shot." His voice had a sullen weight to it.

Mack watched Grier tie his boots. The one thing people like Grier had going for them was heart; the one thing they couldn't tolerate in others was what they perceived as the lack of it.

It wasn't so much that they became friends as that Grier just decided. A week after Grier had bluffed their way out of the bar fight, he drove up to Mack's house with a crate of peaches he'd brought down from Velarde. He stayed for dinner, entertaining Mack and Annie with story after story.

He started making it a regular thing, dropping by a couple of times a week. Grier didn't do anything halfway. When he invited them over for a cookout, Mack's records would be playing on the hi-fi. When the roof of Mack's barn collapsed in a spring windstorm, Grier and his crew were there the next morning and had it blocked and hoisted, tin and beams replaced by the middle of the afternoon.

Grier had a small contracting firm, but it never seemed to get in his way. On a minute's notice he would be there to pull a newborn colt, dig post holes, or sit in on a rehearsal. He even started to teach himself to play guitar.

He was the most stalwart fan Mack had ever had. "Your only

problem, man, is that you're too much of a saint." The way Grier saw it Mack would have been the biggest star in the music world if they hadn't screwed him, and if they had tried that crap on Grier he wouldn't have been such a nice guy about it, he wouldn't have just turned the other cheek and walked away.

It was never dull when Grier was around, but it wasn't always easy. Mack was Grier's hero and heroes were supposed to be flawless. Mack had been famous and Grier seemed to believe there was something literal about fame. Mack was different from the rest of them. Grier's naivete was surprising in a guy so shrewd in so many ways, but there were just things he didn't know. His guitar playing improved to the point where he wasn't half-bad, but if Mack was around, Grier would hand the instrument over to Mack to be tuned.

When Grier first came to him with the idea it sounded terrific. There was an empty theatre downtown and Grier would do all the dirty work, clean the place, set up the lights, tack up posters, and Mack would play a series of Friday-night concerts. Grier turned out to be a natural promoter and the first night was a sellout. At the end Grier came running up on stage to take a standing ovation with Mack, their arms linked. His face was beaming. He had never had anything like this happen to him before in his life.

Thanks to Grier's perseverance, the weekly concerts became the hottest tickets in town. They were pulling in a surprising amount of money, but their success had its complications.

Grier and Annie weren't on the same wavelength and with Grier spending more time than ever over at the house it began to grate. Some of the younger guys in the band grumbled about taking orders from Grier.

Mack came home one afternoon to find Grier on the phone in the kitchen. Annie was out in the patio with Kaia, looking hostile. Grier winked at Mack that everything was under control.

"Well, I don't give a damn what I sound like; this is Mack McLaine," Grier said. "You can tell your boss that if he can't dial his own damn calls he can just take his sleaze-ball contracts and shove them where the sun doesn't shine. That's right. No, you never did hear me talk like that before. Goodbye."

When Grier hung up he was grinning from ear to ear.

"Who was that?" Mack said.

"Nothing to worry about. That was that two-bit music publisher that's been ripping you off."

"Are you serious?"

"Hey, Mack, all I said was what you told me you were going to tell him . . ."

"Damn it, Grier, don't you ever, ever . . ."

"Come off it, Mack. He's no use to you. Hell, I make a better Mack McLaine than you do. Too bad I don't have a voice."

"We're going to have to have a talk, Grier."

"We will, man, sure, but how about later? I got to go see if the printer's got those new posters ready."

They didn't have the talk soon enough. It all blew sky-high the night of the sixth concert, Mack and the band were twenty minutes into it when the lobby erupted.

All Mack could make out from the stage was a lot of pushing and shoving and shouting and Grier bobbing in the middle of it. Everybody turned to look; a few people stood on their seats for a better view. There was a crash, a surge of bodies, the kind of scream you only hear when there's real trouble. Mack ran up the aisle, pushing his way through. The knot of people in the lobby opened and it was all there in front of him at once: the nineteen-year-old Spanish kid writhing on the floor with a broken collarbone, the weeping girlfriend on her knees beside him, Grier being restrained by a dozen hands.

Everybody was shouting something. "He didn't do nothing, man!"

"Move back, everybody, give him air . . ."

"The guy just grabbed him and threw him into the Coke machine."

Mack knelt down next to the boy. The kid's eyes were rolling back and forth in pain. Mack could smell the beer on the boy's breath. Mack brushed his hand across the boy's forehead, trying to get him to lie still. Mack could hear the distant sound of the band, manfully struggling through the old standards, trying to appease the crowd.

Mack looked up at the ring of faces.

"Somebody find out if there's a doctor here."

"He was gate-crashing, Mack, the kid was drunk." Grier spoke quietly, as if it was just a matter for the two of them, as if no one else were there. "He tried to force his way in."

"He wasn't gate-crashing, man, his cousin's in the band, he was *promised* a ticket . . ." Grier's accuser was an agitated high school kid in a glimmery purple shirt.

Grier shouted back at him. "He wasn't on any list of mine, mister, and I don't care whose cousin he is, he's not going to put his hands on me . . ."

The storm of angry voices swirled, cancelled one another. Mack stood up, put a hand on Grier's chest. People were walking out, glancing fearfully over their shoulders, jackets in hand. A bottle smashed somewhere out on the street. A bearded young doctor pushed through, squatted over the injured boy.

Mack raised both hands over his head. "O.K., everybody just shut up for a second! That's it, there's no concert tonight, everybody's going home." There was a chorus of moans and groans. "No, I'm sorry, we didn't come out here to get people hurt. This isn't what it's about."

Mack tried to avoid looking at Grier, but he was impossible to miss, his face flushed, readable as a child's. Grier felt he had been betrayed.

It took more than two hours to get the kid to the hospital, clear the theatre, give people their money back, listen to twelve different versions of what had happened.

It was almost eleven-thirty. Mack was packing up mikes and speakers when he looked up and saw Grier strolling down the aisle of the dark theatre. The piano player saw him too, and slunk off without a word. Grier swung up onto the stage, stood with his hands jammed in his pockets.

"You shouldn't have done it, Mack."

"Done what?"

"Shouldn't have cancelled. People paid their money. We had an obligation."

"There are all kinds of obligations. You don't bust people in two, Grier, I don't care what the kid did."

Grier's face glowed red in the reflection of the fire exits. "I did what I did to protect you, man. The kid was drunk, he shoved me . . ." Grier kicked at the tape marks on the stage floor. "You going to believe me or you going to believe them?"

"I don't know what to believe. I'm just doing the best I can." Mack wound the cord to the mike around his elbow.

"That's not good enough. I stand up for my friends, I expect the same from them. If we're going to do any more of these . . ."

"We're not. That was the last one."

"If that's the way you want it. You're the star. I don't need this any more than you do."

They didn't speak after that. The wounds went deep. There were spasms of doubt when Mack wondered if he had over-reacted. Things that Grier was saying around town inevitably drifted back to him: "I don't see why Mack is such a sacred cow," and "Mack's a nice guy, but he's used to being treated like a star, you can't get around it." Remarks like that only made Mack surer that he'd done the right thing.

They went after it again, each man going his own way. Mack worked the higher part of the cliff. The sun had dropped some and the angle of the light made the outlines of the petroglyphs sharper, more lifelike. They seemed to be everywhere on the upper walls.

Mack searched for another hour, faithful as a monk. Dazed by the sun, he wasn't as sharp, not as thorough. He knew he was inevitably missing things.

The frustration and anger began to build. There had to be a better way. When Tucker had discovered the cave he'd been on his way home, all he was looking for was shelter from the rain; he wouldn't have clambered over wet rock to reach some out-of-the-way hole. If Mack could only think like Tucker. There shouldn't be anything tricky about it. It was probably as obvious as the nose on his face.

Shielding his eyes, Mack saw a series of caves high up, just below the rim of the canyon, and a winding trail of footholds just to their right. Using his hands, he swung between a pair of elephant-sized boulders, found what looked like the trail. He made his way cautiously, crouching in close to the rock. He didn't trust the sureness of his instincts anymore. The trail cork-screwed back, away from where he thought it would take him. He ended up on the canyon rim, overshooting the caves.

A light breeze ruffled through the gnarled branches of the juniper, quickly dried the sweat on Mack's face. He looked down at the gleaming river, at the wilderness of canyons cutting off it. He could see the traces of an ancient kiva, a gently sloping hollow filled with weeds and scattered stones.

Harry had given up and was back at the raft, fooling with one of the fly rods. Rick stood waist-deep in boulders, looking stranded and lost. Only Grier was still at it.

Disappointment cut through Mack like a chill wind. He didn't know if it was aimed at himself or the others. Nothing was ever perfect, nothing ever worked out the way you dreamed it, he knew that. But to look down, from such a height, on those three groping figures, was to know how overmatched they were, why they wouldn't find anything. And Mack had really believed that they would.

Mack turned away. Five feet ahead of him there was a dimple in the earth. He glanced at it without any particular interest, thinking it was a trick of the light or the work of a badger or some other burrower. But as he looked at it he realized that the depression, no more than two feet across, was perfectly symmetrical, like a sinkhole or the pictures he'd seen of sites after an underground nuclear blast. Curious now, Mack got down on one knee, felt the inverted cone of loose earth with his hand. It was the sign of some structural weakness underneath. No animal could have done this; it had to have been some kind of explosion.

Mack stood up, the blood pounding in his ears. He was fully awake for the first time all day.

Mack kicked at the shallow depression. Nothing gave. He scanned the horizon, took his bearings, lined up a timber-covered peak with a series of bare ridges that ran below it. Mack walked back to the rim of the canyon. There was a large shadowed cave set in a sheer wall twenty-five feet below him. A long, bone-white ladder led up to it. Mack didn't remember seeing the cave from below; from the top everything took on a different look. It had to be the one; it was the only cave that was remotely lined up with the far peak. He saw Rick and Grier still searching below him. He wouldn't tell them anything until he was sure.

Mack edged his way down over the rim of the canyon. Peering under his outstretched arm, he searched for footholds below. Huge birds hung on the air currents high above the gleaming river. After two or three tricky maneuvers on the reddish, crumbling rock, he lowered himself onto a narrow ledge. He sidestepped his way quickly toward the cave, pulled himself up into its darkness. He was panting hard.

He snapped on his flashlight and scanned the walls. It was a large cave, big enough to stand up in, but otherwise seemed no different from the other fifty he'd already seen. There was no sign of an explosion. There was a smoke hole carved in the ceiling and dust danced in the single shaft of sunlight.

He ran his hands along the sloping walls, kicked slowly through the dust on the floor. Hope expired as quickly as it had been revived.

Mack finally sat down, leaned against the wall near the entrance. He snapped off his flashlight, picked up a handful of dust and threw it. It was dead-end time again. He felt like a fool. For a minute he had really believed he had something. A raven croaked past, outside in the bright sunlight.

Mack's eyes gradually adjusted to the darkness. Then an impossible thing happened. A section of the back wall began to glow. He knew it couldn't be glowing. The only explanation had to be that it wasn't the same color as the wall around it. It was a circular section, maybe eight feet across, and it was a dull white, not smoke-blackened like the rest. Mack didn't see how he could have missed it before; he hadn't been looking, not in the right way.

He groped for his flashlight in the dust, got back to his feet, bumped his head on a low part of the ceiling. If it wasn't smoke-blackened that meant it wasn't as old as the rest, it wasn't part of the original wall. Hope came roller-coastering back.

Mack shone his flashlight on the gritty, pale rock, ran his

fingers along the almost imperceptible seams. It was immovable, unyielding. A blast could have done this, Tucker's dynamite, but there was no way of being sure. Then something clicked. Mack shone the flashlight on the ceiling, swung the beam of light directly overhead.

The flute player was etched into the smoke-blackened ceiling above him. The curve of the walls made the flute player look as if he were crouched, waiting, as if he had been watching Mack the whole time in the dark.

Mack scrambled to the mouth of the cave and began waving his arms like a lifeguard calling everyone out of the sea. "Hey, get up here! I've found it! I've found it!" Grier and Rick lifted their heads, looking slightly stupefied. At the raft, Harry set down his fly rod. They either didn't believe him or were too tired to move.

"God damn it, you guys, get the lead out! It's no joke . . ."

For a second Mack nearly lost his balance, but he grabbed the top of the ladder to steady himself. Grier and Rick and Harry pushed up over the rocks like resentful converts moving slowly to the altar. They met at the base of the ladder. Mack stared down at the sunburned, skeptical faces. "Start climbing, you lazy bastards, I'm going to make you all rich men."

The beams of the four flashlights all converged on the foot-long etching of the flute player on the black ceiling. Mack tried to explain about the dimple in the earth and the glowing section of the wall, but in his excitement he was garbling it. They were not as convinced as they should have been. They had searched in vain for too long not to be wary. Harry squatted on the cave floor, craned his neck to stare dubiously at the flute player. Rick, drained by the heat, rubbed his eyes with his hands.

"Maybe I'm not explaining this right," Mack said.

As he spoke, Grier drifted to the back wall, felt it with his hands. Grier took out his knife, wedged it into the seam. One violent twist sprayed the cave with tiny bits of rock. Suddenly everyone was silent, watching him. The reflected light off the pale wall made Grier's face eerie, masklike.

"It was an explosion all right," Grier said. He stabbed at the

wall again with his knife. "It's nothing but a goddamned plug of
rock. God knows how deep it goes." Grier's voice was taut with
excitement. "It's going to take more than a knife to get it open,
but we can take care of that." A slow grin came over Grier's
face. "What a bunch of doubting Thomases we got here. Good
for you, Mack. I always said it, the man's got a golden touch.
Maybe next time you guys will believe in him."

They floated out at sunset. The canyon was in shadow again;
only the rim blazed with light. Coming around a wide bend,
they startled some deer that had come down to the water to
drink. The frightened animals bounded back into the woods in
two long leaps.

They were tired, lost in their own thoughts, oddly subdued,
all except Rick, who was racing on extra batteries. He had a
million questions and he didn't see why they couldn't be an-
swered now: how big a plug of rubble did Grier think there was,
what sort of equipment would they need, how could they get
excavating equipment in there without being detected, would
they need dynamite, how could they be sure they wouldn't seal
off the treasure even worse than before?

No one had answers yet, not even Grier. He let the boat drift,
letting the slow-moving current carry them, only leaning on the
oars when he had to get clear of a sandbar. Harry lay back, his
baseball cap pulled forward over his eyes, smiling at Rick's
questions.

A hawk sailed way up in bright sunlight, wheeling high above
the shadowed canyons, a hunter surveying them all. Mack held
the unused fishing poles between his knees. He ran his fingers
down the taut line. We are all locked in together now, Mack
thought, locked in by what we know.

They floated out of the canyon into flat land; the muddy water
became blood-red in the setting sun. Ahead they could see
telephone lines, then the low buildings of the pueblo, then the
bridge.

There was a man leaning over the rail of the bridge. He never
moved. His hat was pulled low, and he wore sunglasses, watching the rubber raft move through the shallow water. Grier

began to work harder, pushing the oars against the gravelly
bottom. Mack saw reflected light flash off the chest of the waiting man. It was the badge of a tribal policeman.

The policeman was middle-aged, very fit in his short-sleeved
khaki uniform, and seemed very good-natured. He waited
while they pulled up to the bank, pushed back his hat as they
struggled to slide the raft up the slope.

"What have you guys been up to?" he said, addressing no one
in particular.

Grier, still bent over the raft, didn't look up to answer. "Little
fishin'."

"Catch anything?"

Harry picked up the tackle box and rods and trudged noncha-
lantly up the slope.

"No, not really," Grier said.

The tribal policeman glanced idly at Rick as he lifted the four
big flashlights out of the bottom of the boat. If he thought that
was odd, or if he noticed their dust-covered clothes, he didn't
give himself away.

"Funny," the tribal policeman said. He pushed on the bridge
of his sunglasses. "The water's been so low and muddy there
hasn't been anyone fishing for a couple of weeks."

"I guess we just thought we could beat the odds," Grier said.
"Shows how much we know."

Chapter Eight

"Picks and *shovels?"* Rick said. "You're trying to tell me we're going to have to dig the stuff out?"

Grier hunched up a little closer to the table, like some plotting pirate. The metal legs of his chair grated across the flagstone. "We are unless you know some way to get a bulldozer through the San Carlos Pueblo without anyone noticing. We've got to go in as light as we can."

Harry lifted the half-empty pitcher of margaritas, poured the foamy, lemon-colored liquid into Mack's glass. On the stone wall behind them were rows of red flowers, some lazily flitting bees.

Mack frowned. "So how are we going in?"

"Horses," Grier said. "You've got two, Harry's got three, right?"

"And what about the raft?" On the terrace above them, waitresses were shaking out a long white lace tablecloth, setting up for a big party.

"We'll use it to float in whatever heavy stuff we need. But if we find what I think we're going to find, I don't want to have to row it out under the nose of any tribal policeman."

Mack took a sip of his drink, felt the bite of the tequila. The table was a wreck, plates piled high, the tablecloth speckled with chili stains and golden streaks of dripped honey. After the second round of margaritas, everything had taken on a glaze of unreality: the talk, the strolling woman guitarist serenading the other diners, the bright orange clusters of apricots in the surrounding trees. But mostly it was the talk.

"I think we need to sit down with a lawyer," Mack said. Rick reached across and stabbed the last morsel of *carne adovada*. Harry lifted up the empty sopapilla basket for the waitress to see. "Somebody we can trust."

Grier shook his head. He doodled on a napkin, his pen embossed with the name of a local lumber company. "No. We're not going to talk to anyone."

"Picks and shovels," Rick said. "How about the banjos and the sourdough bread? There's got to be a better way."

"At least we could find out what the law is," Mack said.

"We know what the law is," Grier said. He went on with his drawing. "The cave is on Indian land. That's what screwed up Tucker. We let anyone in on this and we'll end up with the same kind of circus they had five years ago, with the IRS and the Bureau of Indian Affairs and four hundred of Tucker's relatives breathing down our necks." Grier suddenly froze. "Jesus," he said. Mack turned to look.

A woman had come out on the terrace. She was beautiful, tall and rangy, sunglasses propped up in her shock of red hair, an open, high-cheekboned face. She strode across the restaurant. She had the carriage and confidence of a queen, even in designer jeans. Grier couldn't take his eyes off her.

"I know her, I swear I know her," he said.

"Come off it, Grier," Mack said. "Good God."

The woman sat down at the long, empty table. She noticed Grier staring at her, met his gaze directly, then looked up to chat with a waitress.

"What about dynamite?" Rick said.

Grier fussed a bit more with his drawing. "Tucker tried that too, remember?" he said. "We'll bring some, sure, but there's only certain situations where dynamite is going to do you any good."

Mack glanced at Harry. "This bother you at all?"

"I come from a tribe of the best raiders around," Harry said. "Nothing fazes me, man."

"See this?" Grier said. He held up his napkin. He had made a rough sketch of the cliff and the cave with little stick figures and lines running every which way. "If we brought a couple of pulleys and enough rope, I'll bet I could rig it so we could lift the gold right up to the rim. From there we pack it out on the horses."

Mack was silent for a second. Further up the slope, where the grounds of the restaurant ended, there was an irrigation ditch. He could hear the water running. "And then what?" he said finally.

"Let Rick tell you. Hey, here we go." Their waitress strode between tables with a fresh basket of sopapillas. Just before she arrived, Grier, remembering, slapped his napkin facedown on the table quick as a flash, as if he were concealing state secrets.

Grier and Harry both took hot sopapillas, tore open the delicate puffy pockets of fried bread. Harry got to the squeeze bottle of honey first. The waitress cleared away the stacks of empty plates.

Mack fingered his margarita glass, staring evenly across at Rick. "So?"

Rick waited until the waitress was out of range. When he finally spoke his voice was low, almost laughably solemn, Mack thought. "We take it into Mexico." Rick picked up the napkin with Grier's sketch on it, turned it over, smoothed it out in front of him. "I did a little checking. We're going to need to get ourselves a pedigree, a stamp that says we've mined the stuff."

Harry applied the honey to the sopapilla with the intensity of a teenager applying glue to a model airplane. "And then?" Mack said.

"We take it to the Caymans."

Harry had the dripping sopapilla halfway to his mouth. "The where?"

"The Cayman Islands. They've got all those international banks." A curious wasp circled the table. Harry waved it away. "From there we make the transfer to Zurich."

"Whoa. Hold on," Mack said.

"Switzerland."

"I know where Zurich is. I just want to know if you're serious," Mack said. The wasp came back, landed, its tiny body pulsed over a trail of honey. This time Harry swatted at it with his napkin.

Rick picked up Grier's pen, fiddled with it, smarting from the remark. "It's done all the time, Mack. Maybe you forget, I went to school with the guys who do this for a living."

"No disrespect, Rick, but you're starting to scare the hell out of me. This is real fantasyland stuff."

Rick shrugged, unable to answer.

The red-haired woman raised her hand in greeting to a trio who had just come through the door. They were nearly as striking-looking as their friend. There was a well-built blond woman in a blue jumpsuit and sandals, and a younger woman with short-cropped brunette hair and a lovely Irish face. The man with them had finely chiselled features, and though he was no more than average height, he carried himself with the athletic air of a boxer or skier. Mack stared at him. He was sure he had seen the man before. He just couldn't figure out where. So maybe Grier wasn't making up recognizing the woman.

The red-haired woman got up from her chair, came down the flagstone steps to meet her friends. There were hugs and kisses all around. Others in the restaurant watched them now too, were cowed by their physical grace. Mack racked his brain. He knew the man. It was very disturbing. Arm in arm, they went back and sat down, four people sitting at a table set for twenty.

"All we're doing is having a conversation, Mack," Grier said. "It's not like anything we're saying here is carved in stone. We don't know what's going to happen. You take these things one step at a time." Rick began to jot figures down on the napkin, made a rapid series of calculations, pretending not to be listening. "But I'll tell you one thing, the sooner we get out there the better. I think we could get all the stuff we need together in four or five days, go out next weekend."

Without looking up from his figuring, Rick said, "So what's your idea then?"

"I don't have an idea," Mack said. "Maybe it's not the kind of thing we should be discussing when we're drunk."

"You think we should just leave things the way they are?" Rick said. "Like good little boys?"

"I didn't say that."

Harry reached across and took the napkin out of Rick's hands. Rick didn't object. Harry stared at the columns of figures. "So what is all this?"

Rick pointed to the top of one of the columns with his pen. "As of this morning, an ounce of gold was selling in New York for a little over four hundred fifty dollars. So let's say you've got nice standard fifty-pound bars." Rick's pen moved authoritatively down the neat columns. Grier moved his chair around for a better view. "I don't want to overdo this, but you know when they were searching before they were throwing around figures like forty, fifty, sixty tons. But let's not even talk about that, that would be just jerking ourselves off. Let's be conservative. A pile of a hundred bars, here you go, thirty-six million dollars."

They were all awed into silence, staring at the rows of zeros. "Let me take a closer look at that," Grier said. He took the napkin from Harry, did a quick check of the arithmetic. "Sure beats a sharp stick in the eye."

Rick settled back, resting his case. He looked evenly across at Mack. "So if you've got a procedure for disposing of that in Hobbs, New Mexico, you let me know."

Mack rubbed his forearm. "O.K., I know, I'm being a real pain in the ass. But there's still the big question, isn't there?"

"What's that?"

"Just how much is it possible to get away with?"

A great hubbub rose behind them. They all looked up. An entourage swept into the restaurant, a pair of anxious waitresses leading the way. There were at least a dozen of them, including a no-nonsense middle-aged woman in a tailored suit, bulky portfolios under her arm, a lanky wrangler-type cowboy with a pronounced limp, and an exquisite Japanese woman in a silk print dress. A fat bearded man with several cameras around his neck duck-walked his way around the circle, squatting and rising, laughing every time he snapped a picture. At the center was a small, wiry man in a safari jacket. He had a scruffy beard, dark glasses, and a red bandana tied around his forehead. All the commotion left him unfazed. He took tense little steps and he looked like a jackal.

They moved through the restaurant like the GIs coming into liberated Paris. Waitresses were frozen in deference. The red-haired woman rose from her seat, tripped down the flagstone steps, her arms thrown wide. She embraced the jackal man, her long slender hands pressing against the back of his safari jacket, making it something special. As she drew back, their hands were still around one another's waist. She listened to him intently, her face a little flushed, while all around them the others seated themselves with much switching and banging of chairs.

Grier took it all in, stone-faced. He turned to the waitress standing a few feet away. "Who is that?" he asked.

"Oh, that's Leo Dupree. The director."

"You're kidding."

They all stared. So that was Leo Dupree. The director of a dozen classic Westerns. *The Stalking of Armando Cruz, Renegade, The Outriders.* They were all hard movies, all subject to raging controversy because of the explicit violence. The images stayed with you. The slow-motion shooting of horses, gangs rampaging through small Colorado towns, a spike driven through the chest of a striking railroad worker. They were the kind of movies that left you with nightmares. Mack wouldn't go to see them anymore. To him they were repellent, unreal, a rigged game. All the same, Dupree was famous. Mack kept looking.

Dupree hunched down at the table, making himself even smaller. Everyone was trying to get his attention, but Dupree never smiled, scarcely seemed to acknowledge them. The man with the finely chiselled features stood up at the far end of the table, raised his glass and shouted something. Mack recognized the man now. He was an actor; Mack had seen him in several things. The wrangler with the limp, too; Mack remembered him, he'd been the turncoat in *The Outriders.*

"He's making a film out here?" Grier said.

"That's what they told me," the waitress said. Upstaged, Rick fiddled moodily with his pen.

The bearded photographer scampered around the table like a frisky St. Bernard, snapping more pictures. The entire restaurant was mesmerized, peering discreetly over their shoulders at the celebrities. Mack kept his eyes on Dupree, waiting for some tip-off, some hint of that dark, reflexive violence.

"Maybe we should go over and introduce ourselves," Grier said. "I'll bet he'd like to meet a real Indian."

"Get serious, Grier," Rick said.

"I am serious." A wasp had settled inside Harry's empty margarita glass and lurched along the bottom searching for sugar.

There were gales of laughter from the other table. The blond actress in the blue jumpsuit was telling a story, talking to her hand like it was a snake. It looked very sensual and bizarre. The red-haired woman stood behind Dupree, massaging his neck. Grier still had his eyes on her. Harry clapped his hand down on the top of his glass, trapping the wasp inside. The wasp didn't notice at first.

With the dark glasses, there was no way of knowing for sure what Dupree thought of anything. He kept popping tortilla chips in his mouth. Waitresses scurried back and forth with platters of food, fresh pitchers of sangria. The wasp began bouncing wildly off the sides of Harry's glass.

As the actress massaged Dupree's neck, she leaned forward against him, her mass of red hair falling in front of her face.

"Jesus, look at that," Grier said. "And the guy hasn't made a good movie in ten years." Harry took his hand off the glass. The angry wasp zoomed out, made a couple fast passes over the table and disappeared.

Grier got up from his chair. "I'm going over there."

"Come on, don't be ridiculous," Mack said. "You're going to embarrass me."

"I'm serious. I think they'd really like to get to know us. She was looking right at me, Mack."

"This is a little beside the point, Grier," Rick said.

"No, I think it is the point. If they only knew, right? Who we really were? They'd be dying. Maybe if it all works out, we'll put the money up for their movie."

Grier turned away from them, pivoted on the heel of his boot. He moved across the terrace, rolling from side to side in a near swagger. He put his hand out for a second against the rock wall to catch his balance. Mack wondered how much he'd had to drink.

Grier trudged up the flagstone steps. All the big talk, the scheming, had made him bold. The bearded photographer looked around, startled, tried to block his way, but Grier brushed easily past him, never losing his cool.

Dupree was taken by surprise too. His jackal head jerked up from a plate of chili. Grier reached out and touched him gently on the shoulder.

Mack, Harry and Rick sat silently, watching him. Rick seemed overcome by some melancholic haze, folding and refolding the figure-riddled napkin.

Everyone at the other table watched Grier too; even at fifty feet Mack could see their wariness. Grier stood between Dupree and the red-haired actress, a hand touching each of them. He gestured to the wealth of dishes covering the length of the table. The red-haired actress smiled; Grier had said something that pleased her. Dupree was at least listening. Grier was pulling it off.

Grier suddenly reached down and tousled Dupree's grizzled beard with his fingers. That was astonishing enough, but what he did next was unbelievable. He actually tugged at it, as if he wanted to see if it was real. There was a gasp, shocked silence, and then everyone at the table burst into near hysterical laughter, Dupree laughing right along with them. Dupree reached up and shook Grier's hand; the red-haired actress leaned into him, whispering something. Grier put his arm around her shoulders, staking his claim.

Mack watched as Rick, eyes downward, slipped the napkin into his pocket, laid his credit card on the table. Mack looked back at Grier, poised between Dupree and the actress. It was a perfect tableau. The sun stabbed through the apricot trees behind them, and Grier shone in the dying light, looking like a real hero, acknowledged citizen of another realm. Gold, hell, Mack thought, fifty million or a hundred, the figures didn't matter, it never was about gold.

Grier waved them over. When no one moved, he gestured

again, impatient. Harry looked over at Mack, one hand on the back of his chair, asking the question. Mack shrugged.

Grier still beamed at them, wanting them to come on. Mack shook his head slowly, sardonically. Grier at least thought he knew the answer to Mack's big question. He knew how much they could get away with. Anything. If they had the nerve. The three of them rose reluctantly from their chairs.

Chapter Nine

HARRY STABBED the scarecrow into the porous earth, tenacious as a marine planting the flag at Iwo Jima. It took him three or four tries before it took hold. The pillow head jerked forward and back, the hat with the turkey feathers fell to the ground.

Mack picked it up and handed it back to Harry. Harry set it in place, pulled the brim down at a rakish angle, stepped back to have a look. Streaks of war paint lined the scarecrow's forehead, angled across the soft, rippled cheeks. The arms were extended straight out, like a watchman, and the sleeves of the ancient black coat fluttered in the afternoon breeze. Harry picked up the flint-headed spear, leaned it against one of the arms. For a second the whole rigid figure seemed to shift, as if turning its back to the wind.

"What do you think?" Harry said.

"I don't know if a raven would buy it," Mack said. "But I sure would."

They stood in Harry's vegetable garden protected by a high chicken-wire fence. They were surrounded by cornstalks, the edges of the leaves withered and brown from the lack of rain.

"Well, I guess if it keeps you white folks out of the garden it'll serve some purpose. Maybe if we'd only thought of this earlier we could have turned back a few of those covered wagons. Just line the scarecrows up along the bluffs."

Mack laughed. Harry fingered the soft tassels of the stunted ears of corn.

"You doing all right?" Harry said.

"Middling."

"What does that mean?"

"I don't know." Mack watched a stinkbug tumbling over the dry furrows. "Suddenly everybody's acting like they're real desperados. Dynamiting caves, running trucks across the border."

Harry knelt, examined the underside of one of his tomato plants. "That's just talk, Mack." His yellow dog came trotting out of the juniper. He panted and wagged his tail, exhausted from chasing jackrabbits.

"So far it's just talk."

"Rick called me a little while ago. You know what he was doing? Push-ups. You'd think the guy was in training to be an astronaut."

"I just think we could end up in some real trouble, Harry. We're supposed to be going out there in what, three days, for God's sake."

Stone-faced, Harry gazed steadily at him. "I guess I don't really understand what you're saying. What do you want me to tell you?" The dog put his front paws on the chicken wire, begging to be let in.

"I'm not asking you to tell me anything, I just want to know what you think."

"Let's go into the studio," Harry said. "I want to show you something."

They left the garden, carefully picked their way through the sharp-edged yucca. Far to the south Mack could make out the Cerrillos mine in the Ortiz Mountains. They were strip-mining for gold and the open pit spread against the folds of the mountain like the wings of a tawny hawk. Every time Mack saw it the wings had grown wider.

The mine was at least three hundred years old. In the seventeenth century the Spanish had worked it, using slave labor. The Indians carried out bags of ore hung from their heads and shoulders, climbing ladders consisting of a single notched pole. It wasn't Cibola, but it was something. The mine had played out and reopened a dozen times. The rumor was it was now owned by a South African firm. Mack had read an article about it, about the huge machines that were chewing up the mountain. If they got a third of an ounce for every ton they ground up they turned a profit.

As they crossed the yard Harry bent down to right one of the tricycles. From inside the house Mack could hear the sounds of Harry's kids.

Harry held open the door to his studio and Mack stepped inside. There were great blocks of cloudy alabaster, African wonderstone and Minnesota pipestone lying in the corners like sleeping beasts. Cutting tools and hammers hung lined up on the walls. On the worktable were several of the pipes Harry had built his reputation on, the stone bowls carved into the heads of birds or buffalo.

There were always new things to look at, too: beaded medicine bags and dolls from Woolworth's, a stone bear fetish with a knifelike fragment of bone strapped to its back—a magical supercharger was how Harry explained it. There were Spanish bultos and Hopi kachinas, the poster of Jane Fonda as Barbarella tacked to the wall. It was a magpie's nest, a beautiful jumble, a whole world, smelling of stone dust and endless sanding.

Harry and Mack had met at a party at a friend's house. Mack was telling a story to a group of people. The story was about Mack's being in Oxford, Mississippi, during a college tour and how, after the concert, a famous and hard-drinking Southern writer had corralled Mack and insisted they go sprinkle bourbon on Mr. Bill's grave, Mr. Bill Faulkner, that was. Mack was just getting into the story, about how uneasy he was, huddled in the graveyard at one in the morning, sure that the campus police were coming to arrest them, the writer addressing inebriated prayers of doom to Mr. Bill. "You were the best of us, Mr. Bill, you were the best we'll ever have, because it's all dyin' around us, the South is dyin'."

Harry, who'd been listening intently, suddenly said, "When I die, they'll have to sprinkle white powder on my grave and I'll be born again." With that Harry burst into a maniacal laugh. Maybe it was a cocaine joke, maybe not, Mack wasn't sure. It didn't matter. From the beginning Mack could count on Harry's having a fresh take on things.

Harry had grown up on a reservation in Eastern Montana and had come east for the first time to go to college. It was the time of Vietnam, of the shootings at Kent State, and Harry was as caught up in the violence of those times as anyone. He marched against the war, took dope, read Kerouac's *On the Road*, realized he didn't have to go to graduate school, and took off.

He tried to start a free university in Albany with some friends, took more drugs, started to drink, hung out with bikers, got beaten up pretty badly in a parking lot on Route One somewhere in Jersey. He finally made it back to Montana exhausted, bitter, a real mess.

His parents knew he was in trouble and took him to the spiritual leaders of the reservation for guidance. Harry was skeptical. "All we want is ten days," they told him, "that's all we will ask of you." They sent him on a fast into the mountains, equipped only with a knife and a handful of salt. Mack could never get Harry to describe quite what had happened in those ten days. All he would say was, "It was the heaviest thing that ever happened to me, man, it totally turned my head around." There were times Harry sounded more like a rock star than Mack did.

He needed to be cleansed. All those things he had run away from as a kid heading east to college, he needed desperately to learn. He joined a warrior society, turned to carving and beadwork. His tradition had saved him; now he was going to rescue the ancient ways.

He still walked a fine line. It was hard to know, when you listened to him for a long time, just how much was bullshit and how much was brilliant. They would agree to meet for lunch and sometimes Harry would show up and sometimes he wouldn't. He would tell Mack that Crazy Horse sang to him from the grave and Mack would be sure that Harry believed it and he believed it too, *in some way*. Then would come Harry's wild laugh, "Hey, you going to let me convince you of anything?"

Harry sat down on his stool, picked up a piece of sandpaper off his workbench and tested the roughness of it with his thumb. "You think you want to back out?"

Mack leaned against the workbench, wiped some stone dust off the wood surface. "I don't know."

Harry picked up an alabaster pipe, turned it over, examining it for imperfections. He held it out to Mack. "Here, take a look. This is what I've been working on."

Mack cradled the pipe in his hands. The grinning face of a coyote emerged from the front of the stone bowl. It was smooth-snouted, a little scary, damned sly. Mack held it up in front of the window and light played fitfully through the stone.

"You should see it, Mack, when you smoke it, the fire glows right through the stone. It's beautiful."

"I'll bet."

Harry took the pipe back, went to work on it again with the sandpaper. "You know what Coyote'd say? If you went to him? He'd say, if it glitters, go for it. Go for the flash. Don't worry about being foolish, because you will be, no matter what you do."

Harry worked on the alabaster with long, even strokes, refining, making it even more fluid, as if he could turn the stone into pure light by perseverance alone. The steady rasp of sanding filled the awkward silence between the two men.

"Coyote sees the birds flying so he jumps off the cliff thinking he can fly too and of course he falls and kills himself . . . oh, he's always getting killed." Harry threw the sandpaper aside, stared at the pipe for a second, then set it carefully back on the shelf. "But after a while he comes back to life, hauls himself together the best he can." Restless, Harry stood up, went to the window of the studio and peered out. "Maybe he's missing an eye, so he puts a pebble in the socket and squishes some pine pitch in there to make it stick and he can see just fine through that and he's off again." Harry was silent, just staring out the window.

"What's wrong?" Mack said.

"You believe that story, Mack? You'd believe anything I told you, wouldn't you? Sometimes I get tired of listening to myself talk. Harry Dakota, the Studly Indian Sage. It's too easy. You wouldn't believe how people lap this stuff up, gallery owners, little kids who come up to you at Indian Market, rich women who want to get their fingers in your braids . . . You can just tell 'em anything."

"And what do you get for it?"

"What do I get? Whatever I want. Samples, anyway. Whatever's on the tray. Just as long as I don't make the mistake of thinking I can afford it myself." Harry moved across the studio, ran his hand through the handles of his hammers. "I know, you're worried about breaking some rules once we get out there. I got plenty to worry about without that."

"You're in trouble, Harry?"

"Let's just say I got some problems."

"What kind?"

Harry didn't answer. Mack was leaning back, both palms flat on the workbench, and suddenly he felt the bench trembling. He looked up and saw the hammers rattling on their pegs, the glass vibrating in the window panes. He stared dumbly at Harry.

"What's that?"

Harry laughed. "What do you think, man? It's the mine down at Cerrillos. They're blasting. Every Sunday afternoon. You could set your watch by it. That's how we should be doing it, right? Legal."

Chapter Ten

THE DAY after he saw Harry, Mack played a benefit for a rural Spanish medical clinic that was in danger of going under. The benefit had been badly organized, underpublicized, and the huge auditorium was no more than a quarter full. The organizers were good, decent people, friends of Mack's, but an air of defeat hung over them all.

Mack came on last and he was determined to turn it all around. He surprised even his own band, pulling out all the stops. He shook his guitar as if he was wringing its neck. He nursed it and cursed it, skated across the platform, dipped low, almost driven to his knees by the soulfulness of it all. Harry was sitting down front with his wife and when Mack glanced at him, Harry flashed him clenched-fist approval, urging him on. Behind Mack the band was grinning, the drummer bobbed up and down like a windup monkey. They hadn't seen him like this in a long time. He sang the old hits as if it was the first time. He wasn't going to knuckle under.

It began to work. The couples staggered out onto the dance floor, one by one, first the gentle-souled Mennonite doctor and his wife in their L. L. Bean shoes, then the Spanish director and his new girlfriend, then Harry and his wife. Mack worked as if his life depended on it. By the time Mack started his second slam-bang blues number he had half of them on their feet; by the end, he had them all, shouting and waving.

He fingered the microphone, sweating and out of breath,

waiting for people to quiet down. He cocked his head to one side, smiling, raised a hand in acknowledgment.

"All right now, all right! Thank you . . ." Somebody shouted hoarsely from the back. "Everybody feeling O.K. out there? I'm going to tell you something. Somebody lied to me. Somebody told me the place was empty. It feels pretty damn full to me. You look around for yourself, but I'll tell you what I see. I see a hundred people who came out here because they believed in something. And I don't know anything in the world more powerful than that."

Mack looked out and saw the Mennonite doctor, the director with his arms folded around his girlfriend, saw the other dozen or so other people he knew. They were better people than he was. They were battlers and idealists, people who had been beaten ten times and never given up. Mack felt himself swelling with imperfectly understood emotion. He shook free of the tangled microphone cord. He wanted these people to know how good they were.

"Numbers are funny things, folks. A hundred thousand people turn out to watch the Dallas Cowboys every Sunday, now what does that mean?" The security police lounged against the back wall sipping Cokes, laughing. "People love to talk about heroes, don't they? You know who the real heroes are? You folks right here. You came out, a lot of you worked damn hard to make this happen."

There was applause and a chorus of shrill whistles. Out of the corner of his eye, Mack saw the drummer shifting on his stool, restless and solemn.

Mack didn't know why he was going on like this; all he knew was that he needed to. He stared out across the audience. There was a spotlight glaring in his eyes.

Then he saw at the back of the cavernous auditorium, standing alone, a figure in a familiar white dress. His heart leapt. It was Annie. He squinted, trying to be sure. The dress was an almost ghostly white in the darkness.

Mack was silent, thrown for a second. What could have made her come? He saw the trusting, upturned faces below him, wanting more. Still at a loss for words, Mack fingered the microphone.

"No one can take our hope away," he said finally, his voice trembling. He strained to see through the glaring light. Maybe it wasn't her. She gave him no sign of recognition.

"A couple of weeks ago I met a woman," he said. "An old woman. She lives north of here, maybe an hour from your clinic. She told me a story."

Glancing down, he saw Harry looking dubious. Mack couldn't help himself. He felt a wild, insane temptation to tell everything, his heart full of sorrow and love and too many withheld things. He wasn't even sure now who he was talking to. He was probably making a total ass of himself.

"About losing a little girl. Eight years old. This was a long time ago, you understand, almost forty years ago. She tended her daughter a whole day and a whole night and there were no doctors, no one to turn to . . . She showed me the girl's picture. It could have been my child's picture. Or yours. I don't know why I'm telling you this. Sometimes it seems like things haven't changed that much. But they have changed. They will change."

She was moving now, slipping quickly past the chatting security guards, heading toward the doors. Mack's stomach tightened, he felt a wave of panic. What had he said wrong? He had to find a way to hold her. He tilted the mike even closer to his lips.

"Five hundred years ago the conquistadores came looking for treasure, and I'm going to tell you a secret." The amplifiers sat around him like lurking, red-eyed beasts. Harry dropped his wife's hand, stepping forward in alarm, in outrage. Mack refused to meet his gaze.

"I know where it is," Mack said. Harry ran his hand over his braids, shaking his head in disbelief. "It's in you . . . and in you . . ." Harry was disgusted, waving him off. "And in you." He aimed his words at Annie, across the echoing space, across the sea of kind faces, across the sea of the best intentions.

It was a vain gesture. She entered the brightly lit lobby. For that moment she was illuminated, etched in fluorescent light.

There was no question now that it was Annie. She never looked
back. Mack looked down at his gleaming guitar. It was one thing
to win back an audience, another to win back your wife.

The applause was scattered at first, people weren't sure
whether Mack was finished or not, but then it rose and rose. He
looked at them, feeling pained, embarrassed, a little confused.
"I promise you, we're going to keep that clinic open. One way
or the other." Temporarily lost, he turned back to the band,
looking for help. The applause was still coming. Mack pulled the
microphone to him one more time. "Thank you, thank you . . .
no, come on . . . we'll be back after a break . . . It won't be
long."

Offstage Mack moved swiftly, tripping down the concrete
stairway. Before he reached the bottom, Harry slammed
through a metal fire door and he was furious.

"You goddamned lunatic," Harry said.

"Annie was out there." Mack slipped his head under his guitar strap.

"You are really, really crazy, Mack."

"She was standing in the back." Mack pulled the plastic capo
off his trembling fingers. "Did you see her?"

The musicians trotted down the steps past them, heading for
the dressing rooms. Mack caught the leery sidelong glance of
the piano player.

"No, man, I didn't see her," Harry said. "Listen, Mack, you
can't screw around like that. I'm serious. What did you think
you were doing?"

"I meant every word of it."

"Yeah? People asked you out here to perform, nobody asked
you to preach a sermon."

"Fine. Here." He shoved the guitar into Harry's arms. "You
go play a few songs for 'em. I've got to find her."

Mack jerked open the door to the outside, swung it shut
behind him, left Harry standing. He ran to the front of the
auditorium. A few people had drifted out on the steps to have a
smoke. Mack looked to the left and right, didn't see any sign of
Annie. He felt the bite of cool night air, shook the collar of his
sweat-drenched shirt. A lanky kid sitting on the fire hydrant

recognized Mack and pointed in astonishment. "Hey!" Mack
raised a hand in greeting, turned back toward the parking lot.

The hoods of the cars shone with reflected light. There were a
lot of vans; they all seemed to be silver gray and maroon and a
lot of the pickups had mountain scenes in the back windows.
Halfway across the lot there were three women, walking together. One of them was in a white dress. Mack ran again,
dodging between cars. A bunch of guys huddled together next
to a trailer, passed around a bottle. Mack caught the whiff of
marijuana.

It made no sense. Why would she come and then leave again,
without even speaking? Was there some kind of trouble? The
three women were twenty yards ahead of him, gathered
around a green Volkswagen. One of the women fished through
her purse for keys. Mack slowed to a walk.

The woman in the white dress suddenly heard him coming.
She turned quickly, her face full of fear. It was not Annie. The
woman with the keys froze at the car door.

"Sorry," Mack said. "I thought it was someone else."

No one believed him. The three women climbed hurriedly
into the car; Mack heard the engine sputter and then catch. He
ran a trembling hand over his face, feeling like an utter fool.

He watched the Volkswagen scoot and weave its way out of
the lot. He had seen Annie at the back of the auditorium, he was
sure of it. Even if this wasn't her. He had seen her. He wasn't
that crazy. He turned back, hands on hips, cheeks puffed out in
frustration. Somewhere in the street he heard a bottle explode
with a dull pop. Head down, he began the long walk back.

He didn't know what made him look up. He stopped and
stared down the long rows of cars. His pickup was parked under
some cottonwoods at the far end of the lot. The bright overhead
lights reflected off the windows, but there was something else
too, something moving, like a shadow sliding beneath the surface of the water.

Mack trotted at first, even as the terror began to swell, not
trusting his senses, but then he saw the movement again,
clearer than before. He ran full-out.

Just before he reached the pickup a meaty alarmed face

popped up on the inside of the glass. Something snapped in Mack's head. He yanked open the door of the truck. There were two big men inside. One of them was still on his knees on the floor, his hands full of wires from underneath Mack's dashboard. The contents of Mack's glove compartment were strewn everywhere, road maps and tools and paper cups.

The two big men in Western shirts, taken by surprise, tried to get away, thrashing like baby whales trapped in the wrong size aquarium. One of them tried to kick out at Mack with a cowboy boot. Mack grabbed the man by the leg and pulled him out on the gravel. The man banged his head on the floor of the truck as he came.

The other man shoved open the opposite door, but Mack raced around and caught him as he was coming out, banged him against a station wagon. The guy bounced off and Mack was on him.

The two men rolled on the gravel. Somewhere in the distance Mack heard someone shouting, "Hey, cut it out, you guys!"

Mack punched the man, then punched him again. The man tried to hit back, but mostly he was fending off Mack's blows. Mack hit out in blind fury. For a second he saw the man's face, the whitish scar on one nostril, the fresh blood at the corner of his mouth, the fear in the man's eyes.

"What the hell are you doing, man, what the hell . . ." The voice was almost comically high for such a big man.

Suddenly there was a knee in the middle of Mack's back and the second guy was on him. Mack rolled over, trying to get him off, but he had an arm around Mack's neck and was holding tight. The first man was up now, limping toward Mack. He was looking to hit him, but still a little afraid.

Mack swung around, swung the man on his back the way you'd swing a bag of potatoes, sent him flying into his partner. All three of them went down. They couldn't hold Mack now. Mack grabbed one of them by the leg as he was trying to crawl free; again there was the arm around Mack's neck. Mack fought against it, but the man was squeezing hard; Mack could feel himself starting to black out. He felt a sharp pain in his right ear. The son of a bitch had bitten him.

Mack didn't know what it was that hit them at first; there was just the sudden impact knocking them to the gravel. Mack was on his knees, gasping for breath; his clothes were magically dripping wet. The other two guys hollered and stumbled around in the high-velocity stream of water that did erratic figure eights over them and the nearby cars. Harry stood with the firehose on his hip, the steady force of the water making a hiss like a snake. Somehow Harry had hauled it from the back of the building halfway across the lot and he was laughing his head off.

The two men ran through the cars, disappeared over the embankment. Harry knelt by Mack's side. Mack was trembling all over. He felt his ear. There was blood.

"Can you believe that? He bit me in the ear."

"What the hell are you doing, Mack? Taking on the whole parking lot? You're too old for that stuff."

"They were in my truck, Harry. They were looking for something. They know something."

"Take it easy, man. Don't go nuts on me. Jesus, look at you."

"Somebody's onto us. Rick's talked . . ."

"They were stealing radios, Mack. That's all it was."

Far off Mack could hear the roar of a truck starting up, the squeal of tires.

"Somebody knows. I saw it in their faces."

"You didn't see anything. You're just overreacting."

Mack tasted the blood on his lip. He wiped it away with his hand. "Don't tell me what I saw. I saw what I saw. All right?"

Harry looked away, holding his tongue. Mack's truck stood with its doors open, water dripping slowly off the frame. "All right. Whatever you say."

Chapter Eleven

MACK PICKED up Kaia after her play group and drove up the ski basin road into the mountains. It was one of her favorite places, a thick aspen grove full of pleasures for a two-year-old. They spent almost an hour wading and throwing pebbles into the shallow stream. A dog trotted up from one of the campsites and Kaia fed him a cookie. She toiled up the trail, climbing over the knotted roots, and when she was tired she lifted her arms and cried, "Up-py, up-py!" They found a springy aspen bent low over the trail and Mack sat her on it. Kaia bounced up and down like it was a horse, playing This Is the Way the Cowboys Ride, holding on to Mack's finger for balance. He was perfectly happy.

Through the trees Mack could see out across the desert to the mesas and canyon lands beyond, all golden haze and shadow in the late-afternoon sun. It was an uncanny landscape. He used to worry how he would be able to remember it, when he was away from it. He never knew exactly why that landscape was so important to him. Maybe the stretches and folds, the sheer distances, suggested infinity, God, mystery, who knew what, but it *was* grandeur itself, and Mack always had the feeling that if he only looked hard enough it would yield to him.

In eight hours Mack and Harry and Rick and Grier would be out there, in those canyons, and they would yield, one way or the other. Knowing that had Mack as high as a kite.

Harry had just about convinced him that the incident with the two men he found in his pickup was nothing but a parking lot break-in, a couple of drunks looking for wallets and tape decks. Nothing else made sense. Was Mack really ready to believe that those two guys had overheard Rick or Grier talking in a bar, then followed Mack all the way to the auditorium to search his *glove compartment?* To find what? A treasure map? Come on.

Mack was embarrassed and shaken by what had happened, by the ferocity of his response. He remembered the stories Tucker's wife had told him, of trucks driving up and down the road, day after day, waiting. He remembered the stories and then tried to put them away. He and Harry agreed there was no point in telling Rick and Grier anything that had happened.

Everything was in high gear. For the past twenty-four hours the phone calls had flown back and forth between them. They were running into each other all over town. Mack had spent the morning working on saddles, replacing rings and rotten leather. Then on the way over to borrow his neighbor's horse trailer, he passed Grier on the road. In the sporting goods store he ran into Rick and together they tested twelve varieties of lanterns and flashlights. To the clerk's astonishment, they bought eight. At lunch at The Shed Rick not only picked up the tab, the first time in a blue moon that had happened, he also left a ten-dollar tip under his coffee cup. Everything now had its own natural acceleration. It was like a four-on-one fast break. There was no reason for the ball ever to touch the floor.

Mack balanced his daughter on the springy aspen. She squealed for more and more. On the slope above them, Mack could see some of the aspen leaves starting to turn. At ten thousand feet, summer was already fading. Up here a sign of gold meant the death of a season, summer's end.

I want to make you happy, darling, he thought, you and your mother and me. I don't want to screw up your life, I don't want you to grow up in any damn broken home. I'm going to get your mother to come back, you bet. You talk about breakthroughs; your daddy's going to make a real one, I'm going to bust that wall of rubble wide open and when I come out of those canyons your mother is going to be in for the surprise of her life. Mack took Kaia under her arms and lifted her off the aspen. Tonight I'm going to know, he thought, tonight I'm going to know.

Mack was in a very good mood as he came down the walk. He swung Kaia into the air and caught her, making her laugh. Annie was sitting in the patio waiting for them, but Mack didn't see her at first. It wasn't till she rose quickly that the sudden motion caught his eye. He saw the lean, tense figure flickering through the closely spaced poles of the fence, coming to the gate to meet them. Kaia saw her too.

"Mommy! Mommy!"

Kaia tumbled into her mother's arms. Mack saw the strain in Annie's face.

"Anything wrong?" he asked.

"Not really. You were late, that's all."

"Sorry. I guess we lost track of the time."

"O.K. You know how a person's imagination can run away with them. I was just afraid something had happened to the two of you." Kaia snuggled into her mother's shoulder. Annie smiled, giving a little.

"You shouldn't have worried," Mack said. He patted Kaia's back. "Tell your mommy who threw rocks in the water."

"Kaia did!"

Annie laughed and put Kaia down. There was a brand-new swing, carved in the shape of an airplane, hanging in one of the apple trees. Kaia raced to it, threw herself across it. Mack smiled watching her. He felt Annie's sidelong glance, her re-evaluation. There was a bed of flowers along the wall. Mack hadn't remembered them being there before.

"You plant these?"

"Yes."

"Nice. What are they?" Kaia had moved on, was pitching green apples through the wire fence that overlooked the dry riverbed.

"Begonias. Impatiens."

"I never could remember the names of flowers," he said. It was almost six-thirty and the backyard was streaked by long shadows. Mack could feel Annie's hesitation.

"I bought a steak at Albertson's. It was on special."

"Since when did you start buying steak?"

"Since it occurred to me to ask you to stay for supper."

The offer took Mack by surprise. Kaia was trying to pry a log out of the woodpile. Mack didn't have to meet Harry and the others till ten.

"That sounds great," Mack said.

They were both still for a moment, not quite sure how to navigate the new waters.

"Why don't you play with Kaia for a while?" she said. "I'll get started."

Mack played a game of hide-and-seek with Kaia in the unfamiliar yard, wondering what was up with Annie. Kaia, too young to understand the intricacies of the game, always went back to the same hiding place in the tall weeds, but burst into wild laughter every time she was discovered.

Annie called them in. Settled in her highchair, Kaia cast long, quiet glances at Mack, trying to figure out why he was eating with them. Mack cut up small pieces of his steak to give to her. They were like a family again.

After dinner Mack took Kaia in for her bath. He poured in more than enough bubble bath and he and Kaia worked it into a foaming mountain. She draped her arms with it, decorated his face with a sudsy beard and mustache. She sang and rolled over in the soapy water, pretending she could swim, her body slippery and glistening. Mack knelt by the tub, pouring cupfuls of water over her wet hair. *You have a little girl, take care of her,* Tucker's wife had told him, *it's the most important thing.* In two hours they would be riding out into the canyons. He reached out and cupped his daughter's face in his hand. The gravity of his gaze made her grin back at him.

Mack hadn't heard Annie come in. When he looked up, she was there, watching the two of them. Mack wiped some of the bubbles from his face, trying to look a little less ridiculous.

"I put water on," she said. "Won't you stay and have coffee?"

Mack finished up the dishes, then sat uneasily on the edge of the couch, listening to Annie read Kaia a story in the dark bedroom. He was restless. He thumbed through a copy of *Art Lines,* tossed it away, got up, put some piñon pine in the fireplace, jammed some crumpled pages from *The New Mexican* classifieds under it, lit a fire.

Everywhere there were touches of her, an arrangement of weeds, a familiar kerosene lamp on a side table, the repositioned furniture, all part of her relentless need to make a home. Listening to Annie singing Kaia to sleep, Mack felt it drawing on him too.

He looked at his watch. Harry would be at his house in a half hour to help him load up the horses. Kaia was throwing up her last defenses against sleep, halfhearted demands for juice, a book, a different nightgown. Mack went to the living room window. The moon was just starting to come up. It would be almost full tonight. That would make the riding a lot easier.

"You started a fire. That's nice." Mack turned and saw Annie standing at Kaia's bedroom door, wondering about him.

They got their coffee, came back and sat together on the couch. Annie pulled her leg up under her so she could face him. Her long freckled arm lay across the back of the couch as she sipped her coffee. Mack watched her, remembering what a lovely woman she was.

"I need to ask you something," he said.

"What's that?"

"I gave a benefit for the clinic a couple of nights ago. I thought I saw you."

"You did."

"I wasn't sure." The fire sputtered, a spray of embers bounced off the screen.

"I saw the posters. I had this impulse to see you . . . I thought you wouldn't even have to know I was there. My big chance to be just a fly on the wall."

"But you walked out."

"I couldn't bear listening to any more of it."

"I wasn't sure you were listening."

"Oh, I was listening all right. I got the message."

"I came looking for you," Mack said.

"That wasn't what I intended. I didn't mean to throw you."

She tossed her hair back. "I hope it went all right. The rest of the concert."

"There was a little trouble," he said.

"Really?" She was utterly guileless.

"Nothing serious," he said.

"Something's changed, hasn't it?" she said.

"How do you mean?"

"It's so obvious. Seeing you come down the walk with Kaia, I could just tell. You were looser, maybe. More like you used to be."

"I guess that's good."

"Remember when we met? How you would always tell me that whatever song you'd just finished was the best one yet? How you secretly used to think that you were a genius?"

"I was trying to impress you."

"I don't think so. I think you believed it. I liked that about you." Mack set his coffee cup on the table, leaned back on the couch. "You're not seeing anyone, are you?"

"No," he said, smiling. "And you?"

She rested her forehead against the fingertips of one hand, gave him an amused, girlish glance. "No," she said.

They heard Kaia roll over in her bed, crying out faintly. They were both silent for a moment, a habit they had learned together.

"There's something I want to ask you," she said.

"Shoot."

"Why did you let me leave?"

"Let you leave? You *announced* to me . . ."

"I know."

"You seemed so unhappy."

"But people are always unhappy about one thing or the other. Aren't they? I know I'm not being very clear. But I've been trying to figure out what we have the right to expect from one another. Here we have this child together, we both claim to love one another. I know everyone is supposed to respect everyone else's freedom, no one wants to be oppressive, but do we really think we have no right? . . . For example. What if I were to tell you, tonight, that I wasn't going to let you go? Would I be overstepping my bounds?"

"I don't think so," Mack said.

They stared at one another. Her chin was trembling. Mack reached out and covered her hand. She took her hand away, held it out, fingered the thin gold wedding band.

"I haven't taken it off, see? Funny, isn't it? I still feel very married to you."

Mack moved to her, took her in his arms. They kissed. Both of them were stirred. It had been a long time. Mack held tight to her, buried his face in her hair. She took his face in her hands, wanting to look at him.

"I would love it if you stayed," she said.

He stared into her steady green eyes. Everything he'd said he wanted was right here, being offered to him. He could call Harry, tell him he couldn't make it. They'd all be mad as hell, but what did it matter? They'd all be coming back empty-handed, anyway; it was just craziness. This was his life. Here.

The smell of piñon pine was in the room. The fire crackled, then sang out briefly. He stared at the shadows flickering at the back of the curved adobe fireplace. He leaned forward. For a second he thought he saw it again, the flute player arching over him in the cave.

"Is something wrong?" she said.

"I can't stay. I can't tonight."

"I'm sorry."

"It's not what you think. I'm supposed to meet Harry."

"O.K."

"No, really." He ran his hand over her hair, confused now. He wasn't sure how much he dared tell her. "We're going to float the river for a couple of days." Without knowing why, he decided against telling her about Rick and Grier. "We're going to drive up tonight. We've been talking about it for a long time."

"And you don't want to disappoint him."

"No."

"O.K." She knew him well enough to know he wasn't telling her all of it.

"Let me look at her one last time," he said.

Together they went to the bedroom door. When they pushed it open a band of light fell across their daughter's face, but it didn't wake her. She lay on her back, a stuffed mouse by her pillow, one arm extended through the slats of the crib. Mack reached down and put the arm back inside. He wanted to be sure she was safe. Her skin was incredibly soft.

He put his arm around Annie. Together they stared at their child. "I'm sorry I can't stay," he said.

"Some other time," she said. She looked up at him. "Whatever it is you're doing, be careful. If something happened to you, I don't know what we'd do. We'd be lost."

Chapter Twelve

THE HORSE was spooked. There were four men trying to get him into the trailer and the four men were losing. Buck had his feet set, his nostrils flared; his eyes were wild and rolling. Mack was perched on the metal sides of the horse trailer and had hold of the halter rope. Grier and Harry and Rick were behind. They had the butt line around the rear of the powerful horse. They were digging in with their feet, all their weight against the rope. Grier's cheeks looked like they were about to pop with the effort. The butt line kept the horse from backing up, but he sure wasn't going forward.

"Come on, Buck, get up now, boy, come on," Mack was saying, but Buck wasn't buying it. Every muscle in the big horse was set against them.

Some demon of perversity had gotten into the animal. He wasn't going to be dominated or led anywhere. He didn't trust any of them. Maybe it was the night, the strangeness of the scene. Horses were creatures of habit and these horses were not used to being rousted out in the middle of the night. The lights of Grier's van shone on the trailer, casting long, eerie shadows. Packs lay in heaps on the ground.

The other horses had been skittish, but had been handled. Not Buck. It was as if he sensed something. He wasn't going to be caged. The trailer that Buck had walked into a hundred times before was tonight somehow transformed into a dark trap.

Buck stepped sideways suddenly, banging against the metal

sides. The other horses whinnied. They were stirred up too, banging in their stalls. Buck set himself again, his flanks trembling. Harry and Grier pulled the butt line even tighter. Mack heard Grier curse. He could see the strain and frustration in the faces of the men. It was a standoff.

"It's all right, Buck, fella, come on, big guy." Mack tried to soothe him, tried to finesse Buck into it. He reached out to touch the horse's nose.

It was then that Grier made his move. He took the loose end of the rope and whipped Buck across the rear. It was a mistake. The horse lurched forward, catching everyone by surprise. With the sudden move the butt line went slack. Rick fell to one knee. The horse was free from his tormentors, all except Mack, who still had hold of the halter rope. Buck reared, throwing Mack off balance. Mack was nearly pulled into the trailer with the thrashing animal. He let go of the rope just in time and grabbed hold of the top metal rail to catch himself.

Buck kicked at the sides of the trailer again and again, battering the metal slats in protest. For a second Mack was sure he was going to kick the sides down. The other horses were going crazy.

Suddenly Buck reared again. Mack was still hanging to the side of the trailer. The head of the horse was only inches away. For a moment the horse seemed to defy gravity, its forelegs pawing the air noiselessly, as if it was about to take flight. Framed by the moon, the long, bony head of the horse seemed as ancient and alien as a lizard's; the wide eyes were filled with fear.

Mack stretched out for the halter rope that dangled free, got it, jumped down to the ground. With a quick clatter Buck moved forward into the trailer. Harry slammed the metal door shut behind him.

Mack stared at his boots, taking a second to get control of his anger. He finally looked up at Grier. "You shouldn't have done that. You could have gotten somebody killed."

"At least I got him to move, right?" Grier said. He bent down and picked up one of the bedrolls. "Why don't we get this stuff packed? We're late enough as it is."

It was no small production. The rubber raft was in the back of Grier's van. The trailer with the five horses they hooked to Mack's pickup. It took them a good hour and a half to get everything packed. There were saddles, shovels, buckets, rope, a couple of bundles of dynamite, a small butane cookstove. There was also one disturbing surprise. Mack lifted the saddle blankets to discover a 30.06 rifle and a couple boxes of ammunition. He looked at Grier.

"You didn't tell me about this."

Grier tossed a metal pulley in on top of the sleeping bags in the back of Mack's pickup.

"Be prepared. Isn't that what they teach you in the Boy Scouts? Maybe I'll shoot you some rabbits and cook us up a nice stew."

Rick rode with Mack, Harry rode up in Grier's van. They took the back streets to get out of town. It was late enough that most of the houses were dark. Their only observers, as far as they knew, were a small mongrel dog that came out to bark at the horses as the trailer bounced over the rutted dirt road, and a long-haired hitchhiker sitting on his bedroll at the intersection to the highway. In the flash of headlights Mack saw the hitchhiker's face open in amazement at the midnight caravan. After they passed Mack glanced in the rearview mirror. The hitchhiker was slumped again, resigned to defeat, a small figure receding into darkness.

When they turned onto the highway there were still a few cars leaving the opera. Farther north they had the highway to themselves. They passed a couple of garages, the billboards advertising souvenir shops and candle factories. At Pojoaque there were a couple of low-riders parked at the drive-in, racing their engines.

Turning off the highway everything became even poorer, more marginal. They passed an encampment of trailers, a few houses with dirt yards and ruined cars piled under scraggly apple trees.

They began to move up into the canyons, mounting ridge after twisting ridge. They were entering the maze. In the silvery light they could see down into the canyon bottoms, filled with dark masses of juniper.

Mack's pickup crawled around the hairpin turns, straining with the weight of the horse trailer behind. The truck lights shone off the rock walls. Mack grew more and more excited. It felt as if they were leaving civilization behind, even if it wasn't true. There were still, every mile or two, the chain-link fences, the occasional towers set back off the road, the modest blue government signs.

"You have a nice afternoon with your kid?" Rick said.

"Real nice."

"Must be hard, sometimes."

"It is," Mack said. "You were never married, were you?"

"No. I've been close, though. I lived with a woman once who had kids."

"Kids? Really? I never knew that. How many?"

"One. Then two. I met her when she was pregnant. A terrific person. Beautiful. Her husband had run out on her, another one of those guys off to find themselves. I was like the white knight, coming in to save the day. I was trying to make movies then, my father had cut me off totally, he thought I was a bohemian wastrel. I didn't have a cent."

Rick was silent for a second. Mack downshifted into third coming around a tight curve, felt the horse trailer sway behind them.

"I really loved her. She would cry and say I know it can't go anywhere and I couldn't stand there not being any hope and I'd say, that's not true, everything's going to be all right, even though I had nothing to back it up. It went on for more than a year. The kids started calling me Daddy. I knew I should have cut that off, but I didn't. I know you know what it feels like, Mack, a two-year-old climbing into bed with you in the morning. And at the same time I felt like my head was about to burst, there was this constant pressure. I felt trapped and angry all the time. How could I support this whole family? I knew I had this special destiny, right? I'd have to give up all the things I'd always wanted, what I'd always dreamed about. It seemed so unfair. Then I heard from a friend of mine that they were going to do a low-budget film of a script of mine, I'd have to come to London. I couldn't turn it down. It was the break I'd always been waiting for. She thought we'd somehow go together. I realized I couldn't do it, when push came to shove. It was total emotional panic. I left. It must have been damn hard for her. I know it was; in the couple letters that I got . . ."

"And the film?"

"Well, there's low-budget and then there's low budget. It was a real bust."

"Did you ever see them after that?"

"Once or twice. But it was very hard."

"And what happened to her?"

"She got married. To a very nice person, people tell me." Mack glanced over, caught a glimpse of Rick's brooding face in the dim glow of the dashboard lights. "Weird. I don't know why I've been thinking about all these things. Ever since we found the cave, it's been as if this stuff has just been coming up on its own. I wake up at night thinking about it. What's the point? I guess the point is that only later on could I dare to realize how much havoc I caused, how much pain. I was so caught in my own feelings of being trapped. No one ever sees themselves as being the villain, right? We're that obtuse. In the old neighborhood, her friends would walk by without looking at me. At first I thought it was a mistake, they hadn't seen me. It wasn't a mistake; those people really hated me for what I'd done."

"But it doesn't sound like you could have done anything else," Mack said.

"Maybe not. But where are all those feelings supposed to go? Are they just lost? It was my whole life, Mack." He laughed abruptly. "The usual male remorse, right? But you spend your whole life withholding yourself from life, waiting for some special destiny that never comes and never comes and then it may finally occur to even the densest human being that they may have missed the whole show."

"But it has come, hasn't it?"

"What's that?"

"Your special destiny."

Rick looked across the dark cab, smiling. "I guess it has, Mack."

They stopped at the bridge. The four men worked quickly, hauling the raft down to the river first, then the bigger packs, the pickaxes and shovels, everything that was too heavy or unwieldy to take in on horseback. They worked silently. The only sounds were the low ripple of the water, the occasional impatient snort of the horses in the trailer, the hoot of an owl in the nearby cottonwoods. The moon shone off the surface of the water. There was a wavering beam of a flashlight as one of the men searched for something in the back of the van.

This was the part they wanted to get over with in a hurry. With a pickup and a van and a horse trailer sitting up on a bridge in the middle of the night, it was not a moment when they wanted to run into anybody.

It turned out that working as fast as they could wasn't quite fast enough. Mack was the first one to see the lights descending the mountain.

The others saw it too. The slow-moving headlights disappeared for a moment behind a curve in the canyon road. Mack and Harry were halfway down the riverbank, carrying the heavy metal hoist between them. Rick knelt on the side of the raft, repacking some tools. The lights appeared again, a half mile down the road. It was a rattletrap truck, listing badly to one side, just crawling along.

Grier, up by the van, slid slowly behind the horse trailer, trying to hide himself without looking as if he was hiding. With one quick gesture Grier motioned for them to get down. They were about to be undone by sheer chance. Mack and Harry dropped the hoist they were carrying and walked further down the bank, toward the underside of the bridge.

The fan of light covered the bridge. Mack looked back over his shoulder. Rick was frozen with one knee on the raft, not sure what to do. As the headlights of the battered pickup flashed over him Rick turned his face to one side, covering his eyes.

The pickup never slowed as it crossed the bridge. It couldn't have been going more than thirty miles an hour. It drifted to one side of the road, hit some gravel on the shoulder, wove back to the middle, putted out of sight.

Harry lifted the pulley, boosted it up with a knee. "Drunk," he said.

"Blind drunk, you hope," Mack said.

Above them Grier stepped out into the road, looking to see if the pickup was gone, then ambled down the slope with a bag of tools in his arms. Rick came to join the other three.

"You think he saw us?" Rick said.

"Of course he saw us," Grier said. "How could he miss us?" He shoved the bag of tools in Rick's chest. "Here, see if you can find a place to stick this."

Nothing more was said. They went back to their packing, but they were all a little shaken. They had gotten their first taste of it, what it felt like to need to hide, the uneasy chill of being in the wrong, even before you started. God knew who the guy in the pickup was. Maybe Harry was right, maybe it was some poor drunk trying to make it home in one piece. Even that thought wasn't so comforting. Even if he hadn't seen Rick crouched on the raft, or the rest of them, he could scarcely have missed seeing the van, the pickup, the trailer full of horses. Unless he decided to write the whole thing off as a fit of the d.t.'s, he'd probably mention it to his wife in the morning, and then maybe she'd mention it to her nephew who worked in the sheriff's office, and then someone might take a look. It was an unsettling thought.

It took only ten more minutes to finish loading. The raft sat low in the water; it took all of them to shove it out into the shallows. Harry clambered in, lowered himself into position, reached out to check the oarlocks.

"You sure you don't want to change your mind, Grier, and go in my place?" Rick said. They were standing shin-deep in the water. Mack had a flashlight and the dim light played over the snugly packed raft. In the air above them was the squeaking of nighthawks.

"I don't know what you're worried about, Rick," Grier said. "This is a piece of cake. A nice moonlit night, you and Harry can just let the river do all the work."

"Hope so," Rick said.

"Think of all the saddle sores you'll be saving yourself," Grier said. "Let's go." Grier took Rick under the arm, gave him a boost up.

The arrangements had been Grier's idea. Grier was the one who knew the river and yet he was sending Harry and Rick. The only reason Mack could think of for doing it that way was that Grier wanted a chance to be alone with Mack, wanted a chance to iron things out.

Rick squeezed down gingerly between the shovels and the coils of rope.

"Ready?" Grier said.

"Ready as we're ever going to be," Harry said.

Mack and Grier pushed the raft off, Grier staggering up to his thighs in the muddy water. Harry began to work the oars, shouting something back across the water. Rick was crouched warily, holding on to the sides. The canyon walls, rising black in the moonlight, quickly dwarfed the drifting raft. Grier waded back to shore, wiping his muddy trousers. "Let's go," he said. "They're going to be fine."

They drove the van and the pickup out of the canyon, then along a rough dirt road that ran for almost a mile along the gorge. They pulled into a thick grove of juniper. The horses clattered easily out of their stalls, eager to be on solid ground again.

They packed the horses in the glare of the van, the two men working side by side. They exchanged no more than a couple of words. There was nothing pushy or bullying in Grier now. If anything he showed Mack an almost exaggerated kindness, helping Mack retie a wobbly pack or bridle a skittish horse.

The two men rode out along the rim of the canyon in the full moon. Mack was filled with the presence of Annie, the firelit room, the smell of her hair, a quiet mournfulness and regret. It was hard to believe that had been just a couple of hours ago.

Mack and Grier could see the plain, a ghostly white, below them, and beyond that, the dark shapes of mountains, from the Sandias all the way up to Truchas Peak. The horses were alive, snorting, frisky in the night air. Grier led two of the packhorses and Mack had one. He could hear Grier cursing softly, yanking the lead rope, trying to bring the animals into line. Brush caught at their legs. Mack ducked out of the way of dead branches of piñon. Wordlessly Grier pointed out a low-flying owl.

The night was full of shapes. Mack saw something flitting through the sagebrush, moving parallel to the horses, fifty yards out. At first he thought it was just his mind playing tricks on him, but it didn't go away, a ghostly fluid shadow trotting alongside them for almost fifteen minutes before melting away in the brush. It must have been a coyote out hunting, Mack decided, hunting and curious about these strange intruders.

The night was full of squeaks and scurryings, hunters and foragers, rodents and foxes and marauding birds. The full moon made it easy to spot prey on the bright patches of sand.

It seemed to Mack that they were entering an imaginary landscape. At first, as they rode close to the rim, they could see the lights of Santa Fe off in the distance, a few lights on the distant highway, but then the trail led away from the rim and the lights disappeared. Mack was amazed at where he found himself.

Out of the corner of his eye he thought he saw something leap behind a dark juniper; when he looked directly, he saw nothing. Ahead of him Mack heard Grier still murmuring to the recalcitrant packhorses. We are chasing apparitions, Mack thought. He remembered the flute player. Out here it would not be hard to believe in things like that, in a figure leading you on and on. It must have been on a night like this when Tucker rode out with his partner.

They came to a canyon. It must have been six hundred feet deep; a monster. They couldn't see the bottom.

"Lord," Grier said. The horses moved uneasily, shying from going too close to the rim.

"Don't tell me you didn't know it was here," Mack said.

"I'd never admit to it," Grier said. "You know me. Let's go. Nothing to it but to do it."

Grier led the way, fighting his horse at first to get him headed down the steep series of switchbacks. The trail was so narrow that Mack could reach out and touch the canyon wall. The horses moved cautiously, but even so Mack could hear loose rock giving way beneath their hooves, creating miniature slides, small stones bounding down into nothingness.

There was nothing to do but trust the horses. Once they were under the rim of the canyon and out of the moonlight it was dark; the riders couldn't see anything beyond the ears of their mounts. Swaying with the horse, Mack began to get a touch of seasickness. He pressed his knees into the sides of his horse, found himself reaching for the horn.

They finally came to the bottom of the canyon. There was a thick grove of ponderosa pine and some elder along the stream. They dismounted and let the horses drink. The animals were all lathered up. Mack wiped a handful of white suds from the coat of his horse. The two men squatted on boulders, regathering their strength. Grier's face, under the uncertain beam of the flashlight, had the tired gravity of a hunter.

"How you making it?" Grier said.

"All right. A little edgy. I mean, if we actually find something . . ."

"Oh, you don't have to tell me," Grier said. They both fell silent for a moment. "Rick said that you and Annie weren't together anymore."

"Temporarily," Mack said.

"I hope it works out. I never was real good at talking to her. I guess you know that." The horses browsed noisily in the nearby bushes. "Mack, I'm sorry about what happened between us. It was my fault."

"It's never one person's fault," Mack said.

"You know that kid whose collarbone I busted? He's working for me now."

"You're kidding me!"

"No. I felt real bad about what happened. I went to see him. He's a tough kid. I like tough kids. He's been working for me for the last five months and he does a good job. Though he doesn't quite know how to deal with all the furniture makers and aging hippies I got on the crew."

"That's really amazing, Grier."

"Is it? You really thought I was that bad a guy? I'm just real sorry. It's taken me a long time to figure it out. I guess maybe I just believed in you more than I believed in myself. That's always going to be trouble, isn't it? I saw that you had a gift, something special, and I said to myself, this guy's got it, why hasn't he made it, something's got to be fundamentally wrong. I thought I knew the answer. And I overstepped. In a serious way." Grier stared at his open hands. Moonlight filtering through the trees lit up odd bits of ground as if they were patches of snow. "You don't know how many times I thought about calling you. Couldn't do it. I just wouldn't want what happened back there to be any kind of obstacle."

"I don't see why it should be."

"Well, good. I don't either. And don't be scared. This is going to be the best damn thing you ever did in your life." Grier slapped his thighs. Ill at ease suddenly, he looked back toward the horses. "I guess they're about as rested as they're going to be, aren't they? You ready to ride?"

They rechecked the packs, tightened their saddles, pulled themselves up on the horses again. They rode for almost a mile through ponderosa groves along the canyon floor, crossing and recrossing the stream, the horses' hooves clattering and splashing over the wet rocks. Then they headed up.

Mack and Grier hunched forward in their saddles to give the horses whatever help they could. The animals worked hard, grunting with every step. Switchback followed switchback; Mack could feel the huge muscles of the horse straining under him, his own muscles straining with them, in tune. It was as if they had become one animal. He could hear only the squeak of the saddles, the metallic clicking of hooves, the groans of the horses, the occasional rattle of loose rock.

They moved higher, hugging the wall, never daring to look up or down. Suddenly they were in moonlight again. The horses were drenched in sweat; the smell was strong.

At the top they got off to let the horses recover. Mack heard coyotes crying far out on the mesa, way back in the juniper. Mack, his hand on the wet trembling flank of his horse, stared out at a world of dim canyons stretching away in every direction. Mack was filled with a sweet joy at the wildness of it. They had made it, made a break with everything they had ever known. The night wind was full of new scents. Mack looked over at Grier, who was taking a piss. Grier was grinning.

They rode for another mile, heading west across the mesa top. They came to the remains of an ancient pueblo, low rock walls and dead cholla sprouting from the centuries-old rooms. The horses picked their way among stones and pottery shards that littered the ground. Beyond that they came to a thicket of good-sized juniper, wove in and out of the maze of trees for twenty minutes. Suddenly they were there, at the rim, on a rock that jutted out into the canyon like the prow of a ship. They stared out at the familiar silver band of river. There was no sign of Harry or Rick.

They unloaded the horses, tied them up, gave them oats. Most of the stuff they put under a tarp and tied down; all they were taking with them tonight were the bare essentials. The rest could wait till morning. Mack watched Grier tie his rifle snugly to his pack.

Grier went down first, cautious as a blind man descending a stair. Mack stood on the rim, shining a flashlight down at the fissure in the rock, the narrow string of foot- and handholds. Once Grier was safe on the ledge below, Mack tied the packs to a rope and lowered them one by one.

The two men worked with the dogged urgency brought on by fatigue. In twenty minutes they had everything down that they needed. Together they carried the packs along the narrow ledge into the cave, laid out pads and sleeping bags in the soft dust. The flashlights they propped in the metal frames of their packs cast wavering shadows against the walls.

It was cold. Mack pulled an old band jacket out of his pack. A pair of apples he had tucked in the sleeve rolled out into the dust. Mack held up the fruit.

"Want one?"

"No, thanks."

Mack sat cross-legged on his sleeping bag, watched Grier

meticulously laying out his gear. The rifle went against the wall
behind his bedroll.

"Looks like we beat them here after all, doesn't it?" Mack
said.

"Sure does. I'm going to get some firewood."

Grier slouched out of the cave and was back in fifteen minutes with an armful of dead juniper.

The dry wood caught quickly. The two men sat watching the
fire, the shadows dancing on the arching pale walls. The smoke
gathered, curled slowly through the smoke hole at the top of the
cave.

Mack lay back, stared up at the rippled dome of the cave. The
etching of the flute player was directly above him. In the flickering of the firelight the humpbacked figure seemed to glow for a
second, then fade.

Out of the stillness, Grier said, "You know what I used to do in
the summers, Mack?"

"What's that?"

"Used to work for these contract cutters. When I was nineteen, twenty. Did it for, gee, five summers, I think. We'd start in
Texas in June, work our way up; we'd be cutting in Saskatche-
wan in September. It was good pay, hard work. We'd be running those combines till one in the morning sometimes, trying
to beat a storm. It could be plenty boring, but I always carried a
twenty-two up in the cab so when we'd flush rabbits or pheasant
out of the rows, I'd have at least a shot at it."

Mack felt the pins and needles of exhaustion threading up
and down his legs. Grier's voice seemed to be coming from
someplace far away.

"Harvest the spine of the whole damn continent. All day long,
watching the grain pouring out of those chutes. Close your eyes
at night and you'd still be seeing it. And none of it was yours. It
belonged to these Swedish farmers with their brick farmhouses,
neat as a pin, windrows of Russian olive trees. You couldn't help
it, even with the good pay we were getting, you couldn't help
thinking about how all of that bounty that you'd harvested, it
was never going to be yours. Right through your hands. I don't
know what right I had to think like that. But I've always had the

feeling that I had something coming to me. And now, finally, it turns out that I was right. We are just getting our due, Mack."

There was a cry somewhere out in the canyon. They both heard it.

"What was that?" Grier said.

"I don't know yet."

They both waited. Mack pushed himself up so his back rested against the soft rock wall. It occurred to Mack for the first time just how bad it could be to get trapped in a cave like this. They heard it again, a long, mournful, rising cry. The fire snapped, brushed the walls with light. It came again, the sound rising and falling, a long, complaining bray.

"Burros," Mack said.

"Yeah, burros."

They both lay back in the half-light, laughing out loud. One laugh triggered another, echoing in the dark cave, dissolving their fear. It was perfect. They had it coming. There were herds of wild burros out here only because there had been, in the last hundred years, people as crazy as Mack and Grier, prospectors, fortune hunters, men who, once they got out into these canyons and couldn't find the big strike, just pitched their tools and walked away, let their pack animals go, left them to forage for themselves. The burros over the years had gone wild as deer, formed herds. They were mocking reminders, the only survivors of a century of failed schemes. They were ghosts, all right, four-footed, long-eared, and feisty as hell.

Mack climbed out of his bag, went to the cave mouth, stared up the river. There was nothing but the full moon shining across the canyon floor. A rock face of white pumice on the far cliff seemed to glow as if it were alive. When Mack came back, Grier was still awake, up on one elbow.

"Anything?"

"Nothing," Mack said. "You think we should go looking for them?"

"No. They're all right. They'll show up; give 'em time."

Mack slipped back into his bag, stared at the dying embers, saw them finally blink out. The darkness closed in on them.

Mack could hear the rustle of Grier's sleeping bag as he shifted sides, trying to get comfortable.

Harry and Rick could have tipped the raft over; it would have been easy enough to do in the dark. Or they could have run into someone—night fishermen, poachers, Indian herdsmen, God knows who. Mack thought of the tribal policeman who had been waiting for them on the bridge.

They slept finally, fitfully at first, but then more deeply, Mack dreaming of silver rivers and dim massive curves of canyon walls at night and the feel of horses' muscles wedded to his own.

Mack was awakened by the sound of someone on the ladder. He sat up in his sleeping bag. It was utterly dark and he had no idea how much time had passed. Grier rustled and turned over. He had heard it too.

Mack reached for his pack, trying to find his flashlight. He heard the sharp zip of Grier undoing his sleeping bag.

There was a pale fan of light at the mouth of the cave. Mack heard Grier scrambling. Something heavy thudded into the dust. There was a sharp click and then the sound of metal against metal. The light pulsed.

"Who is it?" Mack shouted hoarsely. He heard the sliding metallic sound of a round being slipped into a chamber.

Suddenly there was a flood of light; the cave was filled with it, blinding them, making them turn their heads away. Mack, on all fours, squinted in the paralyzing brightness, saw Grier on his belly in the soft cave dust, his outstretched hands clutching his rifle the way a drowning man might clutch at a passing spar. Grier, even in the dark, had managed to pull the bolt back.

From behind and above the radiating wheel of light came the familiar voice. "Well, this is a fine howdy-do."

Harry stepped further into the cave, ducking his head. He lowered the flashlight so it wasn't directly in their faces. Rick, looking chalky-white and exhausted, was right behind him. Grier sat up, disgusted, as if it had been some deliberate practical joke. He tossed the rifle away.

"We're your buddies, remember?" Harry said. "Can you believe these guys, Rick? They've been up here sleeping for hours, it looks like."

Rick stooped and put his open palms over the dead fire, searching for the last traces of warmth. Both Rick's and Harry's trousers were muddy to the middle of their thighs.

"You two O.K.?" Mack said.

"We'll survive," Harry said.

"What happened out there?" Grier said.

Rick leaned against the wall, began to unlace his wet boots. Harry glanced over at him, hesitating for a second before speaking.

"Not enough water," Harry said. "At least not to carry all we had with us. The river was so low in that last bend you couldn't have sailed a rubber duck through there. We spent the last two hours trying to hump the raft over sandbars. It got pretty crazy."

Grier was on his feet. "So where is the raft now?" Grier's voice wasn't offering any sympathy.

"Maybe a half mile up, maybe a little more," Harry said.

Grier went to the mouth of the cave. Harry watched him the whole time. Mack reached back and found a pair of balled-up socks in his pack.

"Rick. Here. Put these on." Mack tossed the socks back to Rick. Rick trapped them against his chest.

"We brought it down as far as anyone could have, Grier." Rick's voice was raised as if he were making a general announcement. "We busted our balls."

Grier never moved, still staring out at the canyon. Harry had found a box of raisins in one of the cellophane bags of food. He tore it open, strolled to the front of the cave. He pointed up the river.

"It's just this side of the bend there. We pulled it up under some trees," Harry said. "I hope you tied those horses nice and tight, because that raft's not going to be worth a damn."

Mack pushed to his feet.

"I should have gone with you," Grier said.

Harry poked at the tightly packed raisins, not taking offense. "It wouldn't have made any difference," he said. "No one could have moved that thing."

It wasn't clear that Grier believed that. Mack could see just enough of his face to tell. Rick still sat against the cave wall, pulling on dry socks, his hands trembling from the chill.

"All the same," Grier said. "I would rather have been the one."

Grier could feel Mack watching him. He put his hand on Harry's shoulder. "I'm just sorry you had to go through all that. It's going to be all right, don't get me wrong. There's nobody out there, anyway. Just us chickens." Grier turned back to the cave. Rick still hadn't looked at him. "You did the best you could. We'll take care of it in the morning. You just get yourself into dry clothes and get some sleep, cus we got a day ahead of us tomorrow."

Grier stooped and pulled a thick Irish sweater from the top of his open pack.

"Hey, Rick." Grier flung the sweater and it unfurled in the air like a coarse white net. Rick reached up and snagged it. "Not going to have my partner catch his death of pneumonia on his first night out."

Chapter Thirteen

THE SUN was high in the sky by the time Mack woke. He rolled over and wiped the cave dust from his caked, dry lips and the corners of his eyes. His clothes smelled of smoke. He stared across the tangle of bodies and gear. Grier stood at the mouth of the cave, poised in a brilliant wedge of morning light.

Harry stirred and sat up, cut a bar of summer sausage with his knife. Rick still lay curled in his sleeping bag, one arm outstretched. The sleeve of Grier's bulky Irish sweater came only to his elbow.

"Grier," Harry said. Grier turned. "Breakfast." Harry lobbed a section of the summer sausage at Grier and Grier one-handed it. Mack tried to sit up, his body stiff from sleeping all night on the ground.

"Good morning," Grier said.

"You think it's about that time?" Mack said.

"About that time," Grier said, stripping the skin from his piece of sausage. He nodded at Rick. "What are we going to do about that one?"

Rick's voice was muffled by the sleeping bag. "You're not going to need to do anything. I've been lying here for hours waiting for you guys to wake up." Rick pushed himself up, brushed the dust out of his hair. "Just turn me loose."

After a breakfast of summer sausage and Triscuits spread with peanut butter and strawberry jam, the four men descended the ladder, crossed the boulder field, moved up along the river. It was beautiful in among the trees, a mix of ponderosa and elder, then willow and cottonwood along the water. Morning light played through the branches. There were long-earred squirrels and plenty of birds. Ravens wheeled high overhead, playing on the thermals above the canyon walls. Everything about the morning felt innocent. Harry walked out on the dry sandbars of the river, apart from the other three, leaping across the shallow channels of water.

Three quarters of a mile up they found the raft. At the bend where the river was widest there were a dozen shallow channels weaving through rock and sandbars, washed-up debris and driftwood. The river looked as if it had dropped a good two feet since they had been down it before, and those two feet had been crucial. There was a channel along the east bank of the river where Rick and Harry might have squeezed through, but no one could blame them for missing it in the middle of the night. To get the raft free they would have to somehow work it back up river a hundred yards, then float it back down the right channel.

They slid the raft into the water, sloshed about like a quartet of drunks. They tried to maneuver it through the shallows, but the channel was too low and full of snags, the raft too large and unwieldy. Their next move was to try and carry it across, the rubber hissing as they slid it over the sand. They pulled it through the willow and tamarisk and salt cedar, bulling their way, but the raft kept getting caught or flopping over on them. Mack finally just stopped.

"Hey, fellas, let's think about this," he said. "It would be a hell of a lot simpler if we just carried what we needed. This could take all day." Harry let his end of the raft drop. It made a billowy whomp as it hit the sand. Both Harry and Grier were sweating, sucking for air. "Really. We don't need this."

Grier bent down and pulled up his wool socks, wet with water and sand. "You're right, man." He wiped his hands on his thighs. "I don't know what I was thinking."

They slid the raft under some cottonwoods, then loaded themselves up with buckets, spades, pickaxes, metal ammo boxes. When they set off down the canyon they looked like itinerant peddlers.

They made two more trips up and down the canyon. There were no shirkers, no intimations of blame. They were all aware of how close they were. There wasn't a cloud in the sky and the day quickly began to heat up. They made frequent stops to drink from the canteens, but within minutes their lips and throats were dry again.

The men passed one another on the trail without speaking, staggering under the weight of the coils of rope, another stack of buckets.

It was noon before the real work could even begin. Mack had had no idea it would be so brutally simple. It was peon labor, pick and shovel and bucket.

Grier had to have the first shot at it. When he swung the pickax into the soft rock, an explosion of fragments sprayed everywhere. He turned back to grin at them. Mack missed the joke. The pale wall was unmoved; the mark Grier had made wasn't more than an inch and a half deep, the size of a pencil-sharpener hole.

They took turns. One would wield the pickax until enough chunks and fragments had fallen, then a second would shovel the rubble into a bucket; the bucket would be passed from hand to hand, then dumped over the side of the cliff.

Grier became the self-appointed cheerleader. "Attaboy, Rick, that's the way to swing those buckets. I'll bet this is the first honest day's work you've done in twenty years. Anybody remember any of those old chain gang songs?"

Grier never let up. As a matter of pride he took longer turns with the pickax than anyone else. He worked without his shirt; the huge muscles in his back glistened with sweat. The spray of yellow rock clung to his chest, neck and face like a fine blond fur. When he stopped for a second to dry his hands on his jeans, he still had that mad grin on his face.

"We're getting there, guys, we're getting there. You figure the Spaniards had to make slaves out of the Indians to get 'em to do what we're doing, and we're doing it of our own free will. I guess that's what you call progress, right?"

It did not go fast. After an hour they broke through the huge outer boulder only to discover that they'd just begun. A dark, stale airspace petered out after three or four feet, the shaft filled with smaller rocks, dust and fragments. A number of the rocks they removed by hand, rolling them out, working fairly quickly. They had cleared about ten feet of the passage before they hit another major barrier, a second boulder, immense as the first. They went back to the pickax. No one was complaining, everyone was still giving their best, but the pressure was starting to show.

Light began to creep a few inches into the cave as the sun moved further west. All their faces were masked by fine dust, streaked with sweat. Mack had a series of rock cuts and scrapes on his hands and wrists.

Rick and Harry, buckets in either hand, shoulders bowed from the weight, teetered toward the bright cave mouth and dumped their loads. The rubble cascaded down the side of the cliff. The sound struck Mack as trivial, without consequence.

Rick sauntered back, set his bucket upside down on the cave floor, sat down on it. "Grier, come on, you said you were such a genius with dynamite, I thought you'd be able to figure out a way to blow this thing wide open."

Grier let the pickax rest against his thigh, brushed some of the mixture of dust and sweat off his face with the crook of his arm. "Doesn't work that way, Rick. We'd end up doing just what Tucker did, shut the whole cave off again. You need to get dynamite behind whatever you blow up. And if we could get behind, we'd be there. Get what I'm saying?"

Squatting on the bucket Rick looked up, his eyes all huge dark pupils in the dim light, his thumbs tucked in the palms of his hands, nursing blisters.

"You could give it a try," Rick said.

The hopeless remark stopped Grier for a second. He ran his tongue slowly over his teeth, trying to get some of the grit out. Harry hooked the handle of the shovel with the toe of his boot, flipped it up, caught it. "Rick, Rick," Grier said. "Come on, it could be worse. We could be picking lettuce in California for two dollars a day, right?"

Grier slapped Rick on the back. It was a comradely gesture, but as Rick stood up, Mack saw Grier give him a second, considering glance.

They spoke very little, passing the buckets from hand to hand, finding a rhythm. The soft white volcanic grit worked its way into their shirts, shoes, skin. They labored shoulder to shoulder, sinking into the half-conscious state that fatigue brings on. At moments Mack felt as if the world had narrowed to two pairs of hands, a pair to take a bucket from him and a pair to hand him the next one. The only sounds were the rasp of the shovel, the click of the pickax, the tumble of debris into the buckets. They were like drones in some H. G. Wells science fiction movie, Mack thought, or moles working their way through a mountain. When they took a break they went to the ledge outside the cave, drank from the canteen, their heads back. Water ran down the sides of their mouths, their eyes narrowing in the sudden brightness.

They were slowly making their way. They had dug back fifteen feet, then twenty. There was no way of knowing how far the shaft went. They were working their way into darkness. They placed a pair of lanterns on the floor to make it easier to see.

The passage narrowed. It became harder to take a full swing with the pickax. They came across an ancient timber wedged between boulders, yet another sign that Tucker had been here. It took them twenty minutes to work it free. If anyone besides Mack had thought of the possibility of the shaft caving in behind them, no one was mentioning it. The passage began to slope downward.

When Mack took his turn with the pickax he found himself playing little mind games, the kind of magical thinking he hadn't done since he was a child. On the next blow, or the tenth, or the twentieth, he was going to break through, the treasure would be there, at his feet. Each time he was wrong. The pickax would stab into the soft volcanic wall, Mack would jerk it free. There would be a trickle of pulverized rock and a new two-inch hole. The wall in front of him had become the enemy. He struck at it, blow after blow, his fatigue somehow fueling his rage. He remembered the stories of Rick and Grier, so full of yearning. This was it, what they'd been yearning for, some massive force against which everything would be shattered, their weakness, their self-contempt. Mack was a prisoner, trying to smash his way free.

Mack took a fresh grip, swung even harder. There was a golden spray, and then a small object, dark and glittering, tumbled at his feet. He picked it up, brushed it off. It was a shiny obsidian arrowhead, with a tiny groove running halfway down the center of it. The edges were still razor-sharp.

"Hey, take a look at this," he said. He tossed it to Harry.

Harry turned it over in the palm of his hand. It glistened in the lantern light. The sunlight at the cave mouth was more distant now, a dim reminder of the real world. Harry's eyes were shadowed by the brim of his baseball cap.

"God damn, Mack," Harry said. "Where'd you find this?"

"It just fell out of the wall."

"See this fluting? This is the kind of head they used on the old spear throwers, even before they had bows and arrows." He handed it back to Mack. "Keep it. Maybe it'll bring you luck. In case you run into a mastodon."

The shadows of Grier and Rick returning flickered along the wall.

"Come on, Mack, we can do better than that," Grier said. "Give me that ax."

Mack dropped the obsidian arrowhead in his pocket and passed the pickax to Grier handle-first, Boy Scout style.

Grier went at it again. Mack marvelled at him. Every blow he took was steady and hard, like a long ball hitter in perfect rhythm. Tiny bits of debris sprayed off both Grier and Mack, stinging like hail. Mack stayed close, shovelling out whatever chunks Grier knocked free. The shaft had turned even more sharply downward.

Suddenly Mack saw the earth shift beneath Grier's feet. At first he thought it was just that he was dizzy, his senses playing tricks. Then he was sure. Even in the dim half-light he could see that the ground Grier stood on was sinking, sliding downward, like sand sliding down an hourglass. Grier knew it too, whirling around with the pickax raised high in one hand, like a man snake-bitten.

"Grier!"

Mack reached down for him. There was a long, loud crack as rock and earth began to tear loose. Grier tossed the pickax aside. He was sinking in rubble, lifting his feet in a frightened, farcical dance, trying to reach for some safe place.

"Grier!"

Grier made a leap for Mack, half tackling him. For a moment Mack thought they were both going over, that the cave was going to swallow the two of them. Holding Grier in his arms, Mack wrestled him backward. A second pair of hands held them both as they heard the avalanche of dirt and rock below them. The earth opened up with a roar and at the center of the roar was the clanging of the pickax bouncing off of rock walls further and further away from them.

They lay in a pileup straight out of "The Three Stooges." Grier was in Mack's arms, Harry had pinned both of them, Rick had a grip on Harry's belt.

They lay there for a second, stunned, then began to untangle. Grier still sat on the floor of the cave, right at the edge, knees up, hands covering his mouth. Mack suddenly realized that he was laughing.

"What's the joke, Grier?" Mack said.

"I don't know, I really don't." Grier ran his hand over his dirty face, squinted at Mack. "You know how things can just strike you funny? Talk about the rug being pulled out from under you . . . that just goes to show you, Mack, you can't be too careful. That was close, boy."

"I wouldn't want it any closer."

Mack pulled Grier to his feet. Grier groped for the wall like an old man; he still had the shakes.

"Christ, Mack, let's not do that again, all right?"

A blinding white light wavered behind them. Grier and Mack turned and saw Harry's outline above one of the carbide lanterns.

"Anyone want to take a look?" Harry said.

"Hell, yes," Grier said.

Harry moved carefully along the wall, testing each step, and shone the lantern down into the shaft. Mack, on his hands and knees, came as close as he dared. The light cut through the dust that hung in the shaft. The shaft seemed to head straight down. Mack could see no end to it.

"Christ," Rick said.

"Rick, what do you think?" Grier said. "What do you think's down there? Bats? Tarantulas? A few black widows? Anyone still think Tucker was a liar?"

"Give it a rest, Grier," Rick said.

"A rest? The one thing I'm not going to give it is a rest. We're going down."

They were all unnerved by the shaft's caving in beneath them. Anyone else would have taken some time to get their courage back up. Not Grier. All he was thinking about was how to get to the bottom. If he had sweaty palms he wasn't showing them.

They took the battered timber they had unearthed earlier, wedged it into the narrowest passage of the cave, then lashed the nylon rope ladder to the beam, tied on a long lifeline. Grier tied the lifeline snugly around his middle as the other three watched.

"I'll go first. When I give a tug, the line will be free; you can pull it up and the next guy can go down."

"You're crazy, Grier," Mack said. "You're not going to get me to do this. I'm no rock climber."

"You don't have to be. That's what the ladder is for. It's like climbing out of the hayloft, Mack." Grier winked at him. In the gleam of the carbide lamp Mack could see Harry's and Rick's somber faces.

"Grier, you don't know what's down there," Rick said.

Grier strapped one of the lanterns to his back. "Sure, I do. Gold's down there, buddy."

"And what happens when you run out of ladder?"

"You'll be hearing from me."

"And if it breaks?"

"Then call in the rangers."

Grier picked up the ladder and tossed it over the edge like a fisherman throwing his net into the sea. It unfurled, disappeared in the darkness. They could hear it hitting against the sides of the shaft.

Grier knelt, tested the ladder with his foot. He looked up at them, his whole face alive. Mack was in awe of him. It wasn't a question of bravery. Whatever was driving Grier now was deep and unthinking. Grier was on the scent.

He went down, hand over hand, the rope ladder swaying with each step, but holding. The light on Grier's back bobbed in the darkness, then disappeared. Two minutes later there was a sharp yank on the rope. They hauled it back up.

"I think you're next, Mack," Harry said. "I think that's what we decided."

"I don't remember that," Mack said. "This is not what I came out here for, you know that. I'm a singer, Harry, I sit around all day and try to think up songs about whiskey and wild women . . ."

Harry put the rope in Mack's hands as if it were an award. "Remember to tie it on real tight now, Mack."

Mack strapped one of the lanterns on his back, then looped the lifeline under his legs and tied it around his waist. He took a deep breath and backed onto the ladder. With his first step he felt the ladder sway. He moved very slowly, but it seemed as if any move he made could cause the ladder to twist or turn. The shaft was thick with dust from the cave-in and there were currents of cold air. As he felt the ladder begin to move out from under him, Mack made the mistake of grabbing hold of the lifeline. The ladder pitched violently and he nearly lost it altogether. He lunged for it, caught it, held on. There was a trickle of rubble from above.

"You doing all right down there?" The voice from above was Rick's.

"Oh, yeah, I'm doing just great."

My God, Mack thought, what a bunch of amateurs we are. Even if we get down there, we're never going to get up again. He could feel himself starting to panic, feel his chest tighten. There was no air to breathe.

Far above him he heard Harry singing softly. "The eensy-weensie spider went up the waterspout, down came the rain and washed the spider out . . ."

"Shut up, Harry, it's not funny," he shouted back.

The lantern hung over Mack's shoulder so it didn't interfere with his climbing. The glow reflected off the walls of the shaft around him and Mack, getting his nerve back, finally dared to look beyond his hands. He could see now that the walls were covered with petroglyphs, spirals and lizards, jagged streaks of lightning and feathered serpents. They were everywhere, like the tattoos on the back of a tawny god.

The shaft began to narrow. The lantern on Mack's back scraped against stone and the light, flickering for a moment, made great rocking shadows on the walls like waves on an uneasy sea. Mack couldn't be sure, but it felt as if the shaft was turning, as if he was corkscrewing through the mountain.

Mack, swaying on the ladder, felt with his foot for the next rung, slipped for just a second, and lurched back. There was a crack of metal against rock; the lantern sputtered and went out. He was in utter darkness. "Damn," he said. There was no one to hear him. His heart was pounding.

He stopped to wipe his sweating hands. He had no idea how far he had come. He couldn't think; his brain locked like the wheels of a train. He was losing it, any sense of boundaries, he was Alice tumbling down the hole; if he saw a Big White Rabbit he would have believed it as easily as anything else, Gracie Slick, help me now.

"Mack!"

This time the voice was below him: Grier's voice.

"Yeah."

"You're just about there, Mack. Just a few more feet."

Mack took a quick glance down, saw the beam from Grier's lantern. He waited a moment, gathering concentration, then began to move down. Grier held the bottom of the ladder, talked Mack down it.

"Any spiders down here?"

"None yet," Grier said.

Mack felt Grier's hands helping him down. His boots finally touched solid rock.

"That wasn't so bad, was it?" Grier said.

Mack began undoing the rope around his waist. He had no idea where they were; in the glare of the lantern there was only Grier and him. "Grier, I'm not going to answer that question." He slipped the lantern over his neck, banged on it, trying the switch, but couldn't get it to work. He gave a tug on the rope and it vanished upward, the tail of the rope lashing back and forth like a snake.

It took another fifteen minutes to get Harry and Rick down. The four men stood together, lifting their lanterns, staring at the walls around them. They were in a large chamber and there were a half-dozen thin chimneys of rock leading off in various directions. The floor where they stood was level, though there were fresh piles of rubble created by the cave-in. The chamber seemed to be twelve to fifteen feet high. It was impossible to tell how far it wound around because of jagged outcroppings of rock. There was a distant sound of running water.

"So?" Rick said.

"So?"

"Where is it?"

"Here," Grier said. "Somewhere." If Grier was disappointed that the gold wasn't lying right at their feet, he was hiding it. He turned slowly, scrutinized their surroundings, taking his bearings. "Hey, finders keepers, fellas," he said. He moved along the wall, his lantern in his left hand, feeling the rock with his right.

Mack wasn't going to let Grier work alone. He glanced at Rick and Harry; neither looked like they were willing to give up their lanterns. It didn't matter. Mack moved off carefully to his left, stumbled for a second, caught himself. His eyes slowly adjusted to the dimness. He came to a low ledge, felt his way along it. He realized that he was moving in the direction of the running water. As the ledge curved away, the lanterns of Rick and Harry were not any help. Mack moved in almost total dark. There was a chill current of cold air, then he was through it. He was tapping his way along the ledge when his hand caught on something that was not rock.

It felt like coarse, woven netting. Mack's fingers closed on it, tugged, became entwined. His heart leapt.

"Hey, Grier! Give me a light over here. I think I've got something."

Mack pulled eagerly with both hands, pulled it toward him, sure that he had found it. It was a bag of some kind, with real tumbling weight. His hands trembled with excitement. Their search had ended. He began to tear at the rough fabric like a kid tearing into a birthday present and it ripped easily.

Grier was at his side with a lantern; Rick and Harry were there a second later. The light from their lanterns came up like a wave, shone down Mack's outstretched arms. His hands were clenched in a rush netting, and nesting inside the rough sack were bits of hair and skin, dried bones, a human skull. Mack let go, put his hands to his shirt, stricken.

"Damn," Grier said. "Damn."

Mack wiped his hands slowly over his shirt again and again. Grier held his lantern steady. In the flaring light they could see a half dozen mummies lying in their bags of rush matting as peacefully as dozing picnickers. One was set off from the others, leaned on its side in a cranny in the far wall, as if it had been set up to keep watch.

Across the dusty ledge Mack could see scattered coils of yucca, a stone ax, bits of flint. Alongside the bodies were black and white decorated bowls. Rick leaned over and picked one of them up, gingerly. Inside were ears of corn, feathers, a wrapped leather bundle; grave goods to accompany them on their journey.

Daring to look again at the mummy he had yanked through the dust, Mack saw the shape, the knees tight to the chest like a fetus, the bones held together by ligaments and leathery scraps of skin, everything preserved for hundreds of years by the dryness of their resting place.

Mack was repelled and held at the same time. They should not be here. This was not their place. Terror and awe swelled in him in a way he had not felt since he was a child. Childlike too was the sudden conviction that there was too much in the

world, too much that could not be controlled, some malevo-
lence that might invade him if he was not very careful.

Grier stepped up on the rock ledge, ducking his head. He
moved very deliberately. It was a matter of pride with Grier; he
wasn't going to be freaked out. His lantern threw a web of light
on the sloping walls; shadows slid inside the thin rock chimney
to his right. Grier picked up one of the pots, casually turned it
over, dumped feathers, beads, arrowheads.

"Leave it, Grier," Harry said. "It's not what you're after."

"What's the matter, man? You think it's going to bite you?"

Harry said nothing. Mack stared at the one mummy set off
from the others; it seemed slightly swollen. It sat up like an off-
balance kewpie doll at a county fair. What an odd way to sit,
Mack thought, for seven hundred years. Jesus, get me out of this
hole, let me breathe again. Grier moved across the ledge,
crouched like a wary soldier prowling through a battlefield, a
dream-figure. Mack turned back to Rick for a second. Rick,
gripping his lantern, seemed utterly frozen.

Harry stepped upon the ledge, knelt beside one of the
wrapped figures. He reached down into the dust, lifted a pair of
flutes made of bone. Grier looked back over his shoulder. Mack
still heard the sound of running water. He didn't understand
why none of the others heard it.

Mack watched Harry wipe one of the flutes clean, carefully
tap the dust out of it. Harry fingered it for a moment, then
raised it to his lips. The sweet clean notes echoed in the chamber. The other three men were perfectly still.

Harry played again. The light of the lanterns shone on his
tilted head. His eyes were half-shut, his face solemn, but as he
played Mack saw some change come over him; an awful tenderness came to his face. The sound was piercing, reverberating in
the confined chamber. Ten feet behind Harry, Grier stood,
rubbing his nose with his knuckles, impatient. Mack was ready
to believe anything, ready for one of the rush mattings to stir,
for one of the summoned figures to rise up like Lazarus.

When Harry took the flute from his lips he was smiling. Grier
squatted on his haunches, wiped away the dust on the ledge
with his hands.

"This is it, Grier," Harry said softly. "This is all she wrote. Finale. Goodnight, gentlemen."

"Maybe so, maybe not."

"There's nothing more here. If there ever was, it's gone now." Harry slipped the bone flute inside his shirt.

Mack felt the rock walls press in on all sides, the tons of rock poised above them, the fathoms of darkness. If I were left alone here, Mack thought, without this light, without these voices, I would not exist, there would be nothing to tell me I was alive. "Come on, Grier," Mack said. "Harry's right. Let's get out of here." He heard Rick sneeze behind him.

Grier wasn't listening. He stood up, picked up his lantern. He scanned the walls, tapped them with his knuckles, a man looking for a way out. There was no sign that Tucker had ever been here, no sign of gold.

Grier walked the ledge, forward and back, like a caged animal, stepping over the huddled figures, nudging two or three of them with his foot as if they might be clutching some secret to their bellies, holding out on him.

Rick hung back, one hand on the rope ladder, not wanting to lose touch with the way back. "Come on, Grier," Rick said. "We made a mistake, let's face it."

Grier kicked moodily at the dusty floor with his heel, like a kid trying to break through the ice. He was at the far end of the ledge. Suddenly Grier pulled his knife out of its sheath. He looked in one direction and then the other, as if searching for imaginary enemies. He dropped to his knees and began to stab at the floor of the ledge.

"Grier, what the hell are you doing?"

Grier kept stabbing at the earth, wiping the dust and rock away with his free hand. In the cranny of the wall above him was the one mummy set aside from the others. It looked now like a sentinel, or a winter hawk brooding on a fence.

It was as if Grier had gone mad with rage and frustration. He worked like a fiend. He threw his knife aside and got to one knee. He was gripping something buried in the earth. He began heaving and yanking. Mack saw that he was pulling a buried timber out of the ledge, tearing it out barehanded. Mack felt

Harry stiffen beside him. Grier was ready now, in his fury, to destroy anything. It was a nightmare. They had become creatures of unsettled dust, dim light. Grier rose to his feet, knees bent, cheeks puffed up like a weight lifter. There was a loud crack as the timber came free of the earth.

Harry stepped up on the ledge. "Stop it, Grier, leave it alone before it hurts you." Dust rose in the chamber, swirled in bright, frantic circles in the beams of the lanterns.

Grier knelt again, working with maniacal energy. The second timber came more easily. As it broke free, Grier stumbled and fell with it, falling among the matted still figures. A pot shattered, beads and arrowheads scattered everywhere. Harry moved closer, his long shadow fled up the wall.

"Now, Grier. Stop now," Harry said.

Grier never heard him. He knelt in the loose earth, tearing free what looked like thatching or straw of some kind. It was as if he had come on the remains of some ancient burial platform, but there was no point to what he was doing, Mack was certain, no point except that Grier was possessed.

Suddenly he did stop. He looked down between his knees and plucked something out of the earth. He held it in his palm for just a second, Mack saw the flash of reflected light; then Grier let it drop. Grier looked up at the mummy poised above him and rose slowly to his feet. Harry, thinking with him, moved quickly to stop him. Mack leapt up to the ledge.

Before Harry could grab him, Grier had both his hands in the rough rush matting, tore it open the way you would tear open someone's overcoat. It ripped as easily as paper, burst like a struck piñata. Harry was yanking at Grier's arm; Mack was only a pace or two behind. Mack could see over Grier's shoulder, close enough to see the loose skull rolling forward, gold and silver coins gushing from the mouth and eyesockets like a fountain. It was as if an infection had burst after centuries of pressure. The swollen netting spewed coins, a slot machine hitting jackpot, the past showering down its treasures. The skull tumbled across the ledge.

Harry had hold of Grier by the shirt and was cursing him. Grier tried to throw Harry off, swinging the now empty rush matting like an old sweater. Coins flew off the walls of the chamber. Harry had too good a grip. The two men tripped over one of the loose timbers, fell backward.

There was a loud crack and the ledge gave way beneath them. Mack lunged forward, but this time he wasn't quick enough. He watched, astonished, as the two men fell like elephants falling into an elephant pit. Grier's lantern slid in after them, spinning end over end, the beam waving wildly as it fell. Mack heard Harry scream.

Mack stared in on them. The pit they had fallen into was not more than ten feet down. Harry lay writhing on his back, one knee raised and flopping back and forth like a landed fish. Grier crawled on all fours, heaving to get his breath back. Their pain was real enough, Mack knew that, but the two of them moved with the exaggerated slowness of professional wrestlers.

Mack was staring right at it, and yet it was ten seconds before he realized what it was. The gold bars were stacked, eighty or a hundred of them, on a wooden platform in the center of the pit. They gleamed in the lantern light, looking as obvious and ordinary as a load of lumber or bricks. In the corner of the chamber was a hot spring, mist rising off a shallow rock pool.

Mack swung himself down and Rick slid in after him. Mack bent over Harry and helped him sit up. Grier sat with his back against the rock wall. He wiped blood from his teeth and spat. Mack tried to pull Harry up, but Harry winced, gestured for him to stop. He had hurt his back in the fall.

"Are you all right?" Mack said.

Harry nodded, then slowly lifted his head, staring at Grier. Grier sat now with his legs splayed out in the dust like a Raggedy Ann doll, his head back, eyes closed. Gold or no gold, Harry wasn't through with his anger.

Rick didn't know what to do with himself. He swung around, letting his arms fly, exultant, looking for someone to share it all with. As Mack stood up Rick grabbed him by the elbows. "It's true, Mack, every bit of it turns out to be true." Mack pulled away from him, stared at the walls around them.

Grier and Harry had fallen through a mud roof that was supported by beams and thatching. Mack imagined that it had originally been used as a platform for the dead. Here and there he could spy the gleam of Spanish coins. In one corner were the broken remains of a ladder. At one time there must have been access from one level to the other. Mack's guess was that Tucker had sealed it off to hide his find.

"We did it, didn't we, Mack?" Rick said. "We found where old Tucker tucked it, didn't we? He was nothing but a joker, was he? A goddamned joker."

Jokes, Mack thought. Sure. Real playful. A piece of ghoulish frontier humor. It was like those old-time ranchers Mack had met, the ones his father had told him about, who used human skulls they found out on the range as bunkhouse ashtrays. Tucker must have been a sick man. To stuff a mummy full of coins, set it up there like that, to take the time to do it. For a marker. For himself. Or whoever followed. A great sick joke.

Mack heard Grier move behind him and looked back over his shoulder. Grier sat on his knees, staring wide-eyed at the stacks of gold. There was a shyness in him; it took Mack by surprise. It was something he'd never seen in Grier before.

Grier pushed himself to his feet, picked up the lantern, limped forward. He stood in front of the gold, raised a hand as if to touch it, then let the hand drop. He was like a hungry kid standing in front of a bakery window. But there was no glass in the window. Grier wasn't ready to believe that yet.

Harry stood outside the circle, staring at the steaming hot spring. Mack could see the wet rock gleaming through the rising mist. They had gone as far into the underground as they could go.

Grier finally placed the lantern on the pyramid of gold. The flaring light, only inches away, made his face shine, created the illusion that it was the gold itself that was illuminating him, transforming him into some gilded idol. Grier ran the palms of his hands slowly across the top of the stacked bars, down the sides. Mack felt uncomfortable watching, forced to witness a gesture too private, too intimate. Mack saw Harry watching too, but out of the corner of his eye.

"Look at that," Grier said. "Makes you wish you had a Polaroid, doesn't it?"

Rick shook Mack's arm, beside himself with excitement. "Don't just stand there looking at it, Grier. Count it up, let's see what we've got."

Grier turned angry at the interruption. His eyes were pinched, as if his face had been seared by the light. He had to strain to see them. Mack had a flash of childhood memory, his fundamentalist grandfather warning him, never look on the brightness of God's countenance directly or it will make you blind.

No one said anything. Grier stood alone, as stranded as if he had been cast up on an island. He looked from one to the other of them, trying to smile, trying to act the same as before, even if he wasn't the same.

He picked up a gold bar with his old bravado, hefted it up and down in his hands. "Catch, man," he said. He tossed it underhand. Mack, taken by surprise, tried to make a one-handed catch, but dropped it. He picked the bar out of the dust. It must have been forty, forty-five pounds.

Mack looked up through the ragged hole of thatch. He could make out the twisted rock walls stretching dimly upward, a shining strand of the ladder. The light did not reach.

"So how are we going to get this stuff out of here?" Mack said. Harry hadn't moved. He stood in the half-light, away from the others.

"It's not a problem," Grier said. "Believe me."

Mack said nothing. He felt himself involuntarily shudder. The chamber suddenly felt incredibly narrow. It had changed them. It had scored them the way a bullet is scored by rifling. They had proved to be of softer metal than they thought.

The ascent up the swaying rope ladder to the main cave took at least a half hour.

There was no question of rest. Grier prowled up and down the cave, scrutinizing their gear. The others watched, instinctively deferring to him. Harry, still grim-faced, untangled one of the long coils of rope, rewinding it around his elbow. Not even Harry was going to buck Grier now.

Grier picked up a pulley, spun its wooden wheel, and set it

down again. Rick crouched near the shaft, fist pressed to his lips, attending Grier's every move.

Mack felt like a dumb, useless kid. Grier rummaged through the ammo box of tools, then paused, stared at the packs against the wall. He grabbed Rick's pack and flipped it upside down. A yellow raincoat, blue jeans, some aluminum pans and the fluttering remains of a topographical map spilled into the dust.

"Hey, what the hell you doing?" Rick said.

"Just making do." Grier gave the pack a final shake, dislodged a box of kitchen matches and some underwear. "What is it they say? Necessity—" he braced the pack across his chest, yanked on the aluminum supports "—being the mother of invention? You all going to just stand there staring at me? Let's go."

They worked step by step, under Grier's direction. Mack steadied Harry as he stretched out along the beam that was angled across the shaft. Harry screwed an eyehook deep into the old wood. Grier and Rick threaded rope through the two pulleys, their backs turned against the light, then tied one end of the rope to Rick's empty pack. Mack helped Harry secure one of the pulleys to the eyehook.

When they were done, Mack stepped back and looked down at their primitive piece of engineering.

"You like it?" Grier said.

"I love it," Mack said. "You think it will hold?"

"Damn straight."

"The only other time I ever used a pulley, Grier, we were trying to hoist a piano into a fourth-floor apartment. We ended up breaking every window in the bottom three floors."

"Yeah? Well, at least this time you don't have to worry about the neighbors."

Rick and Mack were appointed to stay up top. Grier and Harry went back down into the shaft again, lanterns draped over their necks. Grier nursed his contraption along with his free hand, edged slowly down into the darkness. Rick and Mack waited. Every few seconds another two-foot length of rope rolled on through the pulley.

It was twenty minutes before the first signalling tug on the line. They began to haul it in, felt the telling weight on the other end. They hauled faster, hand over hand, working into as good a rhythm as any pair of tribal fishermen. The second pulley appeared and then came the bulging pack, floating magically out of the dark. Mack reached out over the shaft and pulled the pack in.

Rick knelt quickly by his side, fumbled with the knotted cords. The bars tumbled heavily to the floor. His face shining, Rick picked one of them up, cradled it like a baby. "Well, hot dog," he said.

He turned it over, ran gentle fingers over the pitted surface. Still on his knees, Rick twisted back toward the mouth of the cave.

Rick tilted the bar of gold up, as if to see if it could pick up the light. At the moment the long streams of sunlight could almost reach them. Maybe Mack was almost imagining it, but it seemed as if he saw the bar glitter dully, showing vital signs after five centuries down.

"No one has ever taken it this far, do you realize that, Mack? Not Coronado, not Tucker, no one. We're the first." Mack said nothing. "You remember when I came to you that day, Mack? With Tucker's drawing? You remember what you thought?"

Even in victory, Mack could feel how needy Rick was. Probably needier than ever. "I thought you were crazy."

"And now?"

"I still think you're crazy. But loaded." Mack stood the pack on end, batted at the fabric to knock some of the dust from it. "Come on, they're waiting for us down there."

The pulley worked like a dream. They moved only four of the fifty-pound bars at a time, not sure how much the nylon fabric of the pack could hold. They cranked their ghostly cargo. A second load came up and then a third. It was as simple as wheeling a bucket out of a well. It almost began to feel like honest labor. With each load Rick's mood soared higher. By the time Grier and Harry came up for a break, there were sixteen gold bars stacked on the floor of the cave.

They were on the ledge outside the cave, drinking in the afternoon brightness. They were all exhausted and covered with dust. Grier's shirt had a ragged tear in it; his chest was marked by a nasty scrape. Harry sat cross-legged, one pant leg rolled up, brooding over the size of the bruise on his shin.

No one spoke at first. They let the sun restore them. There was no more water. Rick thumped the last empty canteen, trying to tease a final drop out of it, while Grier cut pieces of cheese with his knife and passed out the slices. They were like invalids after a long bout of delirium. How odd we must look perched up here, Mack thought. It would be a very weird sight to just happen onto, he thought, like coming on hermit saints creeping out of their desert caves.

Mack sat with his back against the rock, his knees up, his boots half unlaced. He stared down at the canyon floor, at the groves of ponderosa, the thin, shining channels of the river, the sheltering cliffs. Birds glided effortlessly above the rim. The sun sat just above the western lip of the canyon and the stone at Mack's back was as warm as a hearth.

"You know what they should do for us?" Grier said. "After what we've just done?"

"What's that?" Rick said.

"They should carve our faces on the side of the cliff just like Mount Rushmore."

"Maybe one day they will," Harry said. "Give it time."

Everybody laughed. Mack shut his eyes, felt the sun and the light breezes playing across his face. He was very tired and yet at that moment he felt as secure as a cat dozing inside a sunny winter window.

His head nodded forward and he caught himself. He heard the easy laughter of the others. Everything was all right now. The lashing anger of Grier and Harry was forgotten, the dread Mack had felt in the darkness was gone.

All he felt was the sun on his face and there was a kind of immortality in it, he didn't have to wait for Mount Rushmore. He was one with the warm rock, the victorious laughter of his friends, the hazy fathoms of the canyon. He was losing himself, he was ebbing away. He was very tired. All he wanted was to bask in the light while it lasted, to rest, to dream a little longer.

His head grew heavier. He felt as if he were rocking high on the masthead of a ship. He had the illusion that he was slipping and then he realized that it wasn't an illusion. He instinctively caught himself with his hands. In his half-sleep he had pitched forward and when he opened his eyes he was staring down at the dark, jutting rocks far below. One of his boots stuck out over the edge, looking scuffed and faintly ludicrous, like something out of a cartoon escape. Harry's hand was on his shoulder. Mack quickly slid back as far on the ledge as he could.

"Be careful, man," Harry said. "This is no place to be dozing off."

Rick was fifteen feet further down the ledge, sitting on his heels, elbows tucked in close to his body, still warming himself in the golden light. He glanced up at Grier. "How much longer do you think it will take? To get everything up?"

"A couple of hours," Grier said. "If everything goes well, we could take part of it out on the horses tonight, get it loaded on the van."

Harry looked back over his shoulder. "And after that?"

Grier waited a beat. He didn't like being quizzed. "One thing at a time. No point in rushing, right?" He cut another slice of cheese with his knife. "Some things you've got to take on faith."

"The only question is, which ones, right?" Harry said.

Grier held the cheese to his knife with his thumb, slipped it into his mouth. Mack saw him freeze. Grier was staring across the canyon.

"What is it?" Mack said.

"I don't know yet."

Grier pointed with his knife. Mack didn't see anything at first, squinting into the hazy glare, but then he saw movement half-way down the cliff wall. He lost sight of it for a second, then picked it up again. There was a figure scuffling down the switch-backs.

Mack scrambled to his feet. They were all silent, watching.

"Who is it?" Rick said.

"How should I know?" Grier said.

Grier, never taking his eyes off the canyon wall, slipped side-ways past Rick on the ledge. Harry had already melted back into the shadows of the cave.

"You think he's seen us yet?" Rick said.

"I hope not," Grier said. Grier took Rick by the elbow, pulled him further back into the cave mouth. The four men watched the figure descend, not much more than a point of moving light. Straining, Mack thought he could make out a pack on his back. The figure disappeared behind an outcropping of rock, appeared again. A thin tracery of dust hung suspended above the trail.

"What should we do?" Rick said.

"Nothing," Grier said. He snapped his knife back in its sheath. The figure had nearly reached the floor of the canyon. He was moving so fast, he had to be running. Whoever he was, he was in terrific shape. The figure disappeared into the cover of trees.

"Probably some hiker," Harry said. "One of those rah-rah outdoorsman types. Like you, Grier."

For almost a full two minutes they watched together. Grier finally turned and walked away, unbuckling his belt.

"What the hell you doing?" Rick demanded.

Grier didn't bother to reply. He shed his torn T-shirt, found a clean maroon one in his pack, pulled it over his head and tucked it in.

There was no sign of movement on the canyon floor. Rick clenched his fist, stiffened, spun away. "Damn!" he said.

Grier sat down, leaned his head back against the cave wall. "What are you so upset for? I'm not upset." He reached into the side pocket of his pack, pulled out an orange. "Here, peel this, you'll feel better." He tossed the orange to Rick. It took Rick by surprise and he fumbled it against his chest.

Harry never took his eyes off the canyon. Once Mack thought he saw something, but it was only a bird rising out of the willows along the river. Several minutes passed. Rick stood in the middle of the cave, spitting orange seeds into his palms. Grier still leaned against the wall, absently flipping one of the lanterns on and off. Grier was trying to treat the interruption as if it was no more important than Boy Scouts sitting out an afternoon rain. Mack looked over Harry's shoulder.

"You see him?"

"Not yet. Should see him soon. Where can he go? Up the canyon or down, right?"

"Or he could stop," Mack said.

"Now why would he do that?" Harry said.

"Say, if he found the raft."

No one said anything. Grier set the lantern down, wet a finger and then rubbed it into his opposite palm, rubbing off some of the dirt. Despite his act, waiting was not what Grier did best.

"No one knows we're here, right?" Grier said. "There wasn't one of you who just couldn't keep the good news to yourself?"

"Wasn't me," Rick said.

"You're sure?"

Rick wiped the orange seeds into the pocket of his shirt. "Yeah, I'm very sure."

"What about you, Mack?" Grier said.

"Come on."

"I'm not accusing anybody. We should just think hard about it," Grier said.

Harry hadn't moved a muscle. "I know who it is."

"Who?" Rick said.

"Somebody from Mack's band. Mack forgot he had a gig tonight and they came to get the keys to the truck."

"Very funny," Mack said.

Mack left Harry, walked slowly to the back of the cave. He stood over the neatly stacked pyramid of gold. He nudged it with the toe of his boot, but couldn't budge it. It wasn't panic time yet. No one was suggesting that they throw the gold back. It was probably nothing, some harmless kid. They just had to wait it out. Mack picked up the long, coiled rope. He remembered the tribal policeman waiting for them at the bridge. Mack gave the rope a quick yank. The squeal of the pulley made the others jump, their startled faces pale and round in the uneven light.

Fifteen minutes passed and still there was no sign of the hiker. Mack returned to Harry's side.

"Go take a break, I'll watch for a while," Mack said. Harry still didn't turn his eyes away. "You couldn't have missed him?"

"I don't think so."

"How much stuff did we leave in the raft?"

"A couple of canteens. I don't really remember."

There had been a shift among the four of them. Harry now was the unwavering one. Mack looked back at Grier. He sat on his pack, taking apart the butane cookstove, wiping the parts meticulously clean with a blue bandana. He blew dust out of them, then screwed them together again.

"Hell, he's probably a mile down the canyon by now," Grier said. "Harry just missed him. Don't believe what they tell you; the keen eye of the Indian is much overrated."

Rick lay back on his sleeping bag. He spun a short metal bolt up in the air and caught it again, like an edgy teenager. He wasn't saying anything because he knew Grier didn't want him to, but worry rolled off him in waves.

"I want to go down there," Mack said.

"That's dumb," Grier said.

"I don't care. How long are we supposed to wait? If he's found something, I want to know about it. I don't want to have to just assume . . ."

"I told you, Harry just missed him." For the first time Mack saw the light of uncertainty in Grier's eyes. "And what if he happens to look up and see your butt coming down that ladder?"

"The Lord helps those who help themselves," Mack said.

Rick spun the metal bolt high enough that it grazed the smoke-blackened ceiling. It was enough to divert its course. Descending, the heavy bolt tumbled end over end, hit off the tips of Rick's fingers. He had to turn his head quickly to avoid being hit in the face. He sat up on his sleeping bag.

"I think he should go," Rick said. He retrieved the metal bolt, tossed it underhand toward the ammo box. It clanged against the metal lid and dropped in. "I'm tired of this playing around. I want to know who is down there."

"I'm not going to blow it for you, Grier," Mack said. "We haven't done anything wrong, remember? I'm just one of those guys who go bananas over Indian ruins. Come on. You can trust me, Grier, like you'd trust a brother."

He climbed down the ladder, across the boulder field, affecting a deliberate casualness in case he was being watched. Once he was in the cover of the trees, that changed. Without ever being conscious of it, he began to move as quietly as any stalker, his heart beating fast. A shiny black grackle burst from the tamarisk. He did not see a sign of anyone. Maybe whoever it was had just taken a snooze. A backpacker who decided to make camp for the night along the river would complicate things.

There was a small opening in the woods, filled with sunflowers, and on the far side of it, a dense thicket. Mack tried to duck his way through, but the tangle of branches caught at him. He felt thorns stab through his trousers. He freed himself cautiously, taking it a step at a time, breaking through unseen snares. He crouched low to take advantage of a natural tunnel, then parted the blind of vines in front of him.

He could see the raft, right where they had left it, sitting under the cottonwoods. Over the raft stood a young man lifting out one of the oars. He wore a gray ranger's uniform, the familiar green and white patch on his sleeve, a canteen strapped across his chest. His pack was propped against one of the massive, stranded river boulders. He had on short hiking pants and his legs were tanned and strong. The sun had bleached his hair blond and he had round, freckled cheeks and a wide, Howdy-Doody mouth that made him look even younger than he was. Even so, he couldn't have been more than twenty.

When Mack pushed the brush aside, the boy stepped back, startled.

"Hey," Mack said.

"How you doin'?" The boy let the oar drop, rest against the side of the raft, as if he had been caught doing something wrong. Mack kicked through the last restraining vines.

"This is your raft?" the boy said.

"That's right," Mack said.

"You must have had a heck of a time getting it down this far."

"Wasn't easy," Mack said. The kid looked back up the river. Both of them stared at the boot prints, the wavering snakelike patterns in the sand where Mack and the others had battled the raft. The boy took a light punch at the side of the boat.

"You here by yourself?"

"No. Me and my buddies. We floated down yesterday," Mack said.

The boy didn't look like he was sure of that. He squinted through the trees. It seemed to Mack that he was scrutinizing the cliffs, but maybe that was just Mack's paranoia. "You camp here last night then?"

"Yeah."

"Didn't have any trouble?"

"No. Heard some of those burros in the middle of the night. Had us a little spooked until we figured out what it was."

The boy's smile was quick and friendly. "Oh, I know," he said. "I heard a mountain lion night before last. You ever heard one of those?"

"No," Mack said.

"People always told me it sounded like a baby being strangled or something. It really does, too."

Not paying attention, Mack turned, kicked at the loose gravel. He racked his brain for what to do. The ear-splitting scream took him totally by surprise.

Mack whirled angrily, as if he'd been tricked. It was no trick; the boy had meant no harm. Perfectly good-humored, he took his cupped hands from his mouth.

"Isn't that something?" the boy said. "I'm telling you, I just about peed in my pants."

Mack tried to smile, his heart still pounding. The three men in the cave were sure to have heard that. God knows what they would think it was. "You're with the Park Service then?" Mack said.

"Yeah. They send us out every week to patrol the trails."

"Can't be a whole lot of trouble, all the way back here."

"Not much. But you never know what you're going to run into. A month ago there were two girls from Massachusetts, one of them had busted her ankle. That was something. And then, this time of year, you're always looking for fires."

The boy unscrewed the top of his canteen, took a long swig

from it. Mack watched him intently, tasted his own parched lips. He hadn't had anything wet for hours. It must have shown. When the boy finished he said, "Want some?"

"No, that's all right," Mack said.

The boy slipped under the strap, rubbed the plastic spout with his fingers and held out the canteen. "Go ahead."

Mack took the canteen and lifted it to his lips. He tipped it back and drank slowly, swallow after swallow, aware for the first time of the depth of his thirst. His eyes closed. The water was warm and tasted faintly of plastic, but it was everything that Mack needed. He rolled it over his teeth, savored it like some unwarranted blessing. He finally stopped himself, wiped his wet chin with the back of his hand. He offered the canteen back.

"Have some more if you want," the boy said. There was a softness to him that reminded Mack of someone's little brother.

"No, that's fine. That was terrific."

The canteen passed from hand to hand. The boy screwed the top back on. "Everything's been so dry," the boy said. "Last year they lost twenty acres of ponderosa groves over in the next canyon. Such a damn shame. It will take another hundred years to replace all that."

Mack sat down on a felled cottonwood, jammed his hands deep in his pockets. The water whispered in the slender channel. It looked silvery and almost opaque now that the sun wasn't on it. Farther upstream bats darted above the surface, hunting for insects. Mack felt calmer, oddly satisfied. For a second he could almost have forgotten why he'd come. Maybe his real thirst had simply been for the ordinary world.

"You been out here for a long time?" Mack said.

"The last two summers. I'm just seasonal."

"You're still in school, then?"

"Yeah." The boy looked back through the trees, back in the direction that Mack had come from. He did not see any sign of a camp. Mack found a hard, smooth object in the bottom of his right pocket, began to absently finger it without ever thinking to identify it. He did not want to be a threat to this boy. "University of Wisconsin. Got one year left."

"Nice place to go to school, Madison," Mack said. The trick

now was to both reassure this kid and get him moving. A nuthatch performed its nervous pirouettes in a nearby pine.

"It is. Can't wait to get out, though."

Mack stared down at his own dusty boots. He closed his right
hand tight, dimly aware of something hard and razor-edged
cutting into his palm.

"I'd like to work for the Park Service when I get through. It's
so beautiful out here. Some of the ruins up on the mesa, they're
unbelievable, and ninety per cent of them have never been
excavated. People say the Grand Canyon is great, and Canyon
de Chelly, but I don't think you can beat this . . . I just kind of
hope not too many people find out about it."

"I know what you mean," Mack said. He envied this kid. It
would be terrific if the biggest thing you could imagine doing
with your life was working for the Park Service. It would be nice
to have such clean dreams again.

"Probably I should get a master's in range management or
wildlife. They've got a real good department at Utah State.
Maybe you've heard of it."

"No, sorry," Mack said. He had to get this kid out of here. For
everyone's sake. "I hope it all works out for you."

The boy tilted his head to one side, suddenly puzzled. He was
staring at Mack's hands. Mack looked down, saw the obsidian
arrowhead lying in his right hand like a black, glittering heart.
He had been pressing it so tightly there was a thin red line
across his palm. Mack closed his fingers over it again, instinctively wanting to conceal it. The sudden movement didn't pass
the kid by.

He had done nothing wrong; the kid wasn't going to arrest
him for stealing an arrowhead—for God's sakes, everybody did
it. The boy couldn't know that it had come from the cave, no
way.

Mack hadn't been aware of taking the arrowhead out of his
pocket. How long had he been playing with it? It was un-
nerving. Mack wasn't a big believer in the unconscious, but it
sure looked like something was trying to give him away.

Mack put the arrowhead back in his pocket.

"You're boiling your water, I hope," the boy said.

"We've got the tablets."

"Good," the kid said. "You can't be too careful." The boy had lost his perfect ease. "I should be taking off."

He went over and grabbed his pack off the boulder. He leaned forward to shake Mack's hand. The handshake was firm, the boy was smiling, but then the smile disappeared. He was looking over Mack's left shoulder. Mack turned and saw Harry and Rick and Grier standing fifteen yards away.

Grier was in the lead, looking truculent and stunned, like a diver realizing mid-dive that there was no water in the pool. This was not what he had expected. Rick's eyes were squinched up like someone having trouble with his contact lenses. Harry knew they'd blown it. Lagging behind, he absently slapped the trunk of a tree as he passed.

"Well, here they are," Mack said, trying to cover, but the words caught in his throat, sounded oddly lame.

The boy glanced quickly at Mack, his eyes dark with questions. He balanced his pack on the ground in front of him like a bulky shield. Mack smiled stiffly, trying to hide his anger. He had pulled off something delicate and difficult, he had them in the clear. They had not trusted him.

There were still traces of dust on the clothes of the three men, their hair was stiff and dirty, their movements slurred with fatigue. They looked battered and ridiculous, like creatures out of the Wizard of Oz. The boy was not going to mistake them for weekend campers.

"Everything's all right?" Grier said.

"Everything's fine," Mack said.

"We thought we heard a scream," Grier said.

"Mountain lion. He was showing me what they sound like," Mack said.

"Mountain lion," Grier said. "Could have fooled me." Harry tried to suppress a smile. It wasn't really funny, but Harry, at least, saw the comic possibilities.

The boy was the one to extend his hand. "Hi. I'm Wayne Krohn."

Grier shook the boy's hand. "Hey, Wayne."

"He saw the raft," Mack said. "He wanted to make sure no one was in trouble. He's on a trail patrol."

"Oh, yeah?" Grier said. "You see any rattlesnakes?"

"Not this trip," the boy said.

"Man, I hate those suckers."

The canyon was cool now, everything in shadow. The sunlight was more than halfway up the cliff walls. Rick lay back against the side of the raft. Harry sat on the downed cottonwood, examining the lining of his cap. It was an odd little congregation that had been called. Mack was seeing them all now through the boy's eyes and he didn't like what he saw.

"There's this club in Texas," Grier said. "They do things like get into sleeping bags with a dozen of those rattlers. They think it's fun. Saw it on TV. Boy, you couldn't pay me. How long are you out for?"

"A couple of days." The boy glanced sidelong at Harry. "I get back in day after tomorrow."

"And they don't send anybody along to keep you company?" Grier said.

"No." The boy paused, then addressed Mack. "You guys climbers?"

"No," Grier said. "Why?"

"No reason."

Harry had taken his knife out of its sheath and was absently whittling at a broken branch of the cottonwood. He refused to meet Mack's stare.

"So when you're out on these patrols," Grier said. "What exactly is it you do?"

"He was telling me," Mack said. "Last month there was a girl from Massachusetts with a busted ankle, he had to cart her out of here."

"That must have been rough," Grier said.

"Wasn't so bad. The only hairy part was trying to carry somebody like that out of these canyons. Specially in the middle of the day."

He looked up toward the cliffs and Mack followed his eyes. There was a canopy of trees. It was impossible to see the cave from where they now stood. The boy glanced swiftly back at Mack, caught him looking. Mack's gaze faltered.

"Look, I don't want to take up all your time," the boy said. He lifted his pack, slung it over one shoulder. His voice had a new ring to it, an official friendliness. "The only thing I've got to ask you is that you not set any fires. Everything's so dry this time of year and the needles go so deep in these ponderosa groves, you can think you've got your fire out and it'll just smolder under there for hours and then break out half a day after you've gone."

Grier knocked one boot against the other. "I'm just curious," he said. "This isn't even your jurisdiction, is it?"

"What do you mean?"

"Jurisdiction. You know, you don't have any say."

Mack was dumbfounded. Why was Grier challenging the kid?

The boy stiffened a little, then spoke very carefully. "No, I guess not. The river is the dividing line. Indian land on this side, government on the other."

"Christ, Grier," Mack said.

"I was just curious," Grier said. "I always wondered where the line was."

"No, he's right. I don't have any say." The boy slipped his other arm through the shoulder straps. Cooking utensils clanged inside his pack. He looked back at Harry. "Aren't you Harry Dakota?"

Harry laid his knife flat on the trunk of the cottonwood. "Yeah. That's right," he said gently.

"I saw your pipes at the Indian Market. I really think they're super. I bought one for my dad's birthday. He's kinda gotten interested in Indian stuff since they came out to visit last summer." Harry smiled, modest in the face of a compliment. The boy adjusted the straps under his armpits. "Nice talking to you guys."

"Thanks for the water," Mack said. Rick and Harry raised their hands in farewell.

The boy set off down along the river, pausing once to pull up his gray wool socks. The four men watched silently. As he moved further on, they could only catch glimpses of him, fleeting pieces of a puzzle flickering through a curtain of trees.

"A piece of cake," Grier said.

"I don't know what you're calling cake," Mack said. "You're a real idiot, you know that, Grier? You didn't have to get into a debate with him."

"I have a naturally inquiring mind," Grier said.

Rick pushed himself up from the raft, stared down through the trees where the boy had disappeared.

"Did he ask you a lot of questions?" Rick said.

"No. Not many. But I'll bet he's got a lot more now."

"Come on, Mack," Grier said. "That kid never picked up a thing."

"What were we supposed to do? We heard that damn scream. We had no way of knowing," Rick said.

"Turns out he's a fan of Harry's. Real nice," Mack said. "I was doing just fine. It was all taken care of. If you guys weren't such bad actors it would be one thing."

"That part about the rattlesnakes is true," Grier said. "I saw it on TV."

"Don't be pissed," Rick said. "We were worried about you."

"You should have saved your worry. You've got some reason now," Mack said.

"He's gone," Harry said. "Let's leave it at that." A wood-pecker launched a loud attack on one of the nearby trees.

"Now what?" Rick said.

"Give the kid a few minutes. Hell, give him till dark," Grier said. "We've got all the time in the world."

This wait was not like the other. They should have been feeling safe and yet they weren't. Harry went down to one of the shallow channels of the river. He took off his boots and knocked the dust out of them, began to patiently wash his neck and arms. Grier stretched out against a tree, his eyes closed, his hands clasped behind his head. Rick stood poised like a deer ready to jump.

Mack lifted one of the oars out of the raft. The only things they'd left behind were a canteen and an old shirt of Rick's, nothing that would have given them away.

Rick turned and came slowly back to the raft. He was looking at Mack, mute appeal in his eyes, some question he couldn't bring himself to ask. He gave the thick rubber side of the raft a swift, punishing kick, made the entire craft bounce.

Without opening his eyes Grier said, "Just cool it, all right?"

"I'm not doing anything," Rick said.

"Then do less," Grier said.

Mack squatted next to the downed cottonwood, put his head back, stared through the canopy of leaves. The sky began to blur. His eyes had unexpectedly started to tear over.

Ten minutes passed. Then Harry stood up suddenly, water dripping from his face. He was staring toward the cliffs. "Oh, Christ," he said.

Grier sprang to his feet. In three seconds they were all at Harry's side. Looking back from where Harry stood there was a break in the trees and they could see clearly all the way up to the cliffs. The boy stood at the foot of the ladder, looking up.

"Hey, kid!" Grier shouted at him.

The boy didn't hear him. He bent down and picked up a handful of rubble, some of the rubble the four men had spent hours pitching out of the cave. He let it sift through his fingers.

"Kid's not so dumb, after all, is he?" Harry said.

Grier splashed into the shallow water, heading toward the slope. "What the hell are you doing?" he bellowed.

The boy was looking their way, but vaguely, as if he couldn't quite make out what Grier was saying. He raised a slow hand in greeting. Harry sat down, fanned the sand from the bottom of his feet. The boy stared up the ladder again, then slipped out of his pack.

"Oh, shit," Harry said. He yanked on his socks.

The boy began to climb. Grier was on the far side of the water and running. "Hey, kid, don't go up there!"

Rick lurched out into the water and then, halfway across, stopped and looked back in distress, shouted for them to come on. Mack stood stunned. Harry pulled on his boots, but didn't bother to tie them. He stumbled to his feet.

"Let's go," he said to Mack. "We better not leave it to Beaver up there."

The boy was well up the ladder. Grier leapt heavily from

boulder to boulder, screaming something. There was no way he was going to get there in time.

The four men labored up the jumble of rocks, each man for himself. The boy disappeared inside the cave. Grier reached the ladder, propelled himself upward, arms and legs pumping in tandem like the jointed limbs of a clapboard puppet.

Rick slipped and fell in the boulders. When he got up he was limping. No one stopped to help. Harry passed him and then Mack did. As Mack went by he could hear Rick whimpering.

Mack was right behind Harry on the ladder. When he reached the top, Harry turned to give Mack a hand up. Grier stood in the center of the cave, his legs spread wide like the bouncer in a third-rate bar. Mack didn't see the boy at first, his eyes adjusting to the darkness. Then he saw the boy standing ten feet back, not moving, as if he was afraid to come out of the shadows.

Mack heard the ladder rattle behind him, heard Rick heave himself onto the rock floor. The men stood four across in the cave mouth.

"You guys aren't camping, are you?" the boy said.

"Not exactly," Grier said.

The boy ran his hand through his hair. "Lord," he said. "Lord, Lord." Mack looked past him. Far back the stack of gold lay half covered by a tarp. "It's gold, right?" the boy said. "That's what it looks like. For real."

The four men didn't say anything. Then Harry said, "Wayne, let's not make a big deal out of it. There's nothing to worry about."

"I don't know if it was you guys or not, but somebody's done a hell of a lot of excavation here. And the pulley and all that. It's incredible." The boy looked quickly over his shoulder as if it all might somehow have disappeared. "Do you realize how much that must be worth?"

"We realize it, Wayne," Grier said. Harry got down on one knee to tie his shoelaces.

The boy came forward a couple of steps, still incredulous. "Are you guys archeologists or what? You with Indian Affairs? Who *are* you guys?"

"You have to give us a chance to explain, Wayne," Rick said. His voice was less than firm.

The boy stared stonily at Mack. "You told me you floated down yesterday. Sure you did."

"We couldn't let anyone know we were up here," Mack said. "That's just the way it was."

"Hell, tell him the truth," Harry said. He finished tying his boots and stood up. "He's a grown-up. Lay it on the line." Mack glanced at him, not knowing what kind of game Harry was playing.

"We were as knocked out as you are now, Wayne," Grier said. "We don't have to tell you. If word of this got out before it should, you can imagine. Every news team in the country would be down in these canyons."

"Tell him the truth, Grier," Harry repeated.

The boy ran his hand along the wall that still bore the raw scars of their work. He knew when he was being conned. "You guys have permission to be out here?"

Grier bent down and gathered up Rick's strewn clothes, the shredded remains of the topographical map, doing his light housekeeping, trying to make the place a little more presentable. "You mean permits?"

"I said permission, I didn't say permits. Who knows you're out here?"

"We're going to have to tell him the whole story, fellas. Why not?" Harry muttered. God knew what Harry had up his sleeve. Mack hung his head for a second, baffled by shame.

Grier tilted his head back, gazing at Harry. "O.K., you're right. We're not going to try and put anything over on you, Wayne. We're going to tell you. Everything. We've got enough food for old Wayne here, don't we? You can stay and have supper with us."

"I don't think I can," Wayne said.

"Sure you can," Grier said. He tossed the handful of clothes he'd been holding onto one of the sleeping bags.

The boy took a deep breath, puffed out his cheeks, let the air out slowly. "Look, I don't know what's going on. I don't know who you guys are or what you're doing here. But I really just need to get out of here. I'm sorry."

"Wayne, you don't understand," Grier said. "We need your word that you're not going to mention this to anyone."

"If you could hang in there for a minute, Wayne," Harry said. "It would make things a whole lot simpler."

"Look, how can I not mention it?" Wayne said.

"Your word, Wayne," Grier said.

"I'll talk to my supervisor, see what he says, and I promise I won't say anything to anybody else. That's the best I can do."

"Not to anyone, Wayne," Grier said. "We can't let you go until we have your word."

Wayne paused for a second. "O.K., you've got my word," he muttered, without an ounce of conviction.

As he tried to slip between Mack and Grier, Grier put his fingers in the boy's chest, pushed him gently back.

Wayne's face began to color. "I gave you my word!" he shouted.

"Just calm down," Grier said. The boy tried to rush past and this time Grier pushed him back with both hands.

Mack stepped in front, shielding the boy, and gave Grier a shove. "God damn it, don't you put your hands on him!"

Over Mack's shoulder Grier said, "Tie him up."

"What the hell are you talking about?" Mack said. "No!" Grier slid out of Mack's way.

Rick glanced at the others to see what they were going to do. Harry turned away, disgusted, and spat into the dust. "Don't be a fool, Grier," he said.

"I'm serious. Tie him up," Grier said.

"You guys can't do this," the kid said. He took a step backward, stepped on someone's open sleeping bag and slipped down. Rick ran his hand across his chest. His fingers were trembling. His eyes were riveted on the boy.

"This is just wrong, Grier," Mack said. He reached out for Grier's arm, but Grier twisted free. Mack looked to Harry for help. Harry's back was still turned. Mack couldn't believe it. Harry was acting as if it was already over. "You can't bail out now, Harry," Mack said, his voice scarcely audible.

Harry glanced quickly at Mack, his eyes narrow and hard. Mack could see the contempt in his face and yet had no idea of its object. Mack could only stare dumbfounded. The one thing he would have never figured Harry for was a coward.

Rick was at Grier's side, the two men blocking the dim light. They stepped forward tentatively, like partners in a dance neither had danced before. The cave was narrow enough, the boy was not going to get past them. Rick reached out an imploring hand.

"Wayne, it's going to be O.K., believe me."

"You guys are crazy! You guys are in a lot of trouble. I'm a park ranger. This is federal . . ."

Grier stepped forward on his own, grabbed for him. The boy pushed Grier's arm away. Rick, made bolder by Grier's move, grabbed Wayne's other arm and hung on. Grier spun around behind the boy, got him in a headlock. Wayne flailed his arms, his head down. He staggered forward, trying to throw Grier off.

Mack watched with a paralyzed, almost hypnotic attention. *I am letting this happen,* he thought, but what he felt at the same moment was that it wasn't him. There was some stranger watching in his place, some second self.

"Get his legs, man, get his legs!" Grier shouted.

Rick grabbed one leg and when Wayne tried to kick at him with the other, the boy lost his balance. Grier and Wayne fell together in the dust.

Grier was on the boy's back, had the kid's arm twisted up behind him. Wayne's face was pressed into the dust, one eye shut.

Mack moved forward. "Grier!" he shouted.

"Get me a rope, dammit," Grier shouted. "Over there, over there!"

Rick got up off his knees, scrambled for the rope. The boy was still suddenly, knowing it would only hurt more to move now.

"Grier, damn you! We can't do this!" Mack shouted. He grabbed the shovel leaning against the wall. Rick, the rope in his hands, froze for a second. Mack raised the shovel shoulder-high.

"Give me the rope!" Grier shouted.

Mack felt Harry's hand on the shovel, holding him off. Mack looked back at Harry. He could not be sure of anyone now. Harry just shook his head.

Mack stared at Grier expertly winding the rope around the kid's wrists. A hoarse, unintelligible cry came from the boy. Grier lashed the rope around once, twice, three times, tightened it with a series of yanks. Mack struggled to get free of Harry's grasp, but Harry had both arms around him. They were all bound now. Rick sat on his knees, his mouth slightly agape, panting as if he had just finished a long run.

Grier stepped away, left the boy bucking in the dust. Mack flung the shovel against the cave wall. Rick stood up too, wiping the dust from his face, trying to spit the bitterness from his mouth.

Grier avoided their eyes. "Someone help me lift him," he said. Rick was the only one he could have been talking to. The two men lifted the boy by his elbows. Rick batted dust from Wayne's uniform.

"What do you think you're going to do with him, Grier?" Mack said.

Sweat stood out on Grier's forehead. "Jesus Christ, Mack, give me a break, would you?" The boy had started to cough. "I'm not going to do anything to him. I'm going to be as gentle as a fucking lamb, all right? I just don't want him running out until we figure out what the hell we're going to do."

Mack stood mesmerized as Rick and Grier guided the boy toward the back of the cave. He didn't know why he had let it go this far. Unless somehow, somewhere, he really did approve. The boy stumbled, tried to stop his coughing. Grier for a second almost seemed to be lifting him off the ground one-handed. When they got to the back of the cave, Grier sat Wayne down and tied him to the base of the beam. They were in almost total darkness. The kid jerked from side to side, screaming again.

"Don't leave me! They'll come looking for me! You can't get away with this!"

Grier and Rick emerged from the darkness. Grier came slowly, swaggering and yet wary. Rick looked once over his shoulder at the screaming kid. He still couldn't believe what they'd done.

"We've got to talk," Grier said.

"Oh, yeah," Mack said.

The muscles in Grier's face grew taut. "What the hell did you want me to do? You were all ready to let him walk right past us. Everybody except Mr. Badass here. Big fucking help you are! Just get off my back, all right?"

He jabbed a finger in Mack's chest, hard enough to hurt. Mack slapped it away. He was ready to go if Grier was.

"Come on, you guys," Harry said. "Lord A-mighty." He put a hand on Mack, grabbed Grier's elbow and hauled him toward the cave mouth. "Outside, all right? We're not going to get any talking done in here."

They moved almost reluctantly toward the circle of light. The boy was still screaming behind them. "Don't leave me! You guys are going to be sorry . . ."

Rick stopped and looked back. "You sure he can't hurt himself?"

"Staying's not going to help. Move it," Harry said, the self-appointed referee.

They kept hearing the boy's hoarse cries. They descended the ladder, moved out across the boulders, and still they heard him. One after the other of them took the lead, waving irritably for the other three to follow. They were spooked. They moved spasmodically, like chaff blown by gusts of wind.

They did not stop until they came to the remains of the old kiva. There was nothing much left except for a slight circular depression in the earth, cactus growing among the scattered stones. There were still stretches of crumbling low walls, a foot or two high, and on the grass, bits of broken pottery, bones, antlers. The open area was surrounded by some small juniper, low-growing enough that it was still possible to see up to the cave. It was a place for councils.

Grier sat down on one of the walls, crossed his legs in front of him. Mack walked past, too furious to look at him, kicked at the stones, then turned back.

"Tell me, Grier, why you think that had to happen," he said. "I really want to know."

"The boy was walking out, Mack," Rick said. "We didn't have a choice."

"Since when is tying people up a choice?" Mack said. Harry squatted among the flat stones, not looking at anyone.

"I suppose your idea was that we should have just said good-bye to the kid?" Grier said. Despite his bravado, he seemed pale and shaken. Mack heard the boy cry out again, the sound re-fracted and distant. "Nice talking to you, let the whole thing slip right out of our hands? Bull. Every one of you was thinking the same thing. You were just waiting for me to do what I did."

Harry picked up bits of pottery out of the grass around him with the patient curiosity of a collector. He idly tried to fit two of them together.

"We're going to have to let him go," Mack said. "You all know that."

"Maybe we could offer him some part of it, cut him in," Rick said. "We don't have to tell him how much there is."

"Good Lord," Harry said. He tossed away the shards, pieces of an impossible puzzle. Again they could hear the boy cry out.

"I don't want to go to prison," Rick said. "I really don't want to go to prison."

"You're not going to," Grier said. He pushed himself up from the low wall. "There's only one thing we can do." The shadow line had moved up the eastern face of the canyon, was only a few feet below the cave mouth. "We've got at least twenty-four hours before anyone comes looking for him. That's a lot of time. I say we just leave him where he is. We make sure he's got water, that he's tied nice and tight so he doesn't do something foolish and hurt himself. We move all the gold we can. Hoist it up to the rim top, load it on the horses, in two hours we can be back at the van."

Mack's eyes widened in disbelief. Rick ran his hand through his hair, his teeth clenched in a false, frozen smile of anxiety. Harry leaned back on his elbows, shifting over to avoid a prickly pear. His face was a mask. He was not going to tip his hand early.

"We take off," Grier said. Sweat glistened on his forehead. "I've got seventy bucks in my wallet, we'll have enough for gas. In twenty-four hours we can be a thousand miles from here. We call back and tell the rangers where the kid is."

"You're crazy!" Mack said. "That's sheer bullshit. You don't believe it yourself. Not for a minute."

"Don't I?"

"Tell him!" Mack said. "Tell him he's crazy!" Rick looked like he'd just been struck dumb on the spot.

"What other choice do we have?" Grier said. "We let the kid go now and we end up on kidnapping charges and the gold ends up in some FBI vault."

"Maybe we could talk to the kid, Grier," Rick said.

"Talk to him? About what? There is no way we could keep that kid quiet now."

Mack looked across the low rock walls. He saw first one lizard, then another and another. There must have been a dozen, come up to take advantage of whatever heat remained in the still-warm stones.

Harry started to sing. "Goodbye, Old Paint, I'm a leavin' Cheyenne . . ."

"We become fugitives from the law, Grier?" Mack said. "Is that what you're suggesting? I really would laugh, man, if I could."

"My bags are all packed, I'm a off to Montan' . . ."

"Forty million dollars worth of gold," Grier said. "Ten million each. Once we make it out of here we can be whatever we want to be. We can write our own ticket, a clean slate, a new life. You decide if it's worth it or not. But I'll guarantee you one thing, it's the last chance you're ever going to have. It's not going to happen twice."

Mack stared at the dry, littered earth, at the odd bits of sacrificial bone. The ceremonial site was good only for dumb mockery.

"Harry? Rick? You guys could really do this? Just walk away from your lives?" Harry took off his baseball cap and examined the lining.

"Jesus Christ," Mack said.

"I know a guy with a farm in Oregon," Grier said. "The kind of place where nobody's going to ask any questions."

Harry's eyes moved from Grier to Mack and back again, his face impassive, noncommittal.

"Great, Grier, great. All of a sudden we start thinking like guys who knock off small-town gas stations. We're going to be like the guy who jumped out of the plane with the million dollars, D. B. Cooper, right?" Grier and Mack circled the inner walls of the kiva, like animals pacing in a circus ring. Just vanish off the face of the earth. Even if you could get away with it, which you couldn't, no way, you're talking about erasing everything you've been, everything you've done."

"That's what we came out here for, Mack," Grier said.

"Harry? How can you even sit there and listen to this? You're going to spend the rest of your life running and hiding, wiring your family money from Western Union offices? Come on."

Harry looked up at Grier and Mack, gave them both a beaming fake smile. "You know what really blows my mind? That that kid bought one of my pipes. It really freaks me out."

"What do you have to hang on to, Mack?" Grier said. "A wife who won't sleep with you and a record company that won't touch your records?"

"Yeah, I guess that's it," Mack said. Mack glanced bitterly back at Harry and Rick. Rick was staring off into the distance, something absent in his eyes, like the faraway look of a mathematician in the throes of a difficult proof. Harry met Mack's gaze evenly, trying to warn him. Mack felt everyone shifting away from him.

"You know what my problem is, Grier? That I just can't believe you mean this."

"Why can't you believe me?"

"It's like it's somebody else talking. I hear you, but I don't hear you. It's like it's not for real."

"That gold, Mack, is the realest thing that ever happened to me. I'm not going to give it up."

Mack turned and walked away. The canyon was split now between light and shadow. He felt the other three watching him. "A real bunch of cowboys I ended up with. So this is it,

huh? True West, nobody comes out here to live, they come to
steal. Hit it once and you can tell the whole world to go fuck
themselves. Breach clean. Real wildcatters. Congratulations, I
didn't know you had it in you." He thought he heard the boy cry
out again, but he wasn't sure. It could have been an animal or a
bird. Mack whirled.

"You know what I'm going to do? I'm going up and untie that
kid. Right now."

"No, Mack, you're not," Grier said, his eyes widening a frac-
tion, his tone patient and hurt. Rick came and stood at Grier's
shoulder, his face stricken. Mack glanced quickly at Harry.
Harry agreed with him—Mack was sure of it; he could see it in
his eyes—yet Harry never moved.

"We're going to have to get started," Grier said softly.
"There's more rope in the raft; we're going to need it. Why
don't you go get it, Rick? Harry here can get started loading the
bars in the packs. I'll be up in a minute. I want to talk to Mack."

Rick came forward a couple of steps. "I'm sorry, Mack," he
said. "But he's right. There really isn't any other way, I've
thought it through. I think it can work." There was something
stiff and overbearingly sincere about Rick, like a kid at his first
communion. "I've got nothing to lose, you know? That's what it
comes down to. You can understand that, can't you? I want you
with us, Mack. The boy's going to be all right. It's not like we're
going to be hurting anybody . . ."

"Then what are you apologizing to me for? Get the hell out of
here."

Rick kicked over a piece of pottery with his boot, stared at the
ancient black and ochre markings. He was considering saying
something more, but then decided against it. He turned and
headed down toward the river, slowly at first, but then faster,
leaping from boulder to boulder.

Mack looked back at the still-reclining Harry. "So what are
you waiting for?"

"I'm not waiting for anything." Harry brushed off his hands
and rose lazily to his feet. Shaking out his legs, he came down
toward Grier. For a second Grier wasn't sure of him. Harry

slipped his fingers into Grier's hand, twisted it into a soul hand-shake.

"I've got to give it to you, Grier. You sure can talk. I think the guy has outtalked you, Mack, I really do." Harry walked away from both of them, looking up toward the cliffs. "Oh, hell. What are we going to do? What's your idea, Mack?"

"You know my idea," Mack said.

Harry leaped up on one of the low walls, graceful as a cat, his outstretched arms wavering for a second until he had his bal-ance. "You can do better than that, can't you? Your heart's in the right place, Mack, but that wasn't much."

"You go along with this, Harry, I'll break your neck," Mack said.

"You'll probably get that chance." He stepped down off the wall. "Maybe we all aren't so good as you thought we were." He stared at Mack. It was the coldest look Mack had ever seen; there was nothing there that Mack recognized, no warmth, no light. "See, I know what I'm going to do. I'm clear. I like things that way. Load the bars in the packs, isn't that what you said, Grier? Well, you got it. Talk to him, Grier. Talk some sense into him, make the man see the light."

Harry reached out to punch Mack playfully on the shoulder, but Mack grabbed him by the wrist. "You're throwing your damn life away, Harry."

"Just get your hands off me, man," Harry said. He twisted free, started backing away, never taking his eyes off Mack. "Just lighten up a little, would you? Talk to him, Grier."

Harry began to move up the slope. "You son of a bitch, Harry!" Mack screamed at him, but Harry never looked back again, laboring over the rocks with an exaggerated, almost cartoonlike casualness.

Mack spun away, thinking he was done with it, but then he realized he wasn't. He grabbed a rock, whirled and threw it wildly in Harry's direction. "You son of a bitch!" The rock sailed harmlessly off to Harry's left.

Mack turned away, his hands on his hips. Trying to get his breath back, he blinked into floating webs of light, realized that there were tears in his eyes. Grier sat at the far side of the kiva ruins, big-shouldered and quiet, his elbows resting on his knees.

Grier waited for several seconds and then said, "You were really going to hit me with that shovel, weren't you? Back up there in the cave?"

"Yeah."

Grier smiled. "You're really something, you know that?"

Mack faced him. "Say for a second there was no kid up there. Forget about him. Just how smart do you think we are? You know somebody at the border. Rick has the name of some character with a smelter in Mexico. Then we've got these banks in the Cayman Islands and Swiss bank accounts. Come on. How much did you say it was worth? Forty million? Fifty? We're out of our weight class." Grier straddled the low wall. "There are people who will kill you for a fiftieth of what we're sitting on. This was supposed to happen to Coronado, not to guys like you and me, Grier."

Grier scooped up a handful of broken pieces of pottery and spread them on his palm. Mack couldn't tell if he was really listening or not, but he kept on.

"If we were all geniuses, Grier, computer whizzes, something like that, it would be one thing. All it would take would be a couple of electronic blips and zap, twenty million dollars shows up in an account halfway around the world. But we're talking about gold, real bars of it, hard stuff, and you've got to hide it, move it, protect it, and the first time you walk into a pawnshop in Eugene, Oregon, or a bank in Mexico and try to sell the smallest sliver of it, you'll attract sleaze so fast it will make your head spin."

Grier flipped a piece of pottery underhanded, like a poker player tossing a chip.

"The shame of it is we're not equipped to hang on to it. We don't have the tools. All we did was find it. You know what somebody told me once, Grier? I don't know if it's true or not. But they told me the only reason that coyotes have survived so long is that they've learned to avoid poisoned bait. That's what we've got our hands on. Poisoned bait."

Grier sailed a pottery shard toward the river. It dipped

sharply and dived into the grass. "You're thinking about your kid, aren't you?" Grier said.

"My kid. That kid up there."

"I'm going to tell you a story, Mack. When I was growing up in Arkansas there was a man who worked on the farm for us. Named Sid. He and my daddy had a falling out. Sid went to live by himself on the island. It wasn't a real island, except in the spring when the river was out. Someone came over to the house and said that Sid was dyin' over there. This was in the fifties, the time of the polio epidemics. Daddy said he was going to go get him. My mother didn't want him to go, she was afraid he'd get infected, or us kids would."

A squirrel rattled boldly down one of the trees, froze in surprise when it saw them, then whisked out of sight.

"My father went over to the island anyway, and carried Sid out on his back. That was what you did, you see. There was a code." Grier hunched forward, his hands on his knees. "You wonder, sometimes, how you measure up. My father's been dead for ten years now. Before he died the government came and took his eighty acres of farm. There was no Bureau of Indian Affairs to dole out anything. I remember at the end he would say, 'That's all right, son, it doesn't matter.' But I knew it wasn't all right."

Mack stared down at the blisters on his hands, restless, as if they were somehow imprisoned by the broken walls of the kiva. Rick must be back at the raft by now. He didn't understand Harry at all.

"My father would have let that boy up in the cave go, no question. When he had his operations, he always did what the doctors said. He was an obedient, humble man. Obedience is what they send dogs to school for, right? I wanted to grab him and say, do not obey them, you don't have to obey anybody anymore, you are dyin', just tell them no. When he died he had nothing. Nothing to show for it. In this part of the country, you better have something to show. I remember, growing up, the looks in people's eyes, when they saw that you were poor. I remember the jokes, how mean they could be. And I knew that if I ever had the chance for something I would not back away. I

would not be so good a man . . . I know I'm asking a lot, Mack.
But I can't go back now. It would kill me." Grier had begun to
pace. "It's just not fair. We all went into this together. We knew
what we were doing. It's like we've been climbing this impossibly high mountain and we're almost there, we're all roped
together, and one guy decides he wants to go back. But there is
no way back."

"So what do you do?"

"I don't know. Unless you cut the one guy free somehow."

"And you're saying the one guy is me?"

Grier stared at his hands. He was ready. "You're a moral,
decent guy, Mack. But let me ask you something. I'll bet every
night when you go to bed, I'll bet you're just like me. You lie
there and wish you could do it all over again, you feel like you're
just hanging on . . . And I'm saying, let it go. This is your
chance, give yourself a break. Don't be so hard on yourself.
There is nothing I've done that you weren't capable of doing.
People get away with things, Mack, you know they do, most of
the stuff never makes the papers. We're not going to get caught
unless we start acting like idiots."

Restless, Grier slowly began to climb the slope. He stopped on
the rise twenty feet above Mack and looked back down at him.

"It's time to go, Mack."

"Sorry, Grier."

Grier turned away, fed up, looked back toward the cliff. Suddenly the disgust was gone. Grier froze like an animal caught in
the headlights of a car. The curse came low and muttered.
"Aww, shit!" Mack didn't matter any more. Grier began to run.

Mack leaped from boulder to boulder. When he came to the
rise he could see Harry sitting at the base of the ladder. He
looked like he didn't have a worry in the world, slicing away at a
whittling stick with long, hard strokes. His elbows were
propped up on the bone-white rung behind him, his baseball
cap pushed back on his head.

Bewildered, Mack stared at Grier, broad-backed, plunging
doggedly upward. Somehow he wasn't seeing what Grier had
seen. Then he did. He went after Grier, digging, like a
cornerback who realizes he's just blown the zone.

Harry made no motion to greet them. There was a light wind coming out of the canyon. Mack started to gain ground on Grier. The only sounds were their labored breathing and the bright clicks of dislodged rock. As Mack came to the spine of the talus ridge, he could see Rick on the far side of the slope, thirty yards below them. He had a heavy coil of rope draped over his shoulder.

Rick stared up at them, full of wonder, then slipped out from under the rope and began running too, the three men converging on the ladder like flakes of metal spinning to a magnet.

Twenty yards from the ladder, Grier slowed to a walk, wary suddenly, letting the other two catch up. Harry never changed his position, blinking sheepishly at them.

"Is he all right?" Rick said.

"I suppose he is," Harry said. He stood up, tossed his whittling stick away. "I cut him loose."

"You what?"

"I cut him loose."

Grier didn't question it for a second. He was past Harry, already rattling up the ladder. Rick held on, looking from Harry to Mack, waiting for some explanation. Seeing that he would get none, Rick swung himself up on the ladder.

Harry looked ruefully over his shoulder at Mack. "You wanted to break my neck? Well, this is as good a time as any."

By the time Mack reached the top of the ladder Grier was just emerging from the murk at the back of the cave. The loosely coiled rope was draped in his hands.

Harry crawled off the ladder behind Mack, stooped for a second, humpbacked against the glaring sun. Harry rose to his full height, his hands at his sides.

Grier rushed at him, switching the rope to his left hand, swinging wildly at him with his right. Mack and Rick caught Grier, held him back.

"Where is he?" Grier screamed. "You bastard! You candy-assed chicken-shit! Tell me where he is!"

"I don't know, Grier. I really don't."

Grier shoved past all of them, rushed to the mouth of the cave. The others were at his side in an instant. They shielded

their eyes against the setting sun, stared down into the shadowed canyon. It was five or six seconds before Mack spotted
him. The boy had just come scrambling out of the boulder field,
well to the north of them, and was in the open plain, still fifty
yards from the cover of trees.

"I'm sorry, fellas," Harry said. "I thought about it and I just
couldn't let it go any further."

The four men stood silent, the empty cave at their backs.
Mack was dazed for a moment, overwhelmed. He was thinking
several things at the same time. *We have lost everything,* he was
thinking, and *I will never be great,* and yet there was a fierce
gladness in him too, a joy in watching the boy leap down into an
arroyo, buck his way up the other side, zigzag through the
juniper like an animal that had just escaped its hunters. So much
was falling away, Mack wanted to laugh out loud. Watching the
boy run, Mack knew that there were hopes he could never have
back again. He didn't even know if he was sad or happy about
that.

Harry grimaced, rubbed the bridge of his nose, a man not
perfectly at ease with what he had done. Grier twisted the rope
once around his hand, pulled it tight, pitting all his strength
against it. When he finally cried out, it was a sound full of rage
and mourning. He spun, lashed out at the smoke-blackened
wall with the rope, ran to the back of the cave.

"You had no right to do that, Harry," Rick said. "Not on your
own. You can't just decide for everybody like that. You never
even asked us. There it goes. Every damn dream you've ever
had . . ." Rick was weeping.

Mack heard Grier throw his pack aside. The boy was only
twenty yards from the trees. Mack turned and saw Grier with
his rifle in his left hand. Mack and Rick instinctively backed
toward the walls. Harry never moved.

"Don't be nuts, man," Harry said.

"Get out of my way," Grier said.

"It's over, Grier," Harry said. "All you can do is make it
worse."

Grier took the rifle in both hands; Mack heard the safety click
off. Harry stood in a corona of fierce light.

"Don't screw around, Grier," Mack said.

Rick slid down on one of the packs. Grier raised the rifle across his body. Mack didn't know if he was bluffing or not, but this time Mack wasn't going to wait too long. He threw himself at Grier as hard as he could, tackling him around the chest and arms, trying to pin the rifle; but as the two men fell together Mack heard the gun go off. In the enclosed space the sound was deafening and yet through it Mack heard Harry screaming.

Mack rolled in the dust, pushed back to his feet like a line-backer trying to get back in the play. Harry was crawling on all fours toward the mouth of the cave. There was a splotch of blood just above the knee. Rick had pulled back, horrified.

Mack and Grier scrambled to recover the gun that had been knocked free. Mack had his hands on it first, but Grier was lunging over his back; his body seemed electric, impossible to hold. Mack twisted free momentarily, half blinded by the dust. From a sitting position he tried to hurl the rifle down the shaft, but came up short. The rifle clattered against the rock wall and landed at Rick's feet. Rick, lean and wraithlike, recoiled for a second, then stepped on the rifle the way someone might step on a spinning coin on a sidewalk. Grier lunged after it as if it were a loose ball, his body as white with dust as if he had been rolling in flour, a white bear plunging into darkness.

On his feet again, Mack would have gone after it too, but he heard Harry cry out behind him. The cry made him hesitate, look back. Harry had tried to maneuver himself onto the ladder, but his wounded leg couldn't take any weight. He was in trou-ble, clinging to the ladder pole, his body drawn up in pain, etched in sunlight.

Mack was hung up like a runner in a rundown. There was less than a second to decide. The stirred-up dust stood three feet off the floor of the cave everywhere, pale as a low morning fog.

"Damn it, Rick, stop him!" Mack shouted.

Mack ran to Harry, grabbed him under the arms. Harry's body was trembling, slippery with sweat. He cried out again, reflexively trying to fight Mack off. Mack lifted him free of the bone-smooth ladder, staggering with the weight, pivoting back toward the cave.

Through the ash-white haze Mack saw Grier and Rick grappling for the rifle and there was no question who the winner was going to be. Rick was just trying to contain him, block the way.

Mack could see Grier's flushed face over Rick's shoulder. Grier's eyes were dilated, huge and black. He had a look of such deep hurt and betrayal, it was the kind of look Mack had seen only on the faces of children.

Grier wrenched free. Mack's move was pure instinct. There was no time to think about Grier's intent. Mack spun away, trying to shield Harry's body, the two men pirouetting at the lip of the cave like metal toys on a magnetic board, then losing their balance.

They fell in a blaze of light, turning in the fiery air. One of them screamed, Mack didn't know which, and in the scream was all the terror of the newborn, torn from the womb. They hit the first rock outcropping, rolled. Harry's San Francisco Giants baseball cap came off, went sailing on its own. Mack grabbed for a scrub juniper, lost hold of Harry, fell free again, hit a second outcropping of rock. He saw Harry rolling over and over down the slope, trailing a cloud of dust. Mack slid on his belly, his shirt ripping under him, his clutching hands dragging across rock. Then he was in the air again. He landed on his back, his breath knocked out of him; it felt like his ribs were broken. The world began to spin. He couldn't pass out, not now.

He pushed himself to his feet, glanced upward. A figure high up on the cliff wall, he couldn't tell if it was Grier or Rick, screamed something that Mack couldn't understand.

Harry was only ten feet away, lying in the spiky grass, moaning. Along the cliff wall Mack could see the eccentric dark entrances of a series of small caves. If he could get the two of them there they would be safe.

Bent low, Mack scrambled through the brush to Harry, lifted him again.

"We're going to be all right, we're going to be all right . . ." Mack kept muttering reassurances like magical incantations as he dragged Harry through the low-growing juniper. Every time Mack tried to get a better grip on Harry, Harry's knee buckled.

They could have been straight out of a potato sack race. They made one great target. Mack tried to think of prayers, waiting for the sound, the explosion at the back of his head. The sound never came. Mack pulled Harry into a tiny cave in the cliff wall.

Chapter Fourteen

HARRY AND Mack sprawled in the dim, curved space. After several minutes Mack finally raised his head, stared at the mouth of the tiny cave, listening for any sound. The cave was no more than eight feet deep and five or six feet high. It would be a terrible place to be trapped.

Mack heard Harry move, looked over at him. Harry pushed himself up on his elbows, his teeth gritted, then rolled up into a sitting position. Mack stared dully, still too stunned to think. Harry pulled his knife out of its sheath and began to feverishly slash at the knee of his jeans. His hands were trembling.

"Let me," Mack said. He slid over to Harry, took the slashed fabric in both hands, ripped it wide open. The wound was in the lower thigh, just behind the knee. On one side of the knee was a benign-looking puncture, on the other was a tear still welling bright blood. There was no telling what was torn up inside. Harry stared at it, his face as stricken as a little boy's.

"Can you move it?" Mack said.

Harry tried to flex his leg. The pain took him by surprise; he cried out. He bent forward, resting his head gently against the wounded knee, his face instantly beaded in sweat. "I'd be feeling a lot better if you hadn't thrown me into the goddamned canyon."

Mack shut his eyes and opened them. He was seeing spots and couldn't get rid of them. "We're going to have to wash that. You stay here. I'll get you water."

"I wouldn't if I were you," Harry said.

Mack gaped at him, not understanding. "It will be dark in a few minutes, Mack. Wait until dark."

Mack stared out the cave at the lazy, drifting dance of insects in the long grass, and remembered why they were here. He sat on his knees, looked back again at Harry. Harry had both hands cupped around the still bleeding wound. The eyes of the two men met, came to some unspoken acknowledgment.

Mack pulled the shirt over his head and with the knife slashed it into long, ragged bandages. Harry gingerly wrapped one and then another around his upper leg. He pulled the bandages tight, sucking air quickly through his nostrils.

"The kid's going to make it out, isn't he?" Mack said.

"He's out already," Harry said. "He's got a half-hour lead. The shape he's in, no one's going to catch him."

"So we don't have to worry."

"Depends on what you mean by worry. Twenty-four hours from now there will be helicopters and Land-Rovers and rangers with bullhorns. Maybe that worries you, maybe it doesn't." Frowning, Harry poked softly at his bandages. "Everyone's always asking me how much Indian blood I have. I guess now we'll see."

Mack slid up against the cave wall. For the first time he could feel the blows he'd taken in the fall. He ran his hand over his face. He couldn't shake his dizziness.

"That was a real in-your-face kind of move you pulled, Harry. Cutting the kid loose."

"It was." Mack could feel Harry watching him. In the far corner of the cave were small, dark pellets. Mack and Harry weren't the only ones to use this place as a burrow.

"When you walked away from me and Grier out there . . . you were faking? You had the whole thing thought out?"

"You know me, Mack. I never think it all out."

"You could have said something. When Grier first wanted to tie the kid up. We could have stopped it then. I was ready . . ."

Harry lowered himself down on his back. With utter concentration he slowly lifted his wounded leg and propped it against the wall.

"My father told me once, never jump into a bar fight with a

bunch of crazy white men unless you're ready to get yourself killed." Harry rested the side of his face in the dust. "I don't know, Mack. I didn't know what it was I wanted, what I was willing to give up. I don't have principles, like you; it takes me a while to figure things out. Sometimes, Mack, us Indians aren't as noble and pure of heart as you might want."

Mack slumped down so he could get a clearer view of the canyon floor. There wasn't much he could see through the low rock arch: some softly rustling grass, the darkening shadows of boulders, a glimpse of the distant tree line.

Everything had happened so fast there had been no time to think about consequences. There was time now. By daybreak they were all going to officially become outlaws. It was going to take some getting used to.

"You think the boy will tell?" Mack said.

"I think he will tell a story like you can't believe," Harry said. He shut his eyes for a moment, waiting out the pain. "Oh, dammit, Mack, we were just about rich, weren't we? And I screwed it all up."

"No, man, you didn't screw it up."

"How much do you figure I cost you? Five million? Ten?"

"You can make me out an IOU," Mack said.

A chipmunk appeared at the cave mouth, sitting up as if he expected food. Mack threw a pebble at him and he scampered away.

"If Grier came down here now it would be like shooting fish in a barrel," Harry said.

Mack glanced at him quickly. Mack couldn't think clearly. It was as if he was trying to thread beads on a string and kept dropping the string. "Don't get dramatic. Grier is an idiot, but he's not going to come down here and . . ."

Harry was looking at him very oddly. "Mack?"

"Yeah?"

"What the hell is that on your pants?"

Mack looked down and saw that the front of his trousers was soaked in blood.

He yanked the trousers open, saw the wound in his groin, a jagged cut an inch long. There was blood oozing from it. Mack

stared at it as if it were not part of him, as if it was some strange
leech that had secretly fastened itself to him.

"Jesus, Mack, you're gored."

Suddenly Mack remembered. He reached into his pocket.
The whole pocket was wet with blood. He pulled out the obsidian arrowhead. It must have cut him as they had bounced and
rolled down the side of the cliff. He lobbed the arrowhead over
to Harry, who caught it with both hands.

"Are you all right?" Harry said.

Mack leaned back against the wall, pressed the flesh on both
sides of the cut, watched the blood well up and darken. "I
hope."

"Well, damn, damn." Harry gathered in the torn shirt, tossed
it back to Mack. "Welcome to the cave of the walking
wounded."

When Mack took his fingers from the cut, the jagged line
filled with blood again. The wound seemed alien and intimate
at the same time, like something terrible that had happened to
a stranger. Harry slid toward the cave mouth, switching positions, taking up the role as sentry.

"You know," Harry said, "I heard that's how they used to do
prehistoric vasectomies, put arrowheads in the guy's pockets
and push him over a cliff."

"Shut up, Harry," Mack said. Mack tore another strip from his
tattered shirt, dabbed at the torn flesh.

"Mack?" Harry's voice dropped; he wasn't playing anymore.
Head crooked down, he stared out at the canyon like a hound
peering out of a doghouse.

"Mmm."

"I think one of your buddies is looking for you."

Mack slithered quickly to Harry's side. Rick was twenty yards
away, poised and edgy in the boulders, like a bird ready to take
flight at the slightest alarm. He had Harry's baseball cap in his
left hand.

"Where's Grier?" Mack whispered.

"How should I know? You going to talk to him?"

"Yeah," Mack said. He tossed the bloody rag aside, fastened
the top of his trousers, zipped up. "Sure am."

Mack crawled out, rose silently to his feet. Rick didn't see him at first. Mack glanced up the cliff wall, saw no sign of Grier. He moved sideways, a dozen steps to his left, without making a sound. "Rick," he said.

Rick whirled around. When he saw Mack his face brightened in the old way.

"Mack, hey. Oh, God . . . you have no idea . . ." Rick stumbled up through the rocks. "I'm so glad to see you . . ." He stopped short, suddenly not so sure of himself. "Tell me. Tell me about Harry." For the first time he saw the blood on Mack's trousers. "Jesus."

"It's not as bad as it looks. Where's Grier?"

Rick pulled his fingers roughly through his hair. "You don't know the things that went through my head up there."

"Where is he?"

Rick puffed up his cheeks, looking across the canyon, gave a hapless shrug. "He's gone."

"What do you mean? Gone where?"

"I don't know. I . . . He just ran out of the cave."

"He went after the kid? You didn't try to stop him?"

Rick rolled up the bill of the baseball cap. "It all happened too fast, Mack. There wasn't time to do anything."

"But he took the rifle with him?"

"Yes." Rick's voice welled with unhappiness.

"He'll never catch him." Both Rick and Mack turned at the sound of Harry's voice. Setting his jaw like a weight lifter, Harry pushed up onto a stone perch, settled in like some hobbled wizard. His bandaged leg was angled stiffly before him. "No way in the world."

Rick's eyes widened. "You all right, Harry?"

"Fit as a fiddle."

"Christ, man, I'm so sorry," Rick said. Harry didn't bother to reply.

Dusk had descended and even at ten paces their features were indistinct, almost unreadable to one another. The trees along the river were one long, dark serpentine mass.

"You think I should go after him?" Mack said.

"You'd never find him in the dark," Harry said. "And that kid was running like a deer."

"Did you see which way Grier went?" Mack said.

"He was headed straight toward the river," Rick said. "Once he was in the trees I lost him."

"I'm just curious," Harry said. "When you were watching him go, what were you thinking?"

"What do you mean?"

"Why didn't you go with him?"

Rick stared stonily at Harry for several seconds. "You smug son of a bitch." He hurled the baseball cap at Harry. It fluttered wildly like a wounded bird and fell far short. Rick turned away from both of them.

"I came down here . . . because you guys are my friends . . . I was so afraid up there . . ." The words came out in short, choking bursts. "I was praying with all my heart that you were all right . . ." He spun back at them. "But I still can't get over the feeling, the *fact*, that none of this would have happened . . . You had no right to do what you did, Harry! We're going to go to prison because of what you did, you know that. This is your idea of being a hero, throwing other people's lives away? What Grier did wasn't any worse. You must hold us in such contempt."

Harry shifted on his stone seat, rearranged the flaps of his slit jeans. "Rick, I would kick your ass if I had a leg to kick it with. What did you want me to do? Come back and have a roundtable discussion? About what? We were going to work out a treaty that would have made everybody happy? Fuck that shit!"

Agitated, Harry slid to his feet, hobbled a couple of steps toward Rick, nearly fell. "I should have just left well enough alone, right? Tell me where Grier's gone, Rick."

Nighthawks whirled dimly around them.

"Grier lost his head, O.K.?" Rick said. "But he wouldn't . . . He's going to be back any minute. Look, we all know Grier. And you said it yourself, there's no way he could catch him."

"You better hope not."

Mack stepped between the two men, bent down and picked

Harry's hat off the ground. He batted the dust out of it, thrust it into Harry's chest, turned back to face Rick.

"We've got to get Harry to a doctor," Mack said. "I'm going to get the raft, see if I can bring it down and float Harry out of here."

"And what about Grier?" Rick said. "What if he comes back and doesn't find us?"

"Grier made his choice," Mack said. "We're not going to wait on Grier."

"We can't just leave him."

"Rick, all I know is that my friend here has a hole in his leg and if it gets infected and we don't get him to a doctor it's going to be real trouble. I'm going to get the raft. You can come with me or you can stay here with Harry. You choose."

"You know what you're saying?"

"I think so."

Rick was silent, a dark silhouette against the pale wash of the cliff wall. The sky had turned a deeper blue; Mack could make out the first stars. The canyon had filled with night.

Mack felt Rick's steady, skeptical gaze. Mack had made a preemptive move. The only question was whether Rick would let it stand. They both knew the consequences, how much they hadn't even touched on. Rick must have decided this wasn't the place or the time. He pushed away from the cliff wall. "I'll come with you," he said.

The two men made their way down the jumble of boulders, dry stalks crackling under their boots. They skirted the edge of the trees, Mack searching for the path down to the river. Neither of them spoke. Mack batted at a dead branch overhead, sent it swinging erratically, like a gnarled rake.

Rick trailed behind, sticking to the higher, more open ground, like a skittish horse afraid of the plunge into the dark wood. The moon had just come over the rim of the canyon and Rick was in its silvery haze; Mack further down, in the shadows. At every sound Rick would stop and stare, expectant, sure that it was Grier, coming back. Mack could feel Rick's resistance, but refused to acknowledge it, pushing the bone-bruising pace, crashing over the uncertain terrain, over rock and sand and brittle snares of rabbitbrush. With each step their decision became more irrevocable. Glancing up, Mack could see Rick, gaunt and provisional, a ghostly brother, flickering through the picket of dead trees that separated the two men.

Finally they were at the path. Mack headed down into the shadowy tunnel; the dark resinous columns of ponderosa rose above him. He heard Rick fall on the rocks behind him. He turned.

"Rick? You O.K.?"

"Yeah." Rick struggled to his feet, untangling, still in the moonlight at the edge of the trees. Mack moved slowly back toward him. "Look." Rick yanked at something, trying to lift it out of the rocks. He held it out at arm's length. Mack couldn't tell what it was at first, but then Rick shook out one of the long, snakelike coils. It was the length of rope Rick had retrieved from the raft and then dropped on the mad rush back to the cave.

"I promised Grier I'd bring it up," Rick said. He kicked free of the trailing end of the rope. Finding it had pleased him somehow. "I know you probably didn't want to say anything around Harry. But we still have a chance."

"What are you talking about?"

"We have seven, eight hours before the kid makes it back. I'm not saying anything one way or the other; I just think it should be discussed. We got the rope here, we could rig it in a few minutes, now that we know what we're doing. We could have the gold on the rim in no time. Hell, we could be a few hundred miles down the road . . ."

"Come on, Rick," Mack said. "Give it up. You'd make the worst criminal in the world."

Rick held his ground, still in moonlight, winding the rope around his elbow. There was a sudden rush of wind in the pines below them.

"Grier's going to be back any minute," Rick said. "What the hell is he going to think? You know you're just asking for trouble. Grier's not a man you want to provoke. It doesn't make much sense. In the time it's going to take to float Harry out of here, there are going to be cops and rangers all over the place."

Mack kicked at a massive downed tree that had been shattered in some winter snow, long past. "Let's go, Rick."

Rick snapped the coil of rope smartly between his open hands. "I promised Grier the goddamned rope, Mack. And I didn't deliver. Sound familiar? Same old story. Good old Rick. All my life. Nothing but one broken promise after the other."

Impatient, Mack took a step forward, felt the needling pull of the wound in his groin. Rick put out a hand, warning him off. "Don't rush me, man. If you could have heard the way people used to talk about me, Mack, 'That guy, he can be anything he wants. I'd sure like to see what he's up to in ten years.' Well, it's countdown time; we're down to seven hours." Fireflies floated, near and far, in the vast black intricacy of the forest. "I know why you're doing what you're doing. I respect you for it. But what do I have holding me back? Nothing. You can't even call it a gamble."

"You're crazy if you think I'm going to let you go up there and wait for Grier. You don't know what's going to have happened by then."

"And I don't care, Mack! Isn't that terrible? It doesn't matter!" Rick slipped his head under the heavy, coiled rope, adjusted it around his neck as if it were some fibrous wreath.

"You're my friend, Rick. I don't want to lose you."

"Lose me? From what? From the warm, wonderful campfire of humanity? I was never there, buddy! Don't try to save me. And don't try to bully me. Give me some credit. This was my idea, remember? No one would believe me; you all thought I was full of crap. Turned out I was right." Rick slid a hand under the rope where it chafed his neck, pulled himself up even taller, more defiant. "People are always making millions of dollars off of my ideas. Why should I trust you any more than I trust Grier? You can play Mr. Holier Than Thou now, but you held out on me, Mack. After I showed you Tucker's drawing, you went around for two weeks on the sly, checking it all out, never breathed a word . . ." Rick swaggered back and forth on the rocks. He was wound up, as if the moonlight was spurring him

on. "If this is it, I don't want it to end floating down a river
waiting for some police helicopter to pick me up. I'm going to
see something through for once, Mack. I'm going to make a real
run for it."

"I'm not going to let you do it," Mack said.

"You can't stop me."

"No?" Mack pulled on his ear, then came slowly up the slope,
head down. When he looked up he saw Rick, tongue rubbing his
lower lip, almost wanting Mack to try.

Mack grabbed the rope around Rick's neck with both hands,
collaring him, jerking him forward. "Now you listen to me. You
stop feeling so sorry for yourself and think for a minute. We're
going to be all right. You're not going back up there. If you think
for one minute you could get away with it, you're dreaming.
You're going to help me move that raft!"

Rick tried to push Mack away, but Mack held on. They stumbled together, swinging each other halfway around, boulder-
dancing. Their faces were only inches apart as they grappled for
the rope. Mack twisted the rope tighter, trying to throw Rick off
balance. He heard a deep catch in Rick's throat as if he were
starting to choke, and then Rick tripped him. Mack went down
on his back, the wind knocked out of him, and lost his hold on
the rope. Just as he was trying to get up, a blow caught him high
on the cheekbone. He went down again, felt sharp-edged rock
cutting into his shoulder.

Rick stood over him, chest heaving. "If I want to throw my
life away, Mack, it's my own damn business." The rope hung in
long, loose coils around his neck and he was rubbing his right
wrist as if he'd hurt it. His eyes were wide and startled. Rick still
couldn't believe what he'd done. "This was my baby from the
start; no one's going to take it away from me."

Rick backed off a couple of steps, gathering up the trailing
rope, then whirled and fled. By the time Mack got to his feet
Rick had vanished into the darkness and there was only the
slide and click of loose rock somewhere high on the slope, growing fainter and fainter.

Mack shouted Rick's name once, but there was no response.

He didn't shout again. Rick had found his choice. Mack turned and headed down into the dark sheltering woods.

He followed the bank of the river. Water stood in exhausted pools a foot or two deep, eddied in slender channels. It was almost no river at all, as if the hungry sand had sucked up half of what little water there had been in the morning.

He knelt on the sandy bank and drank, then washed himself. He sat on his knees, letting the cool night air dry him, raise goose bumps on his back and chest and arms. The moon continued its slow ascent over the canyon.

Mack trotted easily along the sandbars. A rabbit leapt back in the woods. He heard an owl high in one of the ponderosas. Finally he came to the raft, sitting under the cottonwoods like a glowering bear.

Mack stared for a minute. There had been no sign of Grier. Crazy as he was, Grier should have given up by now; he must have been on his way back. It was important to handle this right, not to waste any more time or energy than he had to. The main channel was forty yards away, and even it seemed narrow, clogged with debris. There was no guarantee that it was deep enough or long enough to do them any good.

Mack meandered up and down, splashing through shallow water, surveying, scheming. The sandbars between channels were brushy and covered with exposed rock. It didn't look easy. Four of them had spent an hour trying to get the raft moving and failed; now Mack was going to try it alone. The difference was that now everything was riding on his being successful.

There was an extra canteen, a tarp and an old shirt of Rick's in the bottom of the boat. Mack quickly put on the shirt, set the tarp, the canteen and the oars under the trees.

He dragged the raft out from under the cottonwoods. It had not been constructed to go overland. Mack pulled it and pushed it, slid it over the sand until he caught it on the rocks or brush. He worked feverishly. The wound in his groin began to throb.

He wrestled with the raft, flopping it end over end, splashing it into one of the narrow channels, falling into the water himself. Finally he heaved it up on the opposite bank.

A bird flew squawking out of the pines. Instantly Mack's heart was pounding. If Grier was anywhere nearby, he could scarcely miss the racket.

Mack dragged the raft on his back like a great inflated shroud. The rubber hissed across the sand, scraped through tamarisk and willow. Finally he pulled it down into the main channel. It sat bobbing on the water. Mack held on to the sides, waist deep in the water, his cheek to the tough rubber, resting for a moment. The moon, sliding out from behind clouds, began to brighten the canyon all around him.

Mack waded through the water, guiding the raft, pulling it off snags, sliding it over the sand where the channel grew shallower. The channel bottom was rocky and uneven; Mack fell in the water again and again. He wasn't sure how much time had passed. The river was the only thing that could carry them home and the river was just toying with him. It was no river anyway. What they needed was some dam release from up above, some commissioner to decide that the farmers needed water for hay. A real flood was what they needed. That or a miracle. Only a state bureaucrat or God would do.

The raft was stuck again. Mack put his shoulder under it, heaved, couldn't make it move. He tried again, staggering sideways, willing the raft off the snag. He heard a snap, the tearing of rubber. The raft slid off his back and Mack fell on his side in the shallow water.

Before he could rise he heard a distant shot, echoing in the canyon to the north of him.

He remained perfectly still. There was no second shot. He wanted to believe that what he'd heard was just his imagination playing tricks on him, but he knew that it wasn't.

Mack felt a sudden flush of warmth in his side. He was bleeding again, down on all fours in the water. He looked up and saw the brightness all around him, saw the long, shining banks of sand twining ahead of him, mocking all his efforts.

He tried to talk his way around it. There were a thousand things that shot could have been: a poacher shining deer, a sheepherder taking a potshot at coyotes. The shot had sounded so far away, so harmless, almost as gentle a sound as a tumbler falling in a lock. They had all agreed that it was impossible. The boy should have been halfway across the mesa.

Mack rose to his knees. The moon hung above the canyon walls. The hysterical need to escape was gone; he felt oddly calm. The most important thing now was knowing what that shot was.

He set off north, along the river, in the direction of the sound. He never questioned the logic of what he was doing. He ran along the gravel banks, in and out of the chokecherry bushes. There was the sharp angry snickering of a bird among the box elders.

What he was doing was crazy. He was willing himself directly into the heart of his worst fear. He caught glimpses of the glowing cliffs through the dark, bending forms of the trees. It was as if he had entered an electrical field and, with every step he took, the waves of force trying to repel him grew stronger, like wind rising in his face. It was a feeling he had only had in dreams.

He had been walking and running for fifteen minutes when he heard something on the trail ahead of him. He froze until he was sure the sound was coming toward him. He pulled back into the trees, crouching down, and waited.

It was almost another five minutes before he caught sight of Grier, running along the bank on the other side of the river, flickering in and out among the trees. He was bare from the waist up and bent slightly forward, trotting like an animal that had been run too long. The rifle swung loosely at his side.

Mack was protected by the angle of the moonlight and the shadows thrown by the cliffs, but Grier seemed oblivious to any danger, stumbling blindly on.

Mack began to run after him. He did not know why. He ran the way a horse runs after seeing another running, without needing to know the cause. He did not want to lose Grier. The two men ran almost side by side, separated by forty yards of low glistening water and dry riverbed.

Mack trotted on the long, luminous stretches of sand, perfectly silent, faithful as a reflection. Grier crashed out of sight for several seconds, appeared again, closer to the littered bank but

further on, stretching the distance between them. Mack let
Grier lead, trailing behind like some guardian angel.

Grier finally tossed his rifle aside, staggered to the water's
edge. He fell to his knees, began to splash water onto his face
and arms. Bent low, his pale skin in the moonlight seemed
silvery, ghostlike.

On Mack's side of the river there was a thicket of tamarisk at
the end of a sandy spit. He moved silently to it, separated the
reeds as delicately as if he were separating a curtain, felt his way
into a sitting position.

Grier scooped frantically at the water, washing his arms, rubbing at the skin between his fingers. Mack could not see his face.
There was a flash of light from the swirling, agitated pool.

Grier finally rose up on his knees. He fumbled through his
pockets. There was a flare of a match as Grier lit a cigarette with
shaking hands. For the first time Mack could see him clearly.
Grier's naked chest and arms were covered with blood. The
match went out. Grier took a single drag on the cigarette,
coughed, tossed the cigarette. The glowing ash cartwheeled
through the air, extinguished itself in the dark grass. Mack did
not move. It was as if he were watching himself in a dream,
doing something terrible that he had no power to stop.

Grier began to rock back and forth on his knees. He was
looking right across the stream, right at the spot where Mack
was sitting. Mack knew that he couldn't be seen. The moonlight
was right in Grier's eyes, it had to be blinding him, and yet
Mack had the eerie sense that some kind of communication had
been established between them.

Grier began to mutter. At first Mack couldn't hear what he
was saying, but then it grew louder. He was repeating over and
over, "Oh, God, save me, oh, God, somebody save me . . ."

It was the moment when Mack could have acted. If he could
have risen out of that thicket, splashed across the shallows,
Grier would have done nothing. If Mack could have forgiven
him. He could not do it. Grier had said, *There is nothing I have
done that you were not capable of doing.* Not anymore. No. He
would not embrace Grier, he would not embrace that possibility in himself. Mack never moved, sitting in his blind of reeds, a

confessor with no absolution to give. He turned his head aside. He could see the luminous walls of the cliffs tapering in the distance. They seemed to meet like glowing gates shutting forever.

There was a rustling in the cottonwoods on Grier's side of the river. Mack and Grier both looked up, saw the staring eyes. There was a whole series of eyes. Then Mack heard a snuffling and the snapping of branches. He saw a dark snout emerge from the darkness, then long, tapered ears. There was a curious herd of burros lined up along the bank watching Grier. They had seen his weakness, seen his shame. They were cursed, sardonic souls trapped in those ungainly animal bodies, witnesses to a million botched dreams.

Grier picked up a rock from the water and hurled it at them. The animals crashed through the woods and were gone.

Grier stumbled out of the water, retrieved his rifle. Mack stepped out of his blind of tamarisk, reeds rattling around him.

"Grier," he said.

Chapter Fifteen

GRIER DIDN'T even turn at first. It wasn't that he hadn't heard. He pulled himself up, letting the rifle slide, the stock thudding into the soft sand. He looked back over his shoulder. "Mack. Hey, Mack." He turned almost gently, facing the stream, one arm crooked across his bare chest.

Mack waded across the shallow stream, the water rippling in widening circles. Grier waited, grave and utterly still, the rifle barrel leaning against his hip. Mack splashed up the bank, shook his boots free of water.

Grier tried to smile. "I don't believe it. Good old Mack. How the hell did you . . ."

"What about the boy?"

"Gone."

"Gone could mean anything."

Grier squatted on his haunches, pressed the barrel of the rifle to his cheek. He glanced sidelong at Mack, his eyes full of appeal. "Dead."

"What do you mean, dead? What could have . . ."

Grier bowed his head, closing in on himself. "I shot him."

Mack walked four or five paces back toward the murmuring stream. "I thought it was impossible."

"I know. I thought it was impossible too." Grier was back on his feet. "If you hadn't blindsided me, Mack, the whole damn thing wouldn't have happened . . ."

Mack picked up a rock. There was an owl hooting again, far back in the woods. Mack threw the rock as far up the river as he

could, heard the harmless splash. "I want you to tell me wha
happened." He whirled to face Grier. "I want you to tell m
everything."

Grier glanced angrily at him, then moved away, swinging th
rifle by the strap. Twice he spun back as if he were about to las'
out. He was like an animal fighting an invisible tether.

"Sure, I'll tell you. Why shouldn't I?" Grier thumbed absentl
at the bolt of the rifle. "Except you probably think you knov
already, don't you? Well, you're wrong. Whatever you're think
ing."

"I don't know anything, Grier." The softness of Mack's voic
seemed to calm him. He looked back at Mack, sizing him up
considering a new possibility. He finally slid down against a tree
covered his face with his hands.

Mack sat down against a pine five yards away, waiting. Grie
was motionless for what must have been two minutes. The rifl
lay on the ground next to him, no more than a couple of fee
away. When he finally spoke, his voice seemed to come out c
nowhere, flat, emotionless.

"I was just trying to figure out what the kid would probabl
do. In his mind, he had to be running for his life. The point wa
speed, to get the hell out. You remember the map? How th
switchbacks angle north from here to the rim? Then there's
fork. To the right the trail is longer and harder, loops around
goes through a couple of good-sized canyons. It had to be two
three hours more. To the left was faster. The only disadvantag
was that it followed the rim south for a couple of miles; he'
have to double back on himself."

Mack scooped up a handful of brittle needles from the fores
floor. They broke in his hand with the slightest pressure. Grie
finally looked over at him.

"You see what I'm saying? Going south was the fastest, bu
he'd be retracing his steps in a way. The only other thing h
could do was bushwhack straight across the mesa, but at night
off the trails, it would be easy to get lost; he wasn't that much o
a mountain man. Scared as he was, he didn't want to be floun
dering in the dark." Grier laid it all out matter-of-factly, with a
certain mildness, as if it were no more than a technical problem

"I know what my choice would have been. I would have taken the chance. Go south, along the rim. He had a good lead, no one was going to catch him from behind. Even if he was going to be coming right back at us on the far rim for forty minutes, he had to figure there was nobody fool enough to try and scale the cliffs in the dark and cut him off. It was one chance in a million."

Mack leaned his head back against the scaly bark of the ponderosa. "But you intended to kill him? If you got there?"

"No!"

"Even though you took the rifle?" Mack wanted to hurt him. "You still didn't know?"

Grier leapt to his feet. "No!" He walked down toward the stream. There was a whisper of wind through the pines. Grier wrapped his arms tight around his chest, staring up through the tangle of branches at the towering pale cliffs. He turned back to Mack.

"It was a hell of a climb. I kept running into dead ends, sheer walls, tent rock. I had to go back and start over I don't know how many times. I really tore my hands up. I have no idea how long it took me. Figured I had missed him. How could it work? Even if I guessed right, he was still probably already past me. It was totally dark when I finally got up to the top." Grier had come up the bank to retrieve the rifle, brushing the pine needles off the stock. He moved restlessly back and forth in front of Mack, gesturing, not wanting to leave anything out.

"Took me more time to even find the path. I sat down in some trees where I could watch the trail. I was shivering. I made up speeches in my mind, what I could say that wouldn't scare him, how I'd step out nice and calm, so natural, say just the right thing so I wouldn't spook him. I made up imaginary conversations explaining why I lost my head, how our lives were on the line. A real basic talk. Then it would hit me that it was over. We'd blown it already."

Mack's trousers and socks were still wet from the river. He leaned forward to wring them out the best he could.

"I imagined him coming in at dawn, all shaky and white, telling the other rangers. They wouldn't believe him at first. But then they would. I imagined the helicopters buzzing the canyons. How do you convince yourself that all of this has really happened? It's like one of those fairy tales where you make a bargain with the devil. You get whatever wish you want, and all you have to do is commit one act that will damn you all to hell."

There was a deep whirring in the branches overhead that made both Mack and Grier start, a heavy, gliding presence, a hawk or an owl, fanning smoothly through the trees.

"I was so sure he was already past me I started running. I had to catch him. I roused up some deer; we nearly scared each other to death. After that I calmed down. If he's past me, he's past me, but I've got to go through with this like I've planned, it's my only chance. I walked back. The only way I could keep going was by telling myself that I'd go just two hundred yards further, and then when I'd gone that, another hundred, another fifty. Then I saw him. He was twenty yards off in the trees, standing right on the rim. It seemed like such a funny thing to do. He must have been sure he was safe."

The story ran on, the river murmuring beneath it. The story was the only place where the boy existed anymore.

"He never suspected a thing. He was looking across toward the cave. Almost like he missed it. There was a glimmer, a glow, you could make it out even at that distance. I couldn't figure out what it was, unless Rick had started a fire. We were both looking at it, neither of us quite convinced that it was real. Blinking like that, it made you feel warm almost. Could have been a thousand years before."

Mack put his head back, stared up at the branches radiating out from their dark trunks, entwined like spokes within spokes. The moon-washed sky seemed impossibly high up.

"It was so quiet and simple," Grier said. "I suddenly got the feeling it was going to work. His face was so peaceful, Mack. 'Son,' I said. He whirled around, all surprised, and he started backing off. 'I'm not going to hurt you,' I said. But he didn't listen. He never gave me a chance. He started running and I started running after. I might have caught him too. But I tripped, went down on my hands, the rifle bounced out on the rock in front of me . . ." Grier was silent for a moment, rub-

bing the stock of the rifle, feeling for nicks. "He was cutting this
way and that. There wasn't going to be another chance. You
know what it's like hunting dove, Mack? How fast it is? You do it
or you don't. By the time I got the rifle back, there wasn't even
time to really get it up, I just shot off my hip. I heard his body go
crashing into the juniper."

Grier stood in front of Mack, hefted the rifle to his shoulder.
Mack couldn't look at him.

"I carried the boy's body down into the boulders. I laid him in
a crevice, covered him with more rocks. Where no one will ever
find him. Hell, a hundred thousand acres of wilderness. People
disappear out here every summer. Fall off cliffs, drown in the
river. They'll search for five days and then when they can't find
anything, they'll give up. It'll be one of those kind of stories."

Grier was finally quiet. Mack shut his eyes, the heels of his
boots dug into the soft, needle-ridden earth. He could see the
boy running and bucking across the bright sunlit floor of the
canyon. What he saw had nothing to do with this story. Mack
opened his mouth, blinked back tears. A stillness filled the trees.
What had been there a moment before was there no longer. A
hole had been torn in the universe.

Grier loitered at the water's edge, absently rubbing at his
bare chest. The telling of the story had reversed their positions.
Grier was calmer, seemed to have partially shaken free. There
was a murmur of wind in the trees, the dark boughs rocked
softly.

Mack was trembling all over, he couldn't control it. He did
not know this man. He was a total stranger. Mack felt as if he
were going insane. All he wanted was to get as far away from
Grier as he could.

Grier turned, swinging the rifle under his arm, careless as any
weekend duck hunter. He studied Mack for a second. "That's
Rick's shirt you've got on, isn't it?"

"Yeah."

Grier came slowly up the bank, kicking at stray stones.
"Where'd you get it?"

"At the raft." Mack got to his feet, brushed off his trousers.

"What were you doing at the raft?"

"I was trying to float out of here." Hands jammed in h
pockets, Mack slipped past Grier, unable to be near him. F
walked to the river, felt Grier's following gaze. "Get Harry t
doctor."

Grier gave a low snickering laugh. Mack stared into the da
slowly flowing water. The boy couldn't be dead. If he was dea
then Mack was cut off from everything he'd ever thought F
was, cut off forever. His mind rebelled. He would undo it som
how. If his will was only strong enough he could bring the b
back.

"And leave me holding the bag?" Grier said.

Mack said nothing, staring up the river. The flash of som
thing far upstream caught his eye.

"So where's Rick?" Grier said.

Whatever it was Mack had seen disappeared for a momer
then reappeared further downstream. It was good-sized, se
eral feet long, rolling over and over in the slow current. Th
water glistened in the moonlight.

"Right where you left him," Mack said. "Doing just what y
asked him to."

"And Harry? What about Harry?" Grier paced the bank, edg
with distrust.

Mack never took his eyes off the river. What he was seein
was impossible and yet it kept coming, Grier's voice was powe
less to stop it. The long slender shape floated, twisted around
snag. A clawlike white limb rolled up out of the water.

It was the boy's body. Grier had not been careful enoug
They were never going to be free of it. The reflection of th
moon lay on the water like a silver coin and the pale tors
floated through it, shattering it into a thousand bright fra
ments. Mack stepped down into the water. Grier's voice wa
somewhere behind him.

"You guys have been going piggyback on me for a long time

The glistening white shape bumped against a sandbar, angle
sideways and caught, lodged firmly. Mack saw it then for what
was, saw the whorls and knots in the bare wood, the stubs
broken branches. It was a log, jarred loose somewhere up

stream. Diverted water poured around the new snag in the shallow stream.

"If we worked together, Mack, we could be out of here by daybreak. No one will be looking for the kid for a couple of days. We have time now. I want you to be with me, Mack."

Mack spun to face him. "I want a favor."

"What's that?"

"Take me to his body. You can do it. I want to see the boy's body."

Grier was silent for several seconds, then came down the bank toward Mack.

"Why? You don't believe me?"

Grier raised his arm. Mack flinched, sure he was about to get hit. In one blurring motion, Grier wiped his forearm and wrist across Mack's mouth.

"You want a taste of it, I'll give you a taste of it. I'll rub your fuckin' nose in it. You're just as deep in this as I am." Grier stepped away, wheeling the rifle across his body, switching hands.

Mack ran his fingers across his lips. Mack didn't know what was in his head and what wasn't anymore, but he tasted the boy's blood, salty and sweet.

"I'm happy you said what you said, man. We should be honest with one another. If you despise me, I got to know that. Oh, yeah." Grier kept backing away, slapping at the stock of his rifle. If Mack had incited him, it somehow seemed to fill Grier with gladness.

"You do what you want," Grier said. "But let me tell you something." He prowled back and forth under the trees. "If I go down, you go down. I'm not going to be the only one to pay. If I serve time, you serve time. You hear me? You go tell Harry that." Grier was strutting and exultant. "You see what I'm saying? I may disgust you, but you don't have a choice. You want to save your ass as much as the next guy. I lose, you lose." Grier hitched the rifle up on his shoulder.

"You're sure of that?"

"I'll tell you how sure I am. I'm going back and see about

rigging those pulleys. You take your time. I know I'll see you. Just don't wait too long, understand? You go talk to Harry."

"I'll talk to Harry," Mack said.

Mack thought he saw Grier smile, but he couldn't be sure. Grier slapped the trunk of one of the ponderosas with an open palm. In his own mind Grier had the confirmation he needed. He turned and moved swiftly into the darkness.

Mack stood at the riverbank for a long time. He finally went to one knee, scooped up a mouthful of water, spat it out again.

He walked slowly down the river, past the raft stranded on the sandbar, beside the point now. Mack was scarcely aware of what he was doing or where he was headed, like a man drugged or half-awake. He drifted up through the pines into the silvery haze of the open canyon. There was a bird singing. It sounded like a robin, as turned around as everyone else, chirping happily in the dead of night.

Halfway across the boulder field Mack looked up and saw a golden flicker three-quarters of the way up the cliff. He stared numbly. The reflected light had the soft, wistful glow of a Christmas tree ornament.

Then suddenly there was a dark figure standing in the light, surveying the canyon. Mack was at least fifty yards away, but it had to be Grier. The figure was waiting. It was Mack now who was the prodigal son, the outcast. Grier was ready to welcome him back into the fold. Mack crouched low in the rocks, afraid of being seen, his teeth still chattering from the cold of the river. He felt a surge of hatred.

The figure raised both hands above its head, stretching, casual, utterly sure of itself. Mack rose to his feet. The figure crossed the mouth of the cave, a wavering, diabolical shadow against the bright inner walls, curling like a dark wick being consumed by the steady force of its own flame. They would go down, one way or the other. Mack was suddenly afraid. There was a new voice in him: what if he just stopped pitting himself against Grier, there would be a kind of hideous pleasure in surrender. It would be so easy to call up to the cave, the most natural thing in the world. The figure turned and vanished.

Mack was suddenly in a hurry. He moved quickly into the darker shadows. There were dozens of caves dotting the base of the cliff. He picked his way from one to the next, searching. He looked up, saw that he was almost directly under the ladder. He stopped, swung around, momentarily confused. There was no sign of Harry. He began to retrace his steps, feeling his way along the gritty rock wall. If Grier had found Harry, if Harry had done something foolish . . .

Then Mack saw the low tracing of light at the base of the cliff, just ten feet ahead of him, like the light under a bedroom door. Mack slithered between two huge boulders. He was on top of the cave before he caught the faint smell of smoke wafting through a two-inch smoke hole. Harry had an uncanny instinct for when to lie low. Mack slipped down into the narrow cave.

Harry lay by a small fire. A heap of snarled kindling, mostly brittle, dead juniper, was jammed against the far wall behind Harry's head. Dark splotches showed through Harry's bandaged knee. If he was surprised to see Mack, he kept it to himself.

"Did you hear a shot?" Harry said.

"Yes," Mack said.

"I thought maybe Grier'd found you."

"No, not me," Mack said. He took a broken branch out of the dust, bounced it into the fire.

"He could have missed," Harry said. "Even if he took a shot at the kid. A guy like Grier, the state he was in, I'll bet he couldn't hit a barn door."

Mack eased down on his side, feeling the slow pull on his wound. He stared into the low flames. "He didn't miss. The kid's dead, Harry."

"How do you know?"

"I saw Grier."

"You *saw* him?" Harry's eyes widened, incredulous.

"Yeah."

The light seemed to swell for a moment. Wincing, Harry struggled to sit up.

"Well, maybe he lied. He was trying to scare the hell out of you, that would be just like Grier. What proof did he have?"

"He had proof, Harry."

The cave was filled with the sweet smell of burning juniper. Harry stared across the fire at Mack.

"You were sitting out there discussing this? I don't understand. He told you how he did it?"

"Yeah." Mack picked burrs from his trousers, flicked them into the flames.

"Where's the kid's body?"

"Grier buried it. Somewhere up on the cliffs."

"Oh, boy, oh, boy," Harry said. Mack's eyes stung from the smoke. He closed them for a second. "Where the hell is Grier now?"

"He went back to the cave. He intends to make a run with the gold, he and Rick."

"And we're just supposed to let the sucker go?"

Mack looked steadily across the fire. "He's waiting for us. He wants us to go with them."

Harry gave a snort of disbelief. "I'm going to break the stupid son of a bitch's neck, I swear to God."

"He said we could do what we wanted. But if he serves time, we'll serve time. He'll take us down with him. He could do it, Harry."

"Oh, he could do it all right."

"I said I'd talk to you."

Harry scrutinized Mack with heavy-lidded, feverish eyes. "Talk to me about what?"

"You've got a choice. Just like everybody else. I'm not going to force you into something you can't do."

Harry spat into the fire. "What the hell is wrong with you?"

Mack stared into the deepest embers. The fragile, glowing structures were tissue-thin, always shifting. There were caves within caves, pulsing like the chambers of a heart.

"That was a good, decent kid," Mack said. "Twenty years old, not even wet behind the ears. You or I could have been his father." Light wavered; shadows ran like dark lizards in the long cracks in the cave ceiling. Mack scooped up a handful of dust. "I should have gone after Grier. I should have forgotten about the raft. I might have stopped it."

"You couldn't have stopped it. The kid should have been long gone. We both thought so. Grier had the rifle, you didn't have a clue to which way he'd gone, for Christ's sake . . ."

"But I should have tried, that's the point."

"Listen to me, man. There was one moment you could have stopped it, *maybe*, but you didn't know, none of us did . . . You're not God."

"But I'm part of this. To even think about going back to my life the way it was, to try and look people in the eye . . ." Mack watched the thin gray line of dust running from his hand like sand from an hourglass. "I'm not quite sure how we go on. I always had a certain conception of myself, Harry. It's not going to work any more."

"So when Grier made his offer . . ."

"I considered it! Standing out there in the canyon just now, it didn't seem like such a bad idea. Erasing your life, right off the board, you botched it so bad you'll never get it right again . . . Yeah, Harry, I considered it!" Mack flung the rest of the dust into the flames. The fire hissed and spat.

After a long minute Harry finally spoke. "I always heard there were hot springs out in some of these caves, but I'd never seen one. I thought they were lying to me." Mack sat, knees up, head buried in his arms. "They say Indians come from as far away as Zuni; it's part of their initiation to spend the night at the bottom of those caves by the hot springs. Their last test. You can see how that would really turn your head around. You come through that and you're a warrior." Harry lifted his bandaged leg, shifting it away from the fire. "Giving up a ton of gold to save a boy's life, turns out that was a breeze. But now the boy's dead, there's nothing left to lose. Not even your good name. It just comes down to what you believe. So it turns out you're not the perfect cowboy; well, all right. But you didn't cop out for forty million dollars and you're not going to cop out because you're ashamed. Besides, asshole, I need you." Harry reached his hand across the guttering fire. "You with me?"

Mack grabbed Harry's hand. "I'm with you."

"Grier really thought he had us?"

"By the balls."

"Can you imagine it, Mack, running roadblocks with Grier in the backseat? We're too ignorant to be anything but good. What about the raft?"

"I tried for an hour and moved it maybe a quarter of a mile. Water's too damn low . . ."

"Well, hell, we may not be able to go far, but we can still go." He fingered the knot on one of his braids. "I told my kid not to bother with these. He's thirteen, he's going out for the football team for the first time. Who wants to be the only kid with braids sticking out of his helmet? When you're that age you want to be one of the guys, right? It's the most important thing. But I always figured when he was older we'd sit down and have a talk about what it means. He could make up his own mind."

"You'll have that talk," Mack said.

"Maybe. Maybe not. If I can't . . . I'm saying just in case . . . I want you to explain it to him."

Mack's face flushed red. "That's ridiculous. What do I know about braids? I'm afraid you're going to have to pass on all that Indian bullshit all by your lonesome."

Harry grinned. "O.K. But I sure would have liked to hear you try." Open-handed, Harry shoveled dirt onto the fire. The mixture of dust and smoke billowed up, filling the small cave. "Once Grier gets the idea we're not going along, this is one place I don't intend to be." Harry coughed, protecting his eyes with his forearm. Sparks flared briefly as the shadows folded over them. "Don't try and think it all out, Mack. Till morning we got nothing to worry about except staying out of Grier's way."

Chapter Sixteen

AT DAWN Mack woke up shaking, chilled to the bone. Harry was still asleep under the tarp that Mack had retrieved. Mack propped himself up on an elbow and with trembling fingers wiped away the dirt and needles pressed to his cheek.

They were in a brushy shelter at the edge of the woods. Automatically Mack stared across the canyon, up at the shadowed mouth of the cave. Then it all came back, like a lock snapping into place. Mack scrambled to his feet. He had no idea how long he'd been asleep.

Muttering curses at himself, he moved quickly along the line of the trees, slid along a blasted cottonwood that jutted out into long grass. He scanned the canyon and the rim in both directions, saw no movement. The morning was overcast and there were storm clouds in the north.

It had been one hard night. Mack had lain in the cold for what must have been two hours, staring up at the fitful flickering of light against the distant cave walls, waiting for Grier and Rick to make a move. None had come. Mack had finally crawled under a corner of the tarp, lying to himself that he was just going to shut his eyes for a second.

There was no fire in the cave now. They must have gone. Unless something was terribly wrong. They had slipped out while Mack and Harry had slept, that was the only possible explanation. It was over.

What Mack had to do now was get Harry out of the canyon.

He thought about the raft with a sinking heart. The only other choice he had was carrying Harry out on his back.

Mack saw the wind coming down the canyon, battering the trees along the border of the woods. In another two seconds he felt the wind cut through his thin shirt. He hunched up, clutching his collar tight to his throat. He was so cold. He could only do one thing at a time. All he wanted now was to get warm.

He slid along the cottonwood, back into the trees. He gathered sticks for a fire, breaking the larger limbs in two with his boot. His arms were full when he glanced up and saw movement in the gray mouth of the cave.

A figure stepped out onto the ledge, hunched forward, adjusted the pack on his back. It was Rick.

Ten feet away Mack saw Harry raise his head, push up from the tarp. Harry had seen it too.

Rick looked quickly back into the cave, then felt his way along the ledge, looking for a way up. Testing one hold and then another, he began to climb. His movements were hampered by the dead weight of the pack and his progress was slow. He slipped, caught himself, pressed against the soft rock.

"What the hell?" Mack said. "He doesn't know what he's doing."

"Oh, Mack," Harry said. "I think he does. He really does know . . ."

There was a shout. Grier stood in the mouth of the cave, the rifle in his arms. He screamed up at Rick. Rick looked back over his shoulder, clinging to the cliff. Grier put one foot on the rock for a second as if he were going after him, but Rick edged higher. Grier set the rifle down, reached up like a cop coaxing someone in off a window ledge.

Again Grier threatened to come up the cliff and again Rick moved upward. The heavy pack lurched to one side, almost taking Rick with it.

Harry had struggled to one knee and Mack stood behind him. Silently they watched the tiny figures jockeying on the rock wall like dark cutouts on a pale felt board.

The wind garbled Grier's angry shouts. He stepped away from the rock, turned back, catlike, the motion fluid as an ani-

mal thwarted by some unexpected barrier. He picked up the
rifle, raised it to his shoulder. Rick cowered above him.

"He wouldn't do it," Mack said. "Not again."

"Don't bet on it."

"Not again," Mack said. "I know him."

Mack moved forward, ducking under a low-hanging branch.
He heard Harry behind him.

"Mack, get back! Forget about them!"

Mack parted the blackberry bushes in front of him, felt the
thorns rake at his trousers. He walked out into the open.

"Grier!" Mack shouted. "Don't do it! No!"

There was no sign that Grier ever heard him. Rick seemed to
shift positions, as if he were trying to look back. Mack kept
walking through the long grass with the uncertain stride of a
sleepwalker. Grier could not do this, Mack was sure of it, he had
to be bluffing, he was the greatest bluffer in the world . . .

"Grier!" Mack shouted.

Rick began to climb again. He was thirty feet above the ledge,
inching upward, his back to Grier.

Grier slowly lowered the rifle with the sadness of a hunter
realizing that a shot was beyond his range. Mack stopped, thinking it was over, feeling almost a beat of gladness. Grier whirled,
hammered the rifle against the rock wall. Holding the rifle in
one hand, Grier shook his finger at Rick, railing at him, moving
along the ledge. He stumbled across something and fell to his
knees. When he stood up he wasn't holding the rifle anymore.

He stooped and picked up a shovel, ran his hand down the
smooth wooden handle. Rick was still crawling toward the rim.
Grier glanced upward and then, taking the shovel by the end of
the handle, hurled it blindly upward, like a ball player hurling
his bat into the stands.

Rick saw it coming. The shovel hit four feet below him,
bounced harmlessly away, but Rick instinctively flinched, put a
hand out to protect himself. He lost his hold. The weight of the
pack pulled him backward, acting almost like the head of a
hammer. He plummeted; his arms cut the air around him like a
man making a point in a furious argument. The shovel sailed
ahead of him, clattered off of boulders. Rick hit on his back on a

jutting fulcrum of rock, the body jackknifed and broke impossibly. Harry and Mack could hear the impact a hundred yards away.

Mack spun, saw the wind tearing at the stand of elders. His eyes smarted with tears. Four or five doves flapped through the trees. Harry crouched by a downed cottonwood, beckoning furiously for Mack to get back.

Mack ignored him, looked again toward the cliffs. Grier squatted motionless on the ledge, staring down, then turned to hide his face against the rock. After several seconds Grier looked out across the canyon, his hands resting loosely on his knees. Mack didn't move. Grier had to have seen him, yet there was no sign, no acknowledgment. Grier was out of reach now, a solitary figure perched on a windswept wall. He rose finally, picked up the rifle, groped along the ledge and back into the cave, carelessly tossing the unused weapon into the darkness ahead of him.

Mack stood for more than a minute, just staring at the mouth of the cave. He heard Harry calling at him again, in a hoarse, angry whisper. Mack turned and walked back slowly through the long grass.

Teeth clenched, Harry tried to stand. He leaned against the cottonwood, favoring his injured leg. "Oh, my God, Mack."

"You saw then? All of it? You saw him hit?" Mack said. Harry nodded. Mack ran his hand across his face, the hollows of his eyes, grimacing. "What do you think his chances are?"

Harry looked at him, bewildered for a second, not sure that he was serious, then looked away. "There are no chances. He's gone."

"And so what are we supposed to do?"

"We don't do anything. We stay as far out of Grier's way as we can. It's all up to him now. He'll make a move, I promise you."

"That's the best that you can come up with? That we do nothing? We sit tight? That's what we've been doing, Harry, sitting tight and watching our lives being destroyed up there."

Both men were silent. Mack stared at the dried weeds, saw a grasshopper leap forward, inches from his boot. It tumbled over, tried to right itself, its soft green belly contracting and expanding like an accordian, filled with clumsy, throbbing life.

"You think he felt anything?" Mack said, more softly.

"Who?"

"Rick."

"Maybe for a second," Harry said. He raised his eyes over Mack's shoulder, suddenly focussed on something far off. "What did I tell you?"

Mack turned. Grier was on the ledge outside the cave, bent forward under a great dark mass. Mack couldn't make out what it was at first. Then he saw that it was the two pulleys and a tangle of rope all hitched over Grier's shoulders. It made Grier look like some monstrous hunchback, as if the pulleys and ropes had finally become part of him, some permanent deformity. Grier felt his way along the cliff and began to climb. He was making his break. One end of the rope unravelled behind him and Grier stopped to gather it in.

"Give me your knife," Mack said.

Harry looked disgusted, tried to wave Mack off. "Just forget it. What are you trying to prove?"

"That there are limits."

"And how are you going to prove that?"

"Grier cut the kid off. Now I'm going to cut him off."

"You don't have time."

"Time enough. Just give me the knife."

Harry gazed steadily at Mack, reassessing, then sullenly took the knife from its sheath and handed it over. "If you get yourself killed I'm really going to be pissed."

Mack patted Harry on the shoulder. "If I'm not back in a half hour, I'll meet you at the raft."

Mack scrambled through the woods, dodging through currant bushes, bending low. There was the hoarse croaking of a raven somewhere nearby. He ran until he was sure the fold of cliff would hide him from Grier's sight. He ran doggedly across the open rocks, not letting himself let up, moving toward the canyon wall.

Everything depended on timing. Grier would rig up the pulleys, but he would still have to go back to load up however much gold he intended to take out. There was no telling how long that would take. If Grier was still at work below when Mack reached the mesa top, that would be one thing. If Grier was up there and had the rifle, that would be something else.

Mack spotted a curving trail of handholds in the cliff wall. He moved upward, using the ancient holds like stirrups. There were little deposits of loose sand in each hold and with every move Mack sent a soft trickle falling below.

When the footholds gave out he had to crawl through a thin chimney of rock. Mack wedged himself into the fault and began to spider his way up. His back was pressed against the rock; one leg was under him, one leg against the opposite wall. He edged upward, finally pushed himself out of the chimney, lay heaving on the prickly grass of the cliff top. He didn't move for a moment, feeling his heart beat against the uneven ground, smelling the chamisa crushed beneath his body.

Mack stood up, circled back into the juniper. Within ten minutes he heard the coarse munching of the horses. He moved up cautiously, saw the rump and swishing tail of the first of them. The horses jerked their heads up, cagey as hawks, staring back at him. There was no sign of Grier. The saddles and blankets were still tucked under one of the piñon trees.

Mack moved slowly among the animals, patting them, feeling the quiver of nerves along their coat. Near the cliff there was a good fifteen feet of rope still coiled, wedged tight under a wide anchoring boulder. It ran back through a pulley rigged to a sturdy juniper tree. From the pulley four strands of the rope travelled along the ground and over the cliff edge. Mack had been lucky.

Working quickly he gathered up the halter ropes of the five horses. Two of the animals were his and as he moved from one to the next, Buck butted him with his head, vying for attention. The horses bunched around Mack, jerking and impatient.

Mack led them fifty yards back into the juniper, leaning an occasional elbow into the massive trotting bodies to keep from getting stepped on. He undid the halters one at a time. Once the horses were gone, Grier could never make it out. What Mack was doing was irrevocable.

The youngest of the horses took off immediately, but Buck and the other three trotted off a few steps and stopped, bewildered by their sudden freedom. Mack hissed at them, waved the halter ropes over his head. They rolled their eyes at him, drifted off a few more steps.

Mack bent down and picked out a handful of stones. Buck was the best horse he'd ever had. Mack ran at them, throwing stones and waving his arms like a crazy man. Buck shied, put his head down, kicked out three or four times. The horses bolted. Mack ran in among them for a moment, still flailing his arms, trying to put the fear of God in them. Let them run for miles; Grier wasn't ever going to get them back. Mack heard the heavy bouncing of the horses' guts, the brittle snapping of branches, the drumming hooves. A horse veered in front of him. There was a splintering of wood like the breaking of boards in a stall. The horse kicked free, unhurt; a broken stump rolled away. The other horses wove in and out of the low juniper, heading across the mesa.

Mack slowed to a walk, finally stopped. He wasn't sure what enough was, but he was sure he hadn't gotten there yet.

On his way back he retrieved the stray halters. He moved toward the cliff edge. There was still no sign of Grier. He stared at the makeshift rigging, the pulley attached to the juniper tree, the slack ropes. He was sure now that Grier had to be below in the cave.

Suddenly the ropes slithered along the ground and grew taut. For a second the pulley was yanked tight, then it fell back against the tree.

Mack took the knife from his belt and walked to the cliff edge. The wind blew the ropes softly over the pale rock. Twice there were tugs on the ropes and each time they would go slack again. It reminded Mack of fish toying with bait.

Grier's hand was the first thing he saw, twenty-five feet below him and a couple of feet to the left of the ropes, fumbling for a secure hold on the porous rock. Then came Grier's shoulder and the top of his head, the barrel of the rifle slung over his back. He labored upward for ten feet, unsuspecting, before he stopped on a narrow ledge to take a breather. Mack slipped Rick's knife back into his belt.

When he looked up and saw Mack he showed no surprise. He steadied himself, squinting upward. Then he began to smile.

"Hey, Mack. Hey. I knew you'd come. I waited all night for you. I told Rick you were coming. I thought for a while . . . Well, that's all water under the bridge. It doesn't matter now." He reached out and gently stroked the ropes. "Nothing matters."

Grier was at a disadvantage and he knew it. It would be next to impossible to get to the rifle and position himself for a shot. The canyon floor was a hundred feet below. Even as Grier talked, Mack could see his eyes darting to the right and to the left, assessing his situation. There was a narrow fault in the rock high to the right of him, but it wasn't anything that could help him now.

"It's all set, Mack. Pull up the rope, see for yourself. It's right there at your feet." Mack glanced at the coil of rope wedged under the rock, four or five feet behind him, then looked quickly back at Grier. "There's nothing to be afraid of. What can I do? Go on. This is like it should have been from the beginning, just you and me."

Grier clung to the soft rock wall, his face tilted up between his hands like a crouching gargoyle. There was a sudden burst of wind that bounced tumbleweeds along the cliff edge. The storm was coming. Mack stared down at Grier, unable to speak.

"Throw me the rope then, man, I'll show you myself."

Mack took a step back, leaned out and scooped up the coiled rope. In two quick yanks he freed it from the boulder. He held the rope in his open palms. It was the same rope that Rick had stumbled across the night before, the rope that had changed Rick's mind. Grier waited below.

Mack threw the rope down. It unfurled, slapped loosely against the cliff wall. Grier leaned out, cat-quick, and retrieved it.

"There you go, Mack," Grier said. "You're not going to believe it. Just check this action."

Grier began to haul in the rope. The lines grew taut again. As they took on their first real weight, there was the fretting sound of ropes rubbing rocks at the cliff edge, the squeal of the pulley.

Looking past Grier, Mack saw a pulley slide out of the cave. Behind it came a bulky pack. The pulley jerked upward like some baited hook and a second pack emerged behind the first.

It took all of Grier's strength to lift his cargo. He worked recklessly, ignoring his precarious perch, heaving like a long-shoreman. Some of his pulls seemed to lift him off his feet, leaving him hanging in the air for a second, as if sheer will would not be counterweight enough. The packs began to move upward. The four strands of rope at Mack's feet slid in alternating directions, surging slowly, fraying at the rock edge, hissing like snakes.

"Look at it, Mack. It's all yours, man, I'm giving it to you, the first load is yours, duty-free . . ." Both packs had been wrapped tight with lengths of rope. They slid past Grier, swayed above his head. There were vultures floating high above the canyon walls. The bars shifted inside the top pack, throwing it off balance. The packs swung and scraped against the cliff. "Take it, Mack, take it, there's lots more where that came from."

The cradled gold rocked higher and higher as Grier talked on in one breathless lullaby, trying to cast a spell, knowing that it was his one chance.

"We're going to put all the rest of it behind us, Mack. We did it, that's all that matters now, we'll have it packed on the horses in no time."

Mack said nothing, shifting from one foot to the other. Grier couldn't know that there were no horses, that that had already been decided. Grier was at his mercy. The only question for Mack was what was demanded of him.

"There wasn't any other way it could have been, Mack. I never laid a finger on you, did I? You got to remember that."

Beyond the hypnotic trolling of the packs it seemed as if the shadowed canyon floor was beginning to sway, going in and out of focus. What Mack remembered was that Rick's body was out there, lying in the long grasses at the edge of the woods.

"Catch it, Mack, give me a hand. It's a gift, Mack, no strings. All you got to do is pick it up. Go on, I'm giving it to you on a platter." The pulley twisted and squealed on the round shoulders of the pack, lurching relentlessly up at him.

Mack reached out and grabbed Grier's pull-rope, stopped it. "Hey," Grier shouted. "What you doin'?"

Mack stared at his hands clenched tight on the rope. He had never seen his hands so clearly before. He saw the small, raised heat blisters, the lines of dirt, the tiny, sun-whitened hairs, the skin around the middle knuckle of his right hand cracked and bleeding. There was no escaping the need to judge. Grier had said it himself. If you're climbing a mountain, all roped together, and one guy decides to go back, there's only one thing to do.

"Come on, Mack, this is no time to play."

Mack slashed at the rope. Grier figured out what he was doing, tried to jerk the rope free. Mack was yanked to one knee, but held fast, slashing again and again. The rope gave with a dull pop, lashed through the singing pulley.

The packs plummeted, hit the wall just above Grier's head. Thrown off balance, Grier pressed against the cliff, crying out. Mack, on both knees, couldn't tell if Grier had been hit or not. The packs twisted one over the other like a bola, crashed on the ledge of the cave. The fabric split on impact, gold bars tumbled free.

Grier scrambled into the crevice high to his right. He disappeared for a moment and then Mack caught a glimpse of him in the rocks, trying to duck under the shoulder strap of his rifle.

Mack had run maybe five steps when he heard the sharp report, the bullet whine just over his head. He slammed on blindly, stumbling over bushes, regaining his balance. His heart pounded like a boxer's fist. He was two hundred yards from the cliff edge when his foot slipped on a pebbly anthill and he flew forward. He sprawled into a headfirst slide and felt the sting of gravel on his outstretched palms.

He lay still, breathing hard, listening for any sound. There was none, except for the sporadic gusts of wind through the piñons.

He sat up, leaned forward to tie the laces on his boots. By now Grier had discovered that the horses were gone. Grier had no way out. He was a man on foot with a caveful of gold and no way to move it. He would go looking for the horses, but it wouldn't take long for him to realize how hopeless that was. After that it was anybody's guess. Maybe he would try to re-rig the pulleys, start all over, hide some of the gold wherever he could.

Or maybe he wouldn't. Mack just couldn't know with Grier anymore. If he could kill Rick, he sure had cause to go after Mack. The kid had been outsmarted, outthought; Mack had to make sure the same thing didn't happen to him. It seemed as if hunting Mack down would be waste motion, at a time when every move counted, but Mack couldn't take anything for granted.

He stood up. Harry would be waiting for him at the raft. All Mack had to do was keep Harry out of Grier's way for a few more hours and they would be all right.

He headed north, staying well away from the rim. Every few minutes he would stop and listen, just to be sure. He walked for almost a mile before descending into a branch canyon. He followed a boulder-choked, dry tributary down to the river, began the trek back.

From the cover of trees he scanned the far walls. He saw no ropes or pulleys, no sign of Grier. Mack walked for thirty minutes before he came to the bend of the river above the raft.

His nerves were wired to the highest pitch. He picked his way silently through a stand of willow, stared out at the raft. It wasn't where he had left it. It was twenty yards down from the sandbar where it had been lodged the night before. It was pulled up now into a bank covered with chokecherry bushes. Wind riffled the surface of the water. There were fresh bootprints out on the sandbar.

Mack stood for several minutes, scanning the trees on both sides of the river, trying to figure it out. He had said he would meet Harry here. Why would Harry try to move the raft on his own? What could have happened to him? There was the sound of a bird flitting in the willows. Mack looked up, saw the weight of the robin's soft, round body waving the young branches like plumes.

Mack took the knife out of his belt, stepped into the open. He was moving toward the raft when he heard the heavy rustle of material. He stared up into the chokecherry bushes and saw the dark, reclining figure, the bulky folds of the tarp.

"Harry?" he said. There was no movement. Fear in his heart, Mack scrambled up the bank, parting the branches. It was not Harry. There was only the stiff shell of the olive gray tarp, wrapped like an empty cocoon. Harry had flown.

He stood for ten seconds, just looking at it, and then a thrown rock thudded against the tarp, rolled harmlessly to the ground.

Mack whirled and saw Grier squatted inside the cavity of a burnt-out tree that rose above him like a charred throne. The rifle was raised and ready.

"Just throw the knife out in front of you," Grier said. Mack let the knife drop.

Grier pushed away from the tree, ran a trembling hand over his face. "You really did a job up there, Mack. I had no idea you had it in you. From here on in, it's going to be one long, hard ride."

Mack stood perfectly still, his hands raised. Grier came to Mack slowly, the way someone would come to an animal caught in a trap. He spun Mack around, pushed him. He was still trying to figure out what to do with him.

"So where's Harry?"

"You tell me."

Grier bent down and picked up the knife. "Don't screw around."

"I'm telling you the truth, Grier, I don't know."

Grier turned the knife over, examined the blade. He did not want to be made a fool of. "He can't be far," Grier said. "Not the way he was moving. Unless he's grown wings. You never know about Indians, right? Catch." Grier tossed the knife under-handed and Mack caught it, dumbfounded. The rifle was still pointed at the middle of Mack's stomach.

"What do you want me to do with this?" Mack said.

"Go down to the raft and cut the tow rope." Mack did as he was told, glancing back over his shoulder to be sure Grier was serious. "Now at one end I want you to make a nice slipknot. Come on. You're good at knots, Mack, I've seen you."

Grier watched as Mack fumbled with the rope. Every so often he would glance up into the woods. Harry was very much on Grier's mind.

Mack held up the finished noose.

"Now put one hand through it," Grier said.

"What is this, Grier? Come on."

"This is not a conversation. Just do what I tell you." Grier gestured with the rifle. Mack obeyed. "Now put it behind your back and slip the other hand in there."

Once Mack's hands were in the noose, Grier moved swiftly behind him, picked up the trailing rope, yanked it tight. Mack felt it cut into his wrists.

"You don't have to do this, Grier."

"Don't tell me what I have to do. Now get down on your belly. Go on!" Grier's voice rose in anger. Mack knelt, lowered himself on one shoulder, fell heavily forward on his chest.

Grier stood over him. Mack glanced up, his cheek in the dirt. The barrel of the rifle was six inches from the back of his head. "You satisfied, Grier? Or are you going to shoot me too?"

Grier jammed a knee into the middle of Mack's back. It took Mack's breath away. Grier was on him, lashing knot after knot around Mack's wrists. The rope tightened, jerk by jerk. Mack was trussed up like a rodeo calf.

"I should fuckin' kill you for what you did up there. I got every reason in the world. You really blew it, man." Grier gave Mack an extra shove in the middle of his back, rose to his feet. He backed off, face flushed. "We got no horses now, Mack. It's a real shame. Because that means you're going to have to be my mule." He picked up the trailing end of the rope, gave it a hard yank. "Come on, mule, let's go."

Mack struggled to his feet.

They moved slowly along the silted bank of the river, past great bundles of stranded debris. Grier stayed five yards back. Six feet of excess rope trailed from Mack's bound wrists, slithered through leaves and sand. It was insane. Grier couldn't be serious. There was no way he could use Mack to help him float gold out of the canyon without it blowing up in their faces, sooner or later. Grier was just improvising. Mack glanced back.

Grier's eyes searched through the tangle of branches. The wild card still to be played was Harry. Grier knew that. Harry could be anywhere. A squirrel scolded them from a nearby tree, its tail rippling with indignation.

"So how much you think you can carry, Mack? Fifty pounds? A hundred?"

"I can carry whatever Rick carried," he said.

Grier was silent. Mack stared up through the trees. The eroded volcanic cliffs stretched on like some tawny, tattered stone dress.

When Grier spoke his voice was soft as ash. "I didn't mean for that to happen," he said.

"What can that matter now? What you meant?" Mack scuffed up plumes of dust with the toes of his boots. He began to work the rope at his wrists, twisting a little left, then right.

They walked on in silence. There was a rush of wind, soothing as surf, and, far-off, the raucous alarm of ravens. Grier strayed up into the woods, checking. When Mack came to the path he stopped and waited for Grier. Grier came on slowly, head bowed, in the grip of a new mood. He looked up, troubled.

"It matters to me," Grier said. "It matters one whole lot."

He gestured with a nod that they were taking the path. They walked side by side, Grier brooding, the gun cradled in his arms. Walking along with his hands tied behind his back it occurred to Mack how weird he must look, like some strolling philosopher.

When Grier spoke again his voice was gravelly, almost broken. "I knew you were coming, see. That was the whole thing. Rick was all crazy and upset. I couldn't talk to him. He was terrified. He would have split right then. But I told him, no, we're waiting for Mack. Everything's going to be all right when Mack gets here . . ."

Mack glanced back at him. Grier pivoted in one direction and then the other, scanning the trees. How could he believe what he was saying? A fidgeting nuthatch maneuvered on a dead ponderosa. If Grier saw Harry, he would shoot to kill in a second.

"We must have waited two hours. We packed the gold that

vas already up. I was so tired. Rick was still going on. I told him
shut up, I know they're coming, I don't want to hear another
damn word out of you. I told him to wake me up when you got
here. I rolled over to the wall and went to sleep."

Long-eared squirrels flowed and disappeared behind fallen
trees, storing up food for the winter. With his rifle, Grier tore
through a spiderweb that stretched across their path, then
wiped the silver strands from the barrel.

"The next thing I know, Rick is shaking me. He's shouting in
my face that we can't wait any more, we've got to get out of
here. I look over and see that it's dawn. 'They're not coming,
Grier, you've got to get that through your head. They made up
their minds and we've got to make up ours.' I go over to the
mouth of the cave and I look down. I'm really feeling bad now,
Mack. It's over. The dream is over. 'We'll be fine,' Rick is saying,
'let them stew in their own juice, it'll be easier this way, we'll be
back at the van in two hours.' 'You think so?' I said. 'Well, let me
ask you one thing. Who's got the key to the van?' He slaps his
pockets, panicking, reaches in and pulls them out."

They had come out of the trees onto the boulders. Wind
battered a huge cottonwood and there was a rumble of distant
thunder. Mack patiently kept twisting the rope around his
wrists.

"I go over to the shaft. I look down. I'm thinking about all the
work it took to bust it open, how together we'd been. He says,
'What are you doing?' I look at him. 'I want to go down one
more time.' 'You're crazy,' he says, 'what for?' I said, 'I want to
take out one more load.' 'We got enough,' he says. 'No such
thing as enough,' I said. 'Those guys can fold on us, but I'm
leaving here a rich man. Four more bars, that's another million
dollars, right? Not bad for twenty minutes of your time.' 'No,'
he's saying, 'I've waited all night, I can't wait any more, there
are too many things that can go wrong . . .' " The more Grier
talked, the more agitated he got.

"All he wanted was to be on the road. I said, 'Rick, I'm sorry,
I'm going to do this.' His face got all funny and then he got
quiet. 'What's wrong?' I said. 'Nothing's wrong, you do what you
got to do.' I get the lantern, we hitch up, swing the pack down. I

tell him, 'It's just like before, I tug the rope twice when it's a
loaded and you pull it up.' He's nodding at me like he under
stands. I go down. I'm feeling fine. Me and Rick were reall
going to do it. I work real quick, load the bars in no time, tie th
pack up tight. I look over at the gold just one last time, trying t
fix it in my mind."

Mack walked on ahead. The trailing rope snagged in th
rocks behind him. He jerked it free. He didn't need to hea
more. He could see where this was going.

"Are you listening to me?" Grier was shouting. "God damn i
You stop and listen to this!" Grier grabbed the end of the rop
and pulled Mack up short. Mack turned. Grier lurched over th
boulders. In that moment Mack felt pity, the pity he might hav
felt for a bird fluttering erratically out of a poisoned field, a
balance and equilibrium gone.

"I tug again. Nothing happens. I try one more time. I thin
maybe he's just being careless; he's wandered off for a second
Again. Nothing. I get scared. Then I think, maybe Mack an
Harry have finally come back, everything's going to be all right
For a second I really believe that, I'm so happy . . . But there
no sound. I scream up the shaft. I grab at the rope ladder
thinking that he's double-crossed me, cut the ladder and
trapped me. But the ladder still holds. I climb back. The cave i
empty. I see one of the packs is gone."

Mack wasn't able to look at Grier any more. He stared up a
the sky. There was a hawk caught in the winds high above th
rim of the canyon and it seemed to be pinioned there, unable t
close its wings.

"I grab the rifle and run to the mouth of the cave. I hear him
climbing. I couldn't believe it. What could be going on in hi
head? What was he afraid of? All I wanted was fifteen minutes
one more load. I could have climbed up and stopped him. Hell,
could have just about grabbed him by the ankle, but I was afrai
of scaring him. Isn't that a great joke? It was ridiculous. All h
was going to do was lose the horse, get himself lost, write
death ticket for every one of the rest of us. All for what? The tw
bars of gold in his pack? He knew what he was doing. I ha
every right. And I couldn't do it. You saw. I looked down tha

barrel and all I could think of was that kid being shot and it just made me sick . . ."

Mack turned away from Grier, stumbled up through the rocks, still working the knots around his wrists. For the first time he could tell that he was making headway.

"I don't know who left that shovel out there. I wasn't trying to hit him. I was angry, sure; who wouldn't have been angry? I didn't even come close. I didn't intend for that to happen."

"Maybe not," Mack said. "But you sat and watched him die and then you walked away like he was nothing more to you than a dog somebody'd run over on the highway. That's what I blame you for, Grier."

Mack climbed the next rise of boulders. Seventy yards ahead of them, along the cliff wall, was the herd of wild burros. They were grazing and they hadn't spotted Mack and Grier yet. The herd of animals drifted slowly toward the two men.

Mack heard Grier clambering over the rocks behind him. "Could you sing me something, Mack? Anything. Hank Williams." Grier began to sing in a hoarse, cracked voice. "Your cheatin' heart . . . will tell on you . . . I heard you do it, Mack. You sing it so beautiful."

Mack kept walking numbly toward the cliffs. Grier was lost now. He was able to see only what he could bear to see. It was no different, Mack thought, from that remarkable ability of the conquistadores to see, across a vast plain, in just the right angle of light, a village of mud dwellings and believe with utter certainty that they were gazing at a city of gold.

Ravens clattered up suddenly from the trees along the river. One of the lead burros lifted his head and then the others did the same. Mack would have liked to see Grier try and get a saddle on one of those. The animals froze, but did not flee.

"Looks like we're finally going to get a little rain," Grier said. Some of the burros put their heads down and began to graze again. "That would sure feel good, wouldn't it? I remember as a kid, you must have done this too, standing out in a rainstorm, just letting it wash over you . . ."

The animals were restless and seemed confused. The herd began to drift, break in two, but a half-dozen animals were still

headed toward Grier and Mack. One of the skittish burros ever
broke into a brief trot, head high, as if startled by something
behind. There was something wrong with the way the animals
were moving. Mack loosened the knots, bit by bit. One or two
strong moves and he could tear free.

Mack remembered something Harry had said once: to hunt
an animal you had to think like an animal, think where they
would go and get there first, get inside their skin.

He was sure now. Harry was in there among the burros.
Harry was just crazy enough. It would never work.

Mack wasn't quite sure what the sequence was after that.
Maybe he tensed and Grier saw it or maybe Grier was just
thinking right along with him. Grier stepped away from Mack
and crouched in the rocks. He raised his rifle, resting his elbow
on his knee for balance. The barrel jumped as he fired. The lead
burro went down like a sack of grain, front legs buckling under
him. Animals were running everywhere, milling in great dusty
circles, braying and screaming. Grier fired again. A second
burro went down, tried to get up, fell heavily on its side.

Mack saw the erect figure, partially shielded by the rock, saw
Harry's baseball cap, a shoulder of his blue shirt bright as any
target. It was too damn easy.

Grier took aim. Mack tried to tear his hands free, but couldn't.
He threw himself clumsily at Grier and knocked him down.
Mack landed hard on his elbows. Grier held on to the rifle,
stepped away and set himself quickly. *Get down,* Mack wanted
to shout, *get down.*

Grier fired.

On his knees, Mack saw the head of the figure explode, saw
the baseball cap blown up, spinning in the air, saw the body
slump, then slide stiffly into the rocks. Honing in, Grier fired
again.

Mack tore his hands free, ran toward the rocks. Grier paid no
attention to him, firing as deliberately as a sharpshooter trying
to win a stuffed bear at the state fair.

Mack began to climb, desperate for a place to hide, to wedge
himself. Above him was a fault in the cliff. In the angled V of the
soft volcanic rock there were scattered hollows of footholds and

mazelike series of shallow eroded caves that wove their way most to the rim top. It was the only hope he had.

He began to climb. He moved quickly, aware of how exposed e was, what an easy target his back would be from the canyon oor. He heard Grier shout; Grier had seen him. Mack froze for second, stretched out on the rock face. He turned his head to ok down. Grier ran over the jumble of boulders, bent low to eep his balance, his rifle in his right hand.

Grier shouted again. "Mack!"

Mack climbed higher, moved into one of the caves. From all urs he glanced up, saw a series of chambers above him, some shadow, some in light. It was his first stroke of real luck. Mack ood, boosted himself up with his hands, scrambled up into a igher chamber.

Time had eroded the ancient walls and ceilings, created a byrinthean network along the cliff surface. As long as Mack ept moving in and out of the twisting chambers it would be most impossible for Grier to get a clean shot at him. The trick as avoiding running into a cul-de-sac; one dead end and it ould be all over.

Pausing to catch his breath, Mack looked through the branch-g corridors of rock, saw the top of Grier's head and shoulders. rier had fallen back and was laboring.

Mack struggled upward, squeezing through eroded smoke oles, going in and out of the light. His hands were raw and loody now from his frantic climb. His left foot slipped for just a econd, sent a rain of sand and loose rock down on Grier's head.

There were petroglyphs all around him suddenly; they eemed to float on the rock like fragments from a dream, spirals nd lizards and feathered watchmen. The past was breaking ree from the walls, fleeing with him like schools of fish. What he hell had Harry been thinking? He must have thought he as invincible. Only gods could get away with tricks like that.)ne idiotic move had cost him his life. Harry was the one erson Mack had trusted not to be taken in, not to be a fool.

Mack could hear Grier panting below him. Mack pulled him-elf through a narrow chimney of rock and suddenly he was out

on the face of the cliff again. Twenty yards to his right was th
ladder. There was nowhere else to go.

If he could get to the ladder quickly enough, he could make
up to the cave. There would be some kind of weapon there
another knife, a pickax, a shovel, something.

Mack spidered his way across the open rock. He stretche
with his foot, tapping frantically for a hold.

"Mack!" the sound of Grier's voice nearly frightened Mack of
the rock. He looked down. He was six inches short of anythin
that even remotely resembled a foothold and the ladder wa
another two feet away. Far below he could see the canyon floo
If only he could wish himself onto the ladder, if only Harr
hadn't . . . He closed his eyes, pressed his face to the ancien
rock, still cool in the morning air. Mack had to will his unwillin,
body to act, just one more time.

He moved his right foot first; his left was moving even as h
felt the right one begin to slip. It was pretty damn fancy, some
thing only a figure skater could have come up with. For a secon
he was sure he was going down. He lunged with his right hand
caught the pole. The ladder rattled and held. He pulled himsel
up. His whole body was trembling, like a swimmer leaving ic
water.

He had hung there for four or five seconds when he heard th
soft voice just below him.

"Don't even think about moving." Mack glanced back an
saw Grier standing at the base of the ladder, the rifle trained o
the middle of Mack's back. Once again, Grier had found a
easier way.

"I've got no reason not to shoot you right now, no reason a
all." Grier was breathless and the barrel of the rifle rose and fe
as he tried to get his wind back. "Don't look at me. Turn around
before you slip. Just do like I tell you. We're going to do this on
step at a time. There you go."

Mack moved slowly upward, heard the rifle clunk against
wooden rung below him. Grier was following him up. The lad
der trembled with the weight of the two men. At the top Mac
reached out for the ledge of the cave.

"O.K., Mack. Don't so much as sneeze. Slide off nice an

gentle." Mack did as he was told. "Stay right where you are.
Attaboy. Now stand back. That's enough. Right where I can see
you."

Mack stood on the ledge of the cave, his hands still raised,
staring at the battered packs, the bars of gold scattered like
bricks on an old construction site. It was as good a moment as he
was likely to get. He glanced back over his shoulder. Grier
lurched up, crablike, resting the rifle barrel on the top rung.
Grier wasn't missing a trick. He was ready for any move Mack
could have made.

Grier climbed off the ladder, moved sideways around Mack,
stepping across strands of rope.

"You must have thought you had me, didn't you? You bet.
Hey, mad dog!" Grier whispered. "Yeah, mad dog! I know what
you're thinking. Go on! Let's hear you say it! Mad-dog killer!"
Grier reached down and gathered in some of the loose rope.
Leaning against the wall were two more packs and a pickax, ten
feet away. If Grier turned his head just once, Mack was going
for it.

"You should know better. Never bet against me, Mack. Every
one of you was just laying for me and I whipped you, one by one
. . ." Grier grabbed one of the packs from the wall and tossed it
at Mack's feet. "Go on. You're my mule, man. They can find you
alive or they can find you dead, I don't give a fuck. Start loading
that up."

Mack nudged the pack with his boot, flipped it over. Harry
was dead. It was unbelievable. Harry would never do anything
like that, Harry didn't make grandstand moves, Harry didn't
need to play hero, not like the rest of them. God damn Harry.

"Go on, Mack. It's the last thing I'll ever ask you to do."

Grier paced behind Mack, whipped up like a bear cornered
by hounds. The ropes at the back of the cave moved softly in
some imperceptible whisper of air. Mack had the feeling that
there was another presence in the cave with them.

Grier's idea of using Mack as a mule, marching him back and
forth across the canyon with a gun at his head, was a joke. They
both knew it. All Grier wanted now was to have Mack bend to
his will.

"Remember how happy Rick was, Mack? When we first found it? Eyes just as big as saucers. What happened to me, Mack? I didn't plan this. All I wanted was what you all said you wanted. I told you, Mack, pick it up!"

Mack never saw the blow coming. Grier smashed Mack across the back of his head with the butt of the rifle. Mack fell to his knees, stunned. Grier circled him. There was a strange, chalky taste in Mack's mouth. He put a hand on the floor of the cave, fighting the closing darkness.

"You too good to get your hands dirty? No one gave me a chance. Everybody stand back and let Grier do it. I thought we'd all agreed. Come on, mule, pick it up."

Mack stared at the scattered gold bars. All Grier wanted was for him to bow down, do reverence, humble himself. Mack couldn't get his head clear.

"Pick it up!"

Mack tried to duck out of the way, but he wasn't quick enough; the butt of the rifle caught him on the ear. Mack grabbed his head with both hands, rocking back and forth. There was a high-pitched singing, coming from deep inside his head. Mack twisted to one side, saw the bending figure of the flute player on the smoke-blackened ceiling. Mack knew now: he would die here.

"Pick it up, mule!"

If he was going out, he was not going out on his knees. He tried to stand, move toward the pickax, but his legs gave way. Grier stood over him, the rifle poised, ready to hit him again.

Mack trailed his fingers in the dust, trying to focus. He stared at Grier's knees, then beyond them. There was something moving at the back of the cave.

It was the ropes or the blow to his head or Mack was going out of his mind. A figure glided silently forward. Grier feinted once with the rifle, brought it up again.

"Pick it up, mule!"

The figure paused, then shambled forward, the slit leg of his jeans flowing around him like a skirt. It was impossible. He had seen Harry die. Harry's braids were undone, his hair long and flowing, his chest bare. Grier never heard him.

As Grier pulled the rifle back, Harry grabbed him, one hand around Grier's throat, the other clamped on the barrel of the gun. The two men toppled together. Grier twisted free, chopped Harry in the chest with the butt of the rifle.

Mack was on his feet, grabbed the pickax from the wall. Grier saw him coming and had the rifle up, blocking Mack's first swing. Mack's hands stung at the impact.

Mack swung again blindly, all over Grier, giving him no room, no time. Grier backed away, parrying the second blow and the third, kicking away a shovel that was underfoot. Mack's rage made him unmatchable. He could see the fear in Grier's eyes.

On the fourth blow the handle of the pickax shattered on the metal barrel. They were near the back of the cave; Mack could see the angled beam across the shaft, five or six feet off.

Mack threw the broken axhandle at Grier and Grier ducked under it. The axhandle tangled in the rope, then fell clattering off of rock as it plunged down the shaft. Mack came up at him like a lineman off the snap. For a second the two men's bodies seemed to lock, strength matching strength, four hands clasped on the length of the rifle between them.

Grier tried to wrest the rifle free; Mack held tight. They had been here once before. The boy had been running across the canyon floor; the boy had been free and Mack had let the rifle get away.

The rage and the sorrow seemed to break inside him and Mack was screaming. He heaved Grier backward, heard the clattering of a bucket as Grier tripped.

Mack saw the look of utter surprise on Grier's face. For the first time Grier gave up the gun, reaching frantically for anything to hold on to. There was nothing. He went backward into the shaft, flailing for the ropes. The ropes rattled and jerked and then there was a long scream. Mack was on all fours when he heard the body hit far below.

Mack backed away from the dark hole, still on his hands, then sat slumped in the dust, holding his knees. He turned his head and stared numbly at Harry limping toward him. It was impossible to register all at once, Grier dead, Harry alive.

"I thought you were gone," Mack said. "I saw you die. I saw your body fly apart."

Harry stared down into the dark shaft, pulled at his nose, eyes smarting. He was just as shaken as Mack was. He finally reached down and pulled Mack to his feet.

"I'm disappointed in you, Mack." He kicked at the battered bucket. "What did you want me to do? On one good leg, what was I supposed to do, come charging in like the cavalry? That scarecrow was the best I could do. When I heard the shot up on the cliff I knew I had to do something."

Mack scooped up one of the lanterns. He switched it on and off and on again.

"Thank God he wasn't hard to fool," Harry said. "I could have stuck two raven feathers up there. He wasn't shooting at me; he was shooting at phantoms."

"But how did you know to come here?"

"It was the one place he had to come back to, right? Just like he figured that you had to come back to the raft."

"We will never be able to tell anyone."

"No."

"We will be looked for," Mack said. He ran his hand along the black plastic of the lantern. Harry stared at him, trying to read him correctly.

"There was nothing else you could have done, Mack. He had it coming." Mack slipped his head under the strap of the lantern. "What are you doing?"

"There's one thing I have to be sure of."

"You're crazy. No way . . ." Harry said.

Mack leaned against the angled beam, yanked hard on the rope ladder, testing it. He gathered in the lifeline, tied it snugly around his waist. Harry watched without comment. Mack stepped out on the rope ladder, felt it sway beneath him.

"Don't be nuts, man," Harry said. "There's nothing down there you don't already know."

Mack looked back at him. It wasn't something they were going to argue about.

Mack moved down into the darkness. There was the familiar smell of dust. The lantern cast wavering circles of light on the walls above him. There was dread in his heart, but it would be worse if he never knew for certain.

He went down and down, focussing only on his hands, and the rungs of the rope ladder. It seemed as if there would be no end to it. He could feel the walls of the shaft closing above him.

Mack stopped finally, hooked an arm firmly into the rope ladder. With his free hand he tried to lift the lantern over his head. The sudden movement made the ladder twist, slide out from under him. Mack held on, riding it out. His leg banged against the rock wall; he swung back.

He shone the light down. Mack was only a couple of rungs from the bottom of the rope ladder. Light slid over the shadowed rock ledges, the reclining shapes of the mummies. The opening in the thatched platform was larger than Mack remembered it; Grier must have torn out beams to make their work easier. Strands of mud-caked thatch hung from the ragged hole like streamers. Grier lay below, sprawled across the bars of gold. Blood welled up from his mouth, his nose, and even, it seemed, from the sockets of his eyes.

The lantern light played uneasily across the body. To have killed Grier was the most immense thing Mack had ever done. There had been no recourse. In the deepest sense Grier had deserved it. But looking down now there was no sense of victory. There was no trace on that broken body of rage or crazed will. In Grier's final transformation he had become what he'd sought all along, an object worthy of awe. Grier had paid his way.

Mack clung tight to the rope ladder, heard the voice somewhere far above. "Hey, man, what you doin' down there?"

Mack hesitated. He had fought Grier for so long. He still felt the fierce, angry tie. There was more to say; he had to convince Grier how wrong he was.

"Mack, God damn it, we don't have all day."

Mack shifted the lantern; shadows fled along the walls. The reclining wrapped figures were waiting for Grier. He would join all those others.

Mack pulled the lantern up. The darkness folded over Grier, like a gentle seal over a raw wound.

Mack hitched the lantern over his shoulder. He climbed quickly. When he reached the top Harry was sitting against the wall. He had pulled one of the sleeping bags up around his shoulders. He'd found one of his old shirts and put it on and was now pulling on a clean pair of socks. He looked drained and sick.

Mack yanked the lantern off, tossed it aside. Harry was watching him out of the corner of his eye. Mack set himself against the angled beam, tugged at the knots that tied the rope ladder, finally worked them free. The ladder collapsed softly, fell into darkness. It took only seconds to do the same with the lifeline. Harry looked dubious, pulling on his boots.

"You trying to tell me something?" Harry said.

"No."

Harry went back to tying his boots. "I hate to be the one to bring it up, Mack, but what the hell are we going to do? You know we can't leave this like this."

"You know what we've got to do," Mack said.

"I suppose so, yeah," Harry said.

"You going to help me?"

"You bet."

Harry shook off the sleeping bag and struggled to his feet. Mack lifted one of the gold bars. He'd forgotten how heavy they were. He duck-walked it to the edge, swung it gently out into the middle of the shaft, watched it plummet.

Harry was right behind him, wrestling with a second bar. "It's been real," Harry said. He gave the bar a final shove with his good knee. The gold tumbled at the lip of the shaft, slid in.

Everything had to go down the hole. They threw down packs, sleeping bags, ropes, tools, laboring side by side. Harry tired quickly. They began to double up on the gold bars, Mack on one end, Harry on the other. Head to head over a bar, they stopped so Harry could catch his breath.

"Someday," Harry said, "I'd really like to tell somebody what this felt like."

"Ready?"

"Say when."

"One. Two. Three. Heave!" The gold clattered down the narrow rock walls.

When Harry began to limp badly, Mack told him to sit down, he'd take care of the rest. Harry didn't object.

He found a jar in one of the packs and huddled against the wall, digging out peanut butter with a knife. With listless eyes he watched Mack work.

Mack was hurrying now; he wanted to get out. Harry finally covered his face with his hands, a man in pain. In fifteen minutes Mack was almost done. He kicked through the cave dust to be sure he hadn't missed anything, then hoisted the last bar of gold. He was at the shaft when he heard Harry groan behind him.

"Oh, God."

Mack looked back, saw Harry peering at him through his fingers. "You all right?"

"Go ahead. Go on." He set the peanut butter jar back on his lap. "Oh, Jesus, every time you do that I think how much poorer we are . . ." He scraped the inside of the jar with the knife. "You come into the world with nothin' and you leave with nothin', isn't that the way it's supposed to be?" Harry licked the knife clean, frowning as if tasting something rancid. Mack stood patiently at the shaft, his arms and shoulders beginning to ache with the weight of the gold. "The thing that makes me so sick, Mack, is that you can't will that kid not to come down that switchback, you can't will Grier off that rim. You can end up holding the whole world in your hands, more power than you ever thought existed right there in your mitts; and the trick is that you can't decide when that moment's going to be, and then when it's time to let it go, you have to let it go, or it will bust you. Go on, Mack, damn, don't listen to me."

Mack let the last bar tumble, end over end, into the shaft. The only thing left was the dynamite. Mack picked it up, turned it over in his hands, walked back to Harry.

"Give me your knife."

Harry offered the knife without protest. "You ever handled that stuff before?"

"I've seen people handle it," Mack said. He set the dynamite down carefully in the dust, reached out and took the peanut butter jar from Harry's lap.

"What the hell are you doing?" Harry said.

"You going to take it with you?"

"No."

"O.K., then." Mack turned and lobbed the jar. It smashed against the back wall of the shaft. He helped Harry to his feet. "Go on. It's going to take you longer than it'll take me. Get out of here. I'll have it all set in a couple of minutes."

Harry conceded, both hands raised, backing away. When he came to the ladder at the mouth of the cave, he looked back.

"One way we could look at it, Mack, we're just putting something away for a rainy day."

"Go on," Mack said.

Harry eased onto the ladder and disappeared from view.

Mack walked along the corridor of the cave, feeling the walls with his hands. Finally he found a depression that was almost big enough. He enlarged it by carving out more of the soft rock with Harry's knife.

He unwrapped the dynamite, took five sticks, cut a narrow slit in one, jammed them in the hole. He cut a five-foot length of fuse. At a foot per minute it would give him time enough.

He picked up the box of caps. It was a neat little box that looked harmless enough, like a tin of Copenhagen tobacco. He opened it delicately and lifted out one of the caps. It was no bigger than a ladyfinger firecracker. A tremor now could lose him an arm. He laid the cap in the palm of his hand as if it were a communion wafer.

He stared at the end of the fuse, then stared at the cap. He didn't have any crimping tools. There was another way; he'd seen old-timers do it.

He stuck the end of the fuse into the depressed end of the cap, put the tip of the cap between his teeth, bit down. He didn't blow up. He rotated the cap half a turn, bit down again, blessed with the luck of the amateur.

Mack slipped the cap into the slit stick of dynamite, tamped the bundle in, shoved loose rock after it. Mack's hands were trembling and it took him two tries to get the fuse lit. He watched it burn down for thirty seconds, making sure it wasn't going to go out.

As he turned to leave, a bright corner of white in the dust caught his eye. He bent down and picked up a plastic laminated card, wiped it clean.

It was the boy's University of Wisconsin I.D. card. The sight of the boy's face caught Mack off guard. It didn't look exactly like him. In the picture the boy seemed slightly bug-eyed and wild, with a look of permanent sophomoric surprise. He was sporting a wispy reddish mustache that hadn't quite come in.

Mack picked at the frayed plastic, stared at the young, hopeful face. The sense of loss was suddenly all over him. The boy's death would never be properly grieved, never properly avenged.

He curled his forefinger along the edge of the card, reached back to fling it the way he might fling a skipping stone, then spun away. He couldn't do it.

He wanted to be rid of it and yet it was impossible. He looked over his shoulder and saw the spark crawling toward the packed wall. He could never separate himself. There was a debt to be paid. He slipped the card into the pocket of his shirt.

He walked to the mouth of the cave. Far down in the rocks to the right were the shattered poles of Harry's scarecrow, still lashed together into a twisted cross, the tattered bullet-torn shirt. Harry sat exhausted thirty yards out from the cliff, his head resting against a boulder, waiting for the blast.

Mack was halfway down the ladder when the explosion went off. The cliff trembled and a great cloud of dust billowed out of the cave mouth, drifted down in flakes of light. Bits of rock rained on Mack's head. It was over.

Harry stood up, waiting for him. Mack helped Harry over the boulders. Harry leaned heavily on him at first, then waved him off, limping forward on his own. The clouds had grown darker and there were flashes of lightning.

They moved through the long grass, across the broken stones of the old kiva, into the trees. They bathed in the river, drank in the shallow pools. Every time Mack put his face in the water and closed his eyes he saw Grier falling back into the shaft; he wanted to reach out and grab him back. Harry, ten yards away, looked over and saw Mack on his knees in the water.

"Leave it behind, Mack. You've got to. We'll tell people whatever we have to tell them. We'll lie like hell. We know what happened. It's for us to remember. No one else."

Mack helped Harry to his feet. They hobbled the last fifty yards to the raft. Mack lifted Harry over the side, propped him up. As he did, the raft slid a little in the low water, then scraped on gravel. Mack retrieved the tarp, wrapped it around Harry.

Harry was asleep within minutes. Mack sat on the bank, watching him sleep, watching one breath follow another. When he was sure Harry wasn't going to wake, he pushed to his feet. He had to get them out, but there was one more thing he had to do.

He walked up across the canyon until he found Rick's body sprawled in the rocks, the head and broken torso soaked in bright blood, the arms still pinned by the straps of the battered pack.

Mack bent to the body, not looking at the face; it was the only way to get through it. He grabbed Rick under the shoulders. On the first move he heaved the body upward, caught it in an embrace.

Mack struggled with the limp body. The bloody head lolled back, fell forward on Mack's shoulder, rested there. Rick's long blond hair tickled Mack's cheek. Mack fought back the nausea rising within him. With the second move he reached down and caught Rick under the back of the legs, lifted him.

Mack staggered under the weight. He moved carefully, one step at a time. The canyon was still; there was one bird singing down in the trees. With the still-warm body against his own, he felt something crushing and repellent, and yet there was also something sad and brotherly.

He came to the mouth of a small cave at the base of the cliff, let the body slide out of his arms. He had to get down on his hands and knees to roll the body into the cave, tugging on it, bending it so he didn't bang the head. When he stood up he realized there was blood all over his shirt and face.

He wiped his face off, went back and retrieved the twisted pack and its two gold bars. He carried it back, clutching it to his chest, then swung it in next to the still body. He began to roll boulders across the entrance to the cave. He performed his task steadily, not asking himself any questions. The body would be sheltered, safe and dry, protected from birds and animals. Mack searched for small rocks to pile around the larger ones.

No one would find Rick, any more than anyone would find the boy or Grier, not unless Harry and Mack led people to the spot. Rock grated on rock, shutting out more and more light. The body lying inside was already becoming shadowlike, insubstantial, part of an old, old story.

Mack cradled the last boulder in his arms, dropped it in place. He kicked it in tight with his boot.

He climbed across the rocks until he found the remains of Harry's scarecrow. He tore away the tattered shirt, wrenched the poles apart, buried all of it deep in a crevice. Only when he turned to go did he see the San Francisco Giants baseball cap on the ground. He picked it up. It looked like something out of a novelty shop, a hole in the front and back, singed circles of blasted stiff threads. Mack jammed it in his back pocket.

He moved down toward the trees. He was exhausted, strung out, and yet he couldn't afford to let down. He had to think of everything. Within a day people would be searching for the kid. The vultures would have picked the bodies of the burros clean by then. Someone would come across stray horses on the mesa, but there was nothing unusual about that. With a start Mack remembered the saddles on the rim top. Maybe, if he dared, he would make a trip back to get them.

One day, maybe not for a long time, there would be a knock at the door. There would be questions about Rick and Grier. He and Harry would have to lie like bandits, and they'd have to be better at it than Tucker had ever been. Someone could put the pieces together. It wouldn't be easy, but if they had a very good reason and were smart, it was possible.

He had come down through the trees. Out of the corner of his eye he caught a flash of something white near the bank of the river. The sudden movement made him start. He turned quickly, wary and ready in a second. It was almost a minute before he saw what he was looking for. There was a great, long-necked bird standing motionless in the shallows. It looked like a sandhill crane or a heron, but it was a pure white, a bird Mack had never seen before.

The great bird began to move, stalking through the low water, searching for prey. It moved with fastidious steps, the long white neck undulating like a snake. It disappeared for a second behind a maze of brush, then came back into view.

Mack began to move toward it, without quite knowing why. He just wanted to get close as he could. The bird stretched its neck upward, tilted its head to one side. Mack began to run, splashing down into the water.

The bird took alarm, flapped out of the shallows with a piercing, flutelike cry of warning. Mack fell forward into the water. The bird flitted through the trees with long beats of white wings, glory pulsing into a tangle of parched vines.

Gladness snuck back like a thief. Mack had been through a bloodbath, killed a man, the future was a question, one long wait, and yet he had had his vision. He had seen himself some sights, no one could take that away from him. What had been lost and what had been saved swayed within him like counterweights in a shaft. He knew where all the treasure in the world lay, he knew how to turn his back on darkness. He had seen Harry come back from the dead and that had been worth its weight in gold. Wonders would never cease, he was sure of it; no matter what happened to him next, they flowed through his fingers like water, never to be held. Somehow he would find a way to teach his daughter that.

He was bone-tired and raving. He stumbled out of the water, made his way back to the raft. He carefully fit the shredded baseball cap on the sleeping Harry's head. He would get them out, but his mind was all jumbled now. He needed to rest.

He climbed into the raft, pulled a corner of the tarp up over him, leaned his head against the inflated black sides. He could feel the rocks through the rubber bottom of the boat. He would just take a moment. When he closed his eyes he was asleep within seconds.

When he awoke there was rain on his cheek. He opened his eyes, stared up at a gray, soft sky. A gentle rain was falling. In the north there were streaming black curtains of mist, a real storm.

Mack stretched his arms out on the raft, letting the rain run down his face, slowly soak into his clothes.

He thought he felt the raft nudge forward. Then he was sure of it. The raft swung to the left, crunched over sand. He grabbed hold of the oarlock, pulled himself up. Water was rippling down the river, swelling into low waves. It curled under parched banks. Shallow tongues of water filled the dry channels of sand.

It was no flash flood, no wall of water, but it was coming faster and faster. Mack felt it lift the raft, bounce it off the willow banks, spin it once all the way around.

Harry had opened his eyes and was smiling, pulling down on the brim of his ruined baseball hat. Mack reached for one of the oars in the bottom of the boat, pulled it free, slid up onto the side of the raft. He dipped the oar into the churning muddy water, felt it press against the plastic blade. On all sides the separate channels were rising, gathering into one powerful stream. Mack lifted the oar out of the water, content to just watch. The river would carry them home, all on its own.